A GENTLEMAN of MEANS

A steampunk adventure novel
Magnificent Devices Book Eight

Shelley Adina

Moonshell
Books

Moonshell Books, Inc.
www.moonshellbooks.com

This is a work of fiction. Names, characters, places, and incidents are a product of the author's imagination. Locales and public names are sometimes used for atmospheric purposes. Any resemblance to actual people, living or dead, or to businesses, companies, events, institutions, or locales is completely coincidental.

Book Layout ©2013 BookDesignTemplates.com
Art by Claudia McKinney at phatpuppyart.com
Images from Shutterstock.com and the author, used under license
Design by Kalen O'Donnell
Author font by Anthony Piraino at OneButtonMouse.com
All rights reserved.

A Gentleman of Means / Shelley Adina—1st ed.
ISBN 978-1-939087-29-4

For Jeff, always

Prologue

Venice, October 1894

Upon her graduation from St. Cecilia's Academy for Young Ladies at the age of eighteen, Gloria Meriwether-Astor had returned to the Fifteen Colonies believing herself to be the epitome of feminine charm, wealth, and beauty, and had been launched upon Philadelphia society with enormous success. When considerable expenditures of money and energy had not resulted in applications for her hand by either the scions of political families or barons of industry, she had swallowed her chagrin, boarded one of her father's airships, and been conveyed back to London.

When the following glittering Season bore similar fruit—or lack thereof—Gloria's father Gerald had expressed his disappointment in no uncertain terms.

"I'll not have you frittering away my money for anyone of lower rank than a baron," he said one morning as she was pulling on her gloves in preparation for making that day's calls. "You're to be a ladyship and that's that. If you can't pull it off by the time the Season ends, you'll go into the business with me and make yourself useful that way. I'm not throwing good money after bad, missy."

Gloria could think of nothing more appalling than accompanying her father from boardroom to warehouse to ship's deck and back again, but despite her best efforts and an attempt to elope with the third son of an earl, she was no closer to a wedding by the age of nineteen than she had been at birth. Indeed, she was much farther away, for the successive waves of Buccaneers, young ladies of wealth from the Fifteen Colonies, that had washed up on England's shores dressed to the teeth and ready to bag a peer had become increasingly younger and the competition consequently more intense.

So Gloria had boarded another of her father's airships and commenced a world tour with him, which had taken her to the Canadas and brought her into renewed acquaintance with her former schoolmate, Lady Claire Trevelyan.

She had not paid much attention to Claire at school. Despite her title and distinguished family, Claire was a brainy, mousy thing who hardly ever spoke, and when she did, it was to say something odd or so distressingly practical that one wondered what kinds of books her father kept in his library. Julia Wellesley, Catherine Montrose, and the other girls in their set despised her, and so Gloria had been content to despise her as well.

A GENTLEMAN OF MEANS

Until the Canadas. Until a young man called Jake Fletcher McTavish had held the merciless mirror of his opinion up to her, and she had been found wanting for the first time in more important ways than merely looks or wealth.

And Gloria's life had changed irrevocably.

If she did not know the full extent of her father's web of intrigue and political aspirations, it was only because he hid them from her. She had been willing to be blind, for to see the truth would have destroyed her world. Or so she had thought, until Lady Claire had drawn her into her confidence and she had helped to save a man's life in the Canadas. And now, more than four years later, as she stood at the viewing port of *Neptune's Fancy*, one of the Meriwether-Astor fleet of undersea dirigibles, she was helping to save a man's life once more.

Two, in fact: Captain Ian Hollys, of Her Majesty's Royal Air Corps, and that same Jake Fletcher McTavish, navigator aboard a former pirate vessel called the *Stalwart Lass*.

She owed him one, and she was determined to see this rescue through.

The tension inherent in doing so, however, was making her nerves vibrate like the strings of a cello.

"Is it not awe-inspiring?" Captain Barnaby Hayes gestured to the undersea view before them—the great gearworks upon which the city of Venice turned, its moving neighborhoods changing places in a clockwork dance of massive proportions every few days. It was Leonardo da Vinci's masterwork, she had been informed by more than one man as they drifted under gears and arms the size of Buckingham Palace. But Gloria to her own forehead, and sank onto the bunk, her knees incapable of holding her up any longer.

She had sent her friends to their deaths.

At the moment of their greatest happiness, when they were looking forward to a rewarding life together—when they had achieved that which Gloria herself wanted most in the world—she had failed at the single task they had set her.

Failed abysmally. Fatally.

Sick, with cold chills of horror running through her veins, Gloria lay on the bottom bunk and wished for the first time in her life that she could die, too. Perhaps she would. Perhaps the shame and the grief would eat at her until she wasted away like a consumptive.

She would deserve nothing less.

A knock sounded at the door. "Miss Meriwether-Astor, are you quite well?"

It was Captain Hayes. With a sigh, she curled up, her face to the iron wall and her back to the door.

"Miss Meriwether-Astor, I am coming in. I am quite taken aback."

Bother the propriety of it. He was captain of this vessel and if he only knew, shared some small part of the murder that lay so heavily on her conscience. She couldn't care less whether he came in or not.

"My dear girl, are you quite all right?" He crossed the cabin to the bunk, but left the door standing open as propriety dictated. "What is the meaning of this merry chase you have been leading us?"

There was nothing for it. She was going to have to tell him. But she must do it like a lady of spirit.

She must do it as Claire might.

She rolled over and sat up, swinging her legs over

the side of the bunk and looking up at the porthole just in time to see a kraken's curly tentacle caress the glass and slip off.

"Oh," she choked, and turned to face him as he knelt next to her, tears springing afresh at the reminder that there could be more than one fate for an underwater swimmer in this most dangerous of cities.

"Do not be afraid," he said, clearly misunderstanding her behavior. "The kraken are curious creatures. Once they realize we are not edible, they tend to leave us alone. But please. You must tell me what is going on, for I am quite at a loss as to how to account for my missing passengers."

She took a deep breath. And then she told him.

Not all of it. Not about the part her father had played—his deal to import convict labor from English transport ships to increase the population of convicts who scrubbed and cleaned the gearworks as the sentence for their crimes. That was too shameful for a word of it ever to cross her lips. But about Jake's and Captain Hollys's wrongful imprisonment … and the rescue that Claire and Andrew had attempted … and their certain deaths? Oh yes.

While she felt a thimbleful of compunction that she was forced to cast him in such a dreadful role, he had brought it on himself. If he had only listened and done as she asked, both of them would not now have the deaths of two—four!—innocent people on their hands.

Captain Hayes groped behind him for a chair and, finding none, folded himself onto the bunk next to her. "I cannot believe it."

"It is quite true. And now also quite impossible to rectify. They are almost certainly dead."

"And if they are not, they will be long before we can turn the ship about and retrace our course. We are ten leagues at least from Venice now." He lifted his head, his eyes wide with shock, his face pale. "Why did you not tell me the truth?"

"Would you have believed it any more readily than the lie?"

Her honesty seemed to shock him, and it took a moment before he could reply. "Possibly not. I am frankly still not quite ready to credit you, my employer's daughter, gently reared and educated, with breaking condemned men out of a Venetian gaol."

"I was not, in fact, to break them out. I was merely to provide the conveyance. And now I must live with the knowledge that my friends' last thought before dying was that I had betrayed them and left them to drown."

He winced, and she instantly regretted the childish urge to lessen her own pain by increasing his.

"I am sorry, Captain. That was unfair when you had no reason to imagine what we were concealing from you."

"Is there anything else?"

"That I am concealing? No," she said bitterly. "Only my own shame and horror, which I will have to live with for the rest of my life."

He was silent a moment. "Then let us have perfect clarity between us," he said at last. "I must tell you in my turn that we are not joining the fleet out in the Adriatic."

"We are not?" Gloria's heart bumped against her ribs with a sudden rush of hope. "Then may we return to Venice? At least we might recover the bodies of my friends and have something more to tell their families than—than—"

"We cannot return." He got up slowly, as though testing his legs' ability to hold him up. "I am very much afraid that we will be taking you to Gibraltar, where an airship is waiting to take us to England."

She stared at him. "England? 'Us'? Are you mad? I have no desire to go to England with you or anyone. Father and I are to return to the Fifteen Colonies once his business here is concluded."

At last the captain's gaze met hers, and in it she saw that he had left horror and shock behind with an effort of will, and had allowed resolve to flow in. "I am afraid not." He reached into the jacket of his uniform and for a frozen moment she thought he would withdraw a gun.

But it was merely a handkerchief, with which he wiped his brow.

"Please make yourself comfortable for the journey," he said. "You will not be locked in, for we have secured the torpedo tubes, and there is no other means of escape."

"But why?" she managed. "What is the meaning of this—this abduction?"

"I am not at liberty to say," he told her. "But rest assured that you have committed no crime and will not be harmed in any way." And with this mystifying pronouncement, he bowed to her and returned to the bridge.

At an utter loss, Gloria sank onto the bunk and wished, not for the first time, that she had never been born.

He slipped an arm around her waist and pulled her to his side. "I am afraid that I may have been rather rash in promising a salon and laboratory when I proposed, having never actually looked into what might be available here."

"Never mind." He should not be downcast on her account. She would live in the attic of a warehouse, as he had done in London, if it meant their being together. "Perhaps there is something closer to the girls' *lycee*, so that they might walk to school."

But the agent was already shaking his head. "I have shown you every available property suitable for a gentleman and lady of your position and connections. There are no more houses."

"What about the unsuitable ones?" Claire asked with interest. "What about Schwabing? It is within the city limits now. And I should love to look at something in the Hohenzollernstrasse."

Oh, dear. She should not have mentioned that bohemian quarter, though she had only been half serious. For he ushered them out with the air of a man seeing his duty through though it killed him, was silent during the ride back, and decanted them outside the gates of Count von Zeppelin's palace with rather more efficiency than completely necessary.

"I believe we've been given the bum's rush," Andrew remarked as the agent's steam landau puffed rapidly away. "Never mind. We shall find someone who specializes in farms. Then I may cause explosions to my heart's content."

"So you shall, without let or hindrance," she told him fondly. "Come, let us have some tea. The girls will be home soon and I want a piece of cake before Lizzie commandeers the lot."

After she removed her hat and gloves, Claire picked up the post from its silver tray in the hall, and followed Andrew into her little sitting room. Count von Zeppelin had allowed them to stay here in this comfortable suite on the ground floor of Schloss Schwanenburg for the past four years while she had attended the University of Bavaria in pursuit of her education. Now that she wore the tiny steel ring on the smallest finger of her right hand that told one and all she was in possession of a degree in engineering, and a trio of pearls set in gold on the fourth finger of her left that informed the observer she had entered into an engagement, it was time to fly the nest and find a place in which to make their home.

Her first home as a married woman. It was a good thing they'd begun the search early. She'd had no idea it would be this difficult.

Had they only wanted to entertain, there were houses aplenty with large, airy rooms. Had they wanted merely a laboratory, there were legions of those in a city that was the intellectual capital of Europe, second only to Edinburgh for the number of engineering minds needing space for experiments.

But a house with both these requirements? That narrowed the pool of possibilities to ... well, they had just frightened off the third agent.

So distressing. She and Andrew were to be married at Christmas. They needed a home by then or they would be reduced to living on her airship. Not that *Athena* wasn't comfortable. She could accommodate a fair number of visitors. But an explosion was not to be thought of.

She poured Andrew's tea, and while he settled in

with the newspaper and the estate listings, she secured a piece of cake and sat back to open the post.

An envelope bearing a cramped, spiky hand that she had only seen once before, more than a week ago, made her sit up. A chill settled in her stomach that even a sip of tea did not help.

Dear Lady Claire,

Thank you for your prompt response, which, if it can be possible, has made me more anxious and perplexed than ever.

Upon receipt of your letter informing me that you, Dr. Malvern, and my daughter Gloria briefly voyaged aboard Neptune's Fancy, an undersea dirigible belonging to my fleet, I immediately sent a message to its captain. The message was returned unopened. I consulted with my other captains and learned that Gloria had requested a small ship in order to take a short sightseeing trip to see the gearworks. Thus far, happily, your accounts match.

They diverge, however, following your departure from the vessel. No one has seen or heard from Neptune's Fancy, and repeated hails by all members of the fleet have had no response.

I issued instructions to the fleet to comb the Levant for any sign of her, to no avail. If she had been vaporized by a lightning strike, she could not have disappeared more completely. I am at a loss. Further, I fear something nefarious may have taken place.

Once again I must ask for your help. Is there a location where you, a young lady of respectability and some fortune, believe she might go? Even if it is only a guess and not a certainty, I beg you will impart the location to me.

Lady Claire, if you can assist in any way in allowing me to discover my daughter, I will be in your debt forever. You have merely to ask and, if it is remotely in my power, your smallest wish will be granted instantly.

I remain your servant,
Gerald Meriwether-Astor

She must have made some sound, for Andrew lowered the paper and frowned. "Is it bad news, dearest?"

"I cannot say." She handed him the letter, and when he reached the three-quarters mark, he made a similar sound. Disbelief. Distress. And perhaps a little confusion.

"Nefarious?" He handed the letter back, and she folded it up. "This from the man who has taken the word to unheard-of depths?"

"My sentiments exactly." She hesitated, then made up her mind. They had been through so much together, had seen each other in the best and worst of circumstances. It made no sense to be anything but utterly honest with the man who was to be her husband. "I must confess, Andrew, that I have been struggling with Gloria's desertion for some days now—since we left Geneva, in fact, and the full import of those moments under the sea was increasingly borne in upon me."

"I can hardly blame you." His hazel eyes, usually so full of humor, held hers with some solemnity. "If we ever see the girl again, I hardly know whether I ought some. I hope you are not bouncing people off the Victor Tor—your shoulder has only just healed."

"Oh, just one of the girls in my mathematics class. She is more annoying than a mosquito at a picnic. And my shoulder is perfectly well."

Maggie, true to form, had taken in the tenor of the room under Lizzie's chatter, her amber eyes moving from Claire to Andrew and finally lighting upon the folded letter in Claire's lap. "Is everything all right, Lady?"

Claire had never kept anything from them save her most personal moments with her intended. A woman's greatest aid was often the truth, so she did not withhold it from these girls, even to protect them. They had proven up to the task of absorbing and understanding the most shocking things, and she would not leave them ignorant now.

So she handed over the letter, which Lizzie read in one hand while she demolished a piece of cake with the other, Maggie hanging over her shoulder from the back of the sofa.

"Do you think something has happened to her?" Maggie took the first cup that Claire poured and handed it to her cousin, then accepted her own. "For I have never believed that she would just abandon the four of you in that dreadful place."

"I know what happened," Lizzie said with such confidence that Claire lifted an eyebrow in surprise.

"You do? Enlighten us at once."

After a swallow of tea, Lizzie said, "It's obvious. She has eloped with the captain of the vessel. You said yourself he was very handsome."

Claire narrowly prevented herself from throwing the

contents of the sugar bowl at her ward. "Honestly, dearest. I am half tempted to forbid your seeing Tigg in any capacity but that of friends and comrades if you are to bring such spoony comments into the conversation. We are trying to be serious."

"I am perfectly serious." Lizzie reached for the cake once more, and Claire moved it out of her reach. "Lady, just one more?" she wheedled. "It's my favorite."

"Anything with frosting on it is your favorite," Maggie observed. "Your corset won't meet in the back anymore if you keep this up."

Sulking, Lizzie subsided into the corner of the sofa with her tea. But she was not yet finished with her theory. "It makes perfect sense, Lady. What else but a handsome man would cause a woman to abandon her friends?"

"You do Gloria a grave disservice, my dear," Andrew said, taking for himself the last piece of cake, thereby forestalling all arguments on the subject. "She is made of finer stuff than that. I would no more believe her capable of such a thing than I would believe you capable of abandoning Claire for Tigg."

"I will someday," Lizzie muttered, clearly unwilling to concede the point.

Claire smiled at her to let her know she had not taken offense. "But it is not likely that you would do so if my life hung in the balance. If indeed you and he are to make a match of it, it will be less a case of abandonment than of a joyful leave-taking, with a lot of cake and throwing of rice besides."

Which sent Lizzie off into a romantic dreamland and made Maggie sigh and roll her eyes. "You should not encourage her, Lady. She is difficult enough to live with when Tigg is right here with us. Heaven help us when he returns to the Dunsmuirs. It will be all dramatic sighs and melancholy gazing at the moon until we are all fit to scream."

"Just wait until your turn," Lizzie said, snapping out of her reverie with vigor. "I shall take great pleasure in pointing out each of your sighs and vapors— preferably in public."

Maggie seemed unperturbed at this dire threat, though Claire wondered if she was, in truth. "I hope you do not expire of old age while you're waiting. I have nary a prospect in sight to entertain you with, thank goodness."

The pink that stained her cheeks made Claire wonder if there was indeed someone who made Maggie sigh, or if it was simply brought on by general feminine modesty about speaking of such things in front of Andrew. She herself had been both unkissed and untried at the age of sixteen. By the next year, however, her life had been turned upside down, not the least because Andrew had given her her very first kiss.

What might the next year bring for Maggie? Claire could only hope that there would be much more peace and far less adventure—if only for her own sake. Claire did not think she could survive another summer like the one just past.

A GENTLEMAN OF MEANS

2

Dear Mr. Meriwether-Astor,

 I was saddened and perplexed to receive your letter with its news—or lack thereof—of Gloria. I had absolutely no idea of her leaving when last we spoke—in fact, we had made plans to see one another again following our brief sojourn to see the gearworks in Neptune's Fancy.

 I am very sorry to inform you that I have no idea where she might have gone. Did she take luggage with her? A change of clothes? She carried only a reticule onto the vessel, which might have held a change of unmentionables at best, a little money, and perhaps her sketchbook and some pencils.

 One member of our party seems to think there

may have been an attraction between Gloria and the captain of the vessel, who introduced himself to us as Barnaby Hayes. I cannot vouch for this myself, as the interaction between them was as civil and cordial as might have been expected between any two persons only recently introduced. He showed no signs of dishonorable conduct in our short acquaintance, and certainly no propensity for kidnapping.

I find myself distressed at the idea that she may not have left of her own volition. But we must keep a positive view of the matter. I will write to some of our school friends in London. There is a possibility, however remote, that she may have contacted one of them and they may be willing to confide in me. If this turns out to be the case, I will inform you immediately.

Gloria is a young woman of resources and intelligence. Whatever has happened, you may be sure that she will do what is right.

Yours sincerely,
Claire Trevelyan

Claire laid down her pen, folded up the letter, and sealed it. A pigeon waited on the balcony outside for it, but she took a moment, in the stillness of her room with its lace curtains and Baroque writing desk, to consider what she was doing.

It felt decidedly odd to be offering comfort, however small and stilted, to Gloria's father—a man who had backed a French invasion of England—who was so evil and heartless that he did not balk for a moment at the prospect of trafficking in human lives and misery.

A GENTLEMAN OF MEANS

Surely a man who owned one of the largest fleets in the world, who had business connections on every continent—though England and Prussia were forbidden to him—had the resources to find his own daughter.

Why should he waste his time inquiring of Claire? She could only hope that once she had heard from Catherine and Julia in London, their correspondence would come to an end and he would turn his investigations elsewhere.

Certainly she was concerned for her friend. But there had to be a reasonable explanation for her behavior. Perhaps Lizzie might even be right. The memory of the dirigible swimming away and leaving her and her friends in abject peril triggered a bubble of anger in her chest, swiftly doused by a surge of compassion.

Gloria could not have left them voluntarily. Their friendship and regard for one another would not have been abandoned so utterly. She was sure of it.

Her father would find her eventually, and in the meantime, she would do what little she could. She enclosed the letter in the pigeon's glossy body, set the numbers and letters of the code for his vessel, and released it into the sky.

Under her breath, as she watched its running lights disappear among the stars, she whispered a prayer for Gloria's safety.

*

The letter that came back from Catherine Haliburton (née Montrose) a week later was unenlightening at best.

What a surprise to hear from you, Claire. I had not supposed you interested in continuing your acquaintance with any of your old friends now that you are forced to earn your living by the sweat of your brow. You are working in a factory, I hear. That must be terribly distressing for your mother. We have not seen her in town for an age, so I imagine that is why.

I was just remarking to Julia the other day as we were lunching at the Orangerie how amusing it is that our old set seems to have done rather well in society—and the roots of our success were clearly visible even in the classroom.

In answer to your rather odd questions, no, I have not seen Gloria. I had a letter from her from Paris a year ago in which she promised to send me some of the fashion plates from the Worth atelier. She still has not fulfilled her promise, so I have washed my hands of her. I have no patience for those who do not keep their word.

I trust you are well, despite your unfortunate circumstances.

Mrs. David Haliburton

With a sigh, Claire tossed Catherine's letter, full of complaints and slights both given and received, into the fire. An envelope engraved with the Mount-Batting crest had come in the same mail, so she opened it with a sense of resignation, expecting more of the same.

Julia did not disappoint.

A GENTLEMAN OF MEANS

Claire, darling, how very amusing that I should hear from you this week, when your name has popped up in conversation repeatedly, though the subject of your family is not one I generally dwell upon.

I have not heard from Gloria recently, outside of a postcard from the exhibition in Venice. Spiteful thing—she knows I was wild to go, but alas, with the renovations to our town house, I am plagued with architects and decorators and simply could not take the time. I am surprised you made her acquaintance there. Goodness, the things she said of you while we were in school—but perhaps that is best left in the past. We are women now, and our school days are behind us.

I see in the society pages that you are to be married at last. What an age you have been about it— quite the last of our class, if I am not mistaken. I myself am delighted to announce that the heir to the Mount-Batting title will be born in the early summer. Amidst all this chaos, I am interviewing nannies and nursery maids, and what a chore it is.

Were you not a governess at some point? If I can find no one for the post when he is old enough, perhaps I shall write to you. I should much rather have someone I know teaching the future earl, and with your odd notions of independence I suppose you will continue to work after you are married. Goodness knows anything would be better than working in a factory.

I must close. They are hanging the chandelier over the grand staircase and my presence is urgently requested.

Julia's letter hit the back wall of the fireplace with rather more force even than Catherine's, and fell into the flames, where the venom embedded therein caught instantly. The offending sheets were consumed in moments, and Claire told herself she must put their contents out of her mind with equal speed.

Some people, as they matured, learned and grew. And some simply never did. She was more grateful than ever for the continued unstinting friendship of Emilie, Lady Selwyn, who wrote faithfully once a month. Each letter was a delight, full of the minutiae of country life in words that fairly glowed with happiness.

Claire looked forward to that same kind of happiness with Andrew. She might have passed up two chances to be the mistress of a great estate—three, if she counted the Kaiser's unfortunate nephew—but what did that signify when she was to become the wife of a man who had earned her respect and admiration as well as her love?

Feeling somewhat restored, she pulled another sheet of paper toward her and wrote another missive to Mr. Meriwether-Astor. It was short and to the point, and would hopefully be the last of its kind.

Dear sir,

I regret very much to inform you that Gloria's and my mutual friends in London have not heard from her more recently than a month ago, and certainly not within the last week.

While I realize that my information brings you no closer to locating her, at least one avenue of investigation is closed so that you may concentrate your not inconsiderable resources on another that might be more profitable.

If there is anything more I might do, I hope you will write to apprise me of it. Please let me know when she is found. I shall be very happy to hear of it, but it will not stop me from giving her a fine talking-to for causing us all so much anxiety.

Yours sincerely,
Claire Trevelyan

*

Lieutenant Thomas Terwilliger, on leave from his service aboard the flagship *Lady Lucy*, gave a final turn of the last screw and set the modified mother's helper on *Swan*'s hardwood floor. The rotary mechanism in its belly that normally contained sweeping brushes was now a sanding device meant to take the peeling, warped planks back to their original state so that they could be varnished and restored to beauty.

"There she goes," he said with satisfaction, as the mother's helper buzzed slowly across the expanse of the salon, a track of sanded wood spooling out behind it.

"That will save us a lot of elbow grease." Alice Chalmers watched it with the approval of one who has sanded plenty of floors. "Thanks, Tigg. Well done."

"It was nothing," he said modestly, because truly, it was a trifle compared to the mighty Daimler 954C engines he had been working on down in *Swan*'s engine room. But still, he took pleasure in a job well done. That was something he'd learned from the Lady, who took as much pleasure in a mother's helper behaving as

about it ent going to change what happened."

"It might help us understand, though."

"I ent putting that in your heads. Bad enough it's in mine."

"So you and the captain are content to jump like mice every time the steam pipes clank? To wake in the middle of the night in a puddle of sweat? To stare off into space and not come back no matter what anyone says to you?"

Jake's mouth tightened, as though he might be reining in his temper with an effort of will. That was different—he was learning control.

"Do you blame us?" Tigg went on. "What happens when we're in an air skirmish and you go into that trance, Jake?"

"I won't."

"You can't say that. Are you willing to put Alice's life in danger because you're too proud to admit you've got the megrims?"

He barely saw Jake's fist in time to throw up his arm and block it. With a twist and a movement of his foot, he had him on the cabin floor, leaning on him gently, the offending fist twisted up between his shoulder blades.

"You forget I've had advanced training from Mr. Yau," Tigg told him softly. "Don't swing on me again or I won't be so gentle next time."

Jake was fuming with rage as Tigg let him up. "It's none of your business," he snarled. "If you ent got the sense to let me keep the ugliness to myself, you deserve what you get."

Tigg, on the alert in case he took another poke, said, "I'm trying to be your friend, you numpty. We're a flock, remember? We help each other."

He could see the struggle going on behind the other boy's eyes, as green as those of Snouts. The struggle between the horrors of the megrims and the belief that a man kept his fear to himself. The struggle to trust someone other than Captain Chalmers. Well, Tigg could understand that. Alice had made a man out of an angry boy, but that didn't mean a man could live without friends.

Especially friends who knew all about the ugliness that their lives had been before the Lady came.

"Think on it." Tigg turned and shrugged into a shirt and his uniform jacket. "I saw what little I saw, and only a fool wouldn't have the megrims."

Jake only grunted. But through dinner on *Athena*, Tigg kept an eye on him and saw the effort he was making to be normal. The only time he seemed to soften was when he spoke to Maggie.

Maybe she was the key.

After dinner, when the gentlemen had joined the ladies in the large salon for the latest variation of cowboy poker, he waylaid Maggie at the door on her way back from fixing a pin in her chignon.

"Got a sec, Mags?"

Her smile warmed her amber eyes, making Tigg wonder for about the fortieth time why no one had spoken for her. Yes, she was young, but didn't they have eyes in their heads at that fancy school she and Lizzie went to? There should be a steady stream of young gentlemen traipsing through the park bringing her Flanders chocolates and flowers. But Maggie didn't seem to mind.

Perhaps she was like the Lady had been, and had

bigger fish to fry than the opinions of young gentlemen.

"I have all the time in the world for you," she told him. "What is it?"

"I'm worried about our Jake."

The smile faded, and she glanced to where Jake sat hunched protectively over his cards—as though he expected someone to take them from him. "I am, too. It's been weeks since we were in Venice, and he's perfectly safe here, but still … he reminds me of the way he used to be. Remember?"

Only too well. "I think we should get him to talk about it. Him and the captain both, but Alice is the best one for that job."

"I think so too. But how?"

"You could ask him to escort you out into the garden."

Maggie raised an eyebrow with an expression that clearly said, *Are you mad?* "He'd laugh in my face."

"Tell him you're afraid of villains. It won't be far wrong—we've had our share here."

"That's true." She thought for a moment. "All right. And you'll find us out there? Because I don't want him to think—" She hesitated, and color washed into her cheeks. "I wouldn't want to give the wrong impression."

"I don't think he's sweet on you, if that's what you mean."

"You don't?"

Well, blow him down if she didn't look disappointed. Crushed, even. If Tigg could have backed away and run for it, he would have. This was Lizzie's department, not his. Before he opened his big mouth again, he'd remind himself he belonged in the engine room with a wrench, not in a drawing room.

"I'm no expert," he finally said, sounding as lame as he felt. "But I bet he'll go with you."

At least he turned out to be right on that score. Jake might not be a gentleman, but Tigg had never known him to refuse Maggie anything, even though his pride might put up a fight first.

As Tigg followed them down the gangway trying to look as though he was merely out for a stroll, Lizzie slipped up behind him and took his hand. They fit together so well that his fingers entwined with hers without his even needing to think about it.

"Something is up," she said without preamble. "You were distracted at dinner and hardly heard me. What is it?"

Trust his Liz to get down to brass tacks.

"I've asked our Maggie to talk to Jake. His mind is still locked in that Venetian prison, and if anyone can give him a key to get out, it's she."

"So you're out here to prevent their being interrupted?"

"No." He squeezed her hand, hoping she would understand. "I'm going to join them. I'm hoping that between the two of us, he'll open up."

"He won't open up to you."

"Whyever not? I'm his mate. And I've already brought it up once today."

"Didn't get very far, did you?"

"No. He told me to shove off. But I could see in his face that it's driving him mad."

"You haven't asked for my advice, but I'll give it anyway. Maggie sees things that the rest of us don't. I think you should leave her to it. If she can't get him to confide in her, then nothing any of us can do will work, and he'll have to come to terms with his memories himself."

"But—" Tigg almost couldn't voice the fear that lay deep down. But this was Lizzie. They'd never kept anything from one another, and now was no time to begin. "What if he hurts her?" he finished reluctantly.

Lizzie stopped dead in the white gravel of the walk. "Hurts her? Is there some danger of that?"

"He took a swing at me this afternoon for getting too nosy. I just wondered—it's why I wanted to be there."

"Surely not." Lizzie sounded a bit winded. "Not our Jake."

"He's not the same as he was, Liz. Or rather, he's become all too much as he used to be. Before the Lady. Remember?"

"That was a long time ago, when we were children."

Tigg had no reply.

In the twilight, he heard Lizzie take a deep breath. "If you truly think so, then perhaps we'll just take a walk through the park. We'll give them a wide berth— wide enough that they can't see us, but close enough that we can help if she cries out." She choked. "I cannot believe I am even saying such a thing about Jake."

"Are you warm enough?"

"Yes, I brought a shawl. And you will keep me warm if that fails."

He passed an arm about her shoulders and drew her close to his side. "Don't let the Lady hear you say something so wicked. She might think you were drawing me in."

"I didn't let her, did I? She and Mr. Malvern are beating Alice and the captain at cards. I let Mr. Stringfellow know where we were going, but no one else."

Near the lake in the middle of the park, they could hear the murmur of voices, and Tigg made out the two figures pacing slowly along the gravel walk—one tall and rangy and looking perpetually underfed, and one straight and graceful, her sleeves puffed in the new fashion and her skirts trailing now that the Lady had allowed both girls to let their hems down.

One girl had saved the life of a future king, and the other had prevented a foreign invasion. It did not seem sensible to keep the Mopsies looking like children when anyone with eyes in his head could see that they were not.

Tigg wondered if these two girls who meant so much to him had ever been children. If any of them had.

"Do you ever wonder what life might have been like if we'd grown up like normal people?" he mused aloud.

"I am a normal person," Lizzie said crisply.

"But do normal people get tipped out of a burning airship into the Thames and grow up as street sparrows?"

"Well, if you must put it like that ... no, I don't think of it. For if I did, I should be filled with hatred toward my father for taking my mother's life. For taking Maggie's and my lives away from us—twice—and there is no profit in that." She glanced up at him, though it was getting increasingly dark. "Why? Do you?"

"I can't imagine it," he said after a moment. "My earliest memory is holding a spool of ribbon for my mother as she trimmed a bonnet. Then it's a blank until the next memory—the madam giving me a wallop for crying while my mother was with a man. But how she went from being a respectable milliner to a—" He couldn't say it. "To working there is just dark. And then she died, and I never had the chance to ask her."

"Have you ever known your father?"

He shook his head. "Just shadows—moments that might have been memories, or something my mother told me in a story. I know he was an aeronaut, and he must have been a Nubian, for my mother was as fair as you."

She slid her hand into the crook of his arm, tugging her paisley shawl with its peacock pattern more closely around her. "I'm glad we've had the lives we did. For I wouldn't trade what I have now for all the jewels in the Queen's treasury."

His smile held quiet content. "I wouldn't either. In fact, I—"

He stopped, and she looked up at him curiously. "Tigg?"

"Have you seen the sentries?"

The count's guards paced the walks and boundaries of the park twenty-four hours a day. There were usually always two within view, even if they were off in the distance. Now Lizzie's keen eyes swept the park, the lake, and the trees. "That's odd."

And then a shot rang out.

3

Claire lifted her gaze from the contemplation of her cards. "What was that?"

Alice had abandoned her hand on the tablecloth altogether, allowing everyone to see that she would have been the first to fold. "Sounded to me like a rifle."

"A rifle? In Munich? In the count's own park?" But despite his reluctance to believe it, Andrew was already pushing back his chair.

"Where are the girls?" Claire said suddenly. "Have they gone back to the palace?"

"Allow us to look," Captain Hollys told her. "Do not distress yourself, Claire."

She was about to tell him she was not in the least distressed—that when one heard gunshots, one customarily looked to the safety of those for whom one was responsible—when they all heard a second shot.

At this confirmation of reality and not imagination, the salon was abruptly abandoned. Claire dashed into her cabin and snatched the lightning rifle off its brass rack on the wall, thumbing its cell into life in the same motion. Andrew waited for her at the base of *Athena*'s gangway, his face tense.

"Mr. Stringfellow says that the girls are walking with Tigg and Jake in the park."

"Good heavens," Claire breathed. "Two shots—"

"Do not think it, dearest. Come."

Where on earth were the sentries? Had the entire company been set upon? Rendered unconscious? Killed? And what of the count and the baroness and their visiting grandchildren?

No, no. She must not let her fears run away with her. The most immediate necessity was to find the girls and make sure they were unharmed. But where would they be? The park was enormous—acres and acres of grass and gardens, the lake, the trees, all artfully laid out to look as natural as possible.

A flash of white caught her eye by the lake. A swan, startled out of sleep? Or—

"Andrew, it's Maggie!"

She gathered up the skirts of her evening dress in one hand and set off at a run. A moment later she found Lizzie and Maggie both crouched behind a statue of Zeus, breathing hard, as though they had been running, too.

"Girls!" The lightning rifle in her other hand was no barrier to the embrace she gave them both. "Tell me what has happened at once."

"Two shots, both from behind *Swan*," Lizzie said

without preamble, and Claire realized that between walking with the young gentlemen and meeting her, they had been scouting. She should have expected nothing less, and her earlier concern seemed foolish. "Something has happened to the sentries."

"I noticed that too." Since it was now fully dark, she used the light in the glass globe of the rifle to scan their forms quickly. "You are not hurt?"

"No," Maggie said. "Jake and Tigg have gone to flush them out, whoever they are."

"Excellent. The pheasant shall find the hunters waiting at the butts."

Another shot whistled over their heads and took a chip off Zeus's noble ear. Why, the nerve!

Claire had clearly seen the muzzle flash, there beneath the trees. She sighted through the notch in the lightning rifle's flared barrel and squeezed the trigger.

The grass, the trees, and the intruder were all illuminated in the blue-white flash before it engulfed the man standing there, flickering along the barrel of the gun still pointed at them, and causing it to explode in his hands as the cartridge caught fire. The charge made short work of his clothing—his body—his hat. The charred remains slumped to the earth.

"Nicely done, Lady," Lizzie said with admiration.

Claire could not rejoice at any man's death, though he had clearly meant theirs. "The question is, how many are there?"

"That was the third, all from different directions," Maggie told her. "But it was the first shot to be directed at human targets. The others seem to have been shooting at poor *Swan*. Don't they know that they would need many more bullets than that to damage a fuselage?"

"Unless they meant to draw us out, in which case, they succeeded," Claire said grimly. "The other villains will have seen the bolt, so we must be careful in our examination of the corpse. Come."

Lizzie shared her dark shawl with Maggie so that the white lace of her waist would not draw undue attention. Claire was thankful that her own gown was sapphire blue—close enough to black in the dark to make it easy to blend in with the shadows.

She pulled a fold of it over her nose and mouth as they approached the remains of the gunman. The smell of charred flesh was dreadful, and it was all she could do to circle the body enough to ascertain that all hints of identity had been burned away.

Andrew joined them a moment later and she turned gratefully into his arms. "Claire, dearest, you frightened me to death, haring off into the night in that manner."

"I am sorry," she said meekly into his shirt. "I saw the girls and every thought but reaching them fled my mind."

"I saw the shot, and your return fire. I suppose I should be used to it, but ..." His arms tightened about her. "There is no possibility of your becoming an ordinary *hausfrau*, is there?"

"I do not think so," she confessed. "Would you love me more if there were?"

Softly, he said, "I do not think it possible to love you more. I should simply explode."

She might have expressed her complete agreement with this view in more concrete terms had Lizzie not whispered, "Lady! Bring the light."

With a sigh, Claire forced herself to recollect the danger of their situation. They might not have much time. There had been no further shooting, but that might only be because the villains were triangulating their position.

By the clear glow of the lightning globe, within which tendrils of energy flickered restlessly, waiting for the next depression of the trigger, Claire examined what the girls had found.

It was a rucksack of the kind that walkers used in the Alps. It contained half a sausage in waxed paper, a shirt, a box of ammunition, and in an inner pocket, a medallion.

"What can this be?" She turned it over, but other than a pin on the back, it revealed nothing. The front contained an etched design. "Are these cats?"

Lizzie frowned as she took the bit of brass, the size of a sixpence. "A lion, it looks like, and a leopard with spots, and a dog? No, a wolf. All three with circlets on their heads."

"Is it a coin?" Maggie asked. "A medal?"

"Never mind," Andrew said urgently. "We must find the others—to say nothing of the two villains who remain."

The words were no sooner out of his mouth than there was a fusillade of shots from the woods surrounding the clearing in which *Swan* was moored.

"Tigg!" Lizzie squeaked.

Claire grabbed her just as she leaped to her feet. "You must not!"

"But Tigg—"

"Tigg is a trained aeronaut. Dearest, we must have help. Run to the palace and alert the count that we are under fire from persons unknown. Quickly—you and Maggie are the fastest of us all."

Despite her fear, Lizzie's practical nature told her that this was the necessary and most helpful course. She grabbed Maggie's hand and they took off like athletes at the starting gun in the direction of the palace, where lamps were coming on all over the ground floor.

"Nicely done," Andrew said. "They will both be safe."

"Until they accompany the sentries back here," Claire said wryly. "Come. Let us resume our hunt for the hunters."

But by the time they reached the area from which the sounds of fighting had come, the battle was over. Alice and Tigg knelt next to the lifeless bodies of two men, whose lack of knowledge of the park might have contributed to their undoing.

"It was me they were after," Alice said grimly, rifling pockets for some sign of identity. "Look at this." She held up a second medal, the cast figures identical to the one Tigg had found. "I've heard about these. I knew I'd have a price on my head when I fled Venice, but not that they'd come so far, nor take to shooting when they got here. But all they accomplished was to put a few more holes in *Swan*'s fuselage for Jake to patch tomorrow, and give us all a run around in the dark."

"I don't know about that," Tigg said, dusting off the knees of his uniform trousers as he stood. "If it hadn't been for me, this one would have dropped you for sure. He had a clear shot."

"Then I owe you my life." She grinned at him, but it was belied by the sparkle of tears. "Again." Her smile faded as her gaze took in her company. "Say, where is Ian?"

"I thought he was with you," Tigg said. "And where

is Jake?"

"Here." Jake stepped out of the trees and picked his way over to Claire. "I checked quite a distance out, but there don't seem to be more. And no indication of how they came, either. They might have rappelled down from a lampless airship on ropes." He paused. "Where are the girls?"

"Gone to the palace to get help," Andrew said. "We must find Ian. I do not relish being mistaken for an assassin, and he might know the significance of the medal."

"Medal? You mean like these?" Tigg and Alice both held out similar brass pieces, and Tigg went on, "Not a scrap of paper to indicate who they are, but they all carried these—as though they belonged to a club."

"Let me see." Jake tried to take it from Tigg's hand, but the young lieutenant shook his head.

"I can hear the count's men. Come. We must get out in the open and identify ourselves. If something happened to the sentries on duty tonight, the others will be on edge."

Spoken like a true military man, Claire thought with quiet admiration. How easily Tigg took command, with both logic and concern for those under his protection. She was more convinced than ever that Lizzie was a fortunate young woman. If ever two souls were meant to match each other in bravery and resources, it was they.

The sentries were indeed on edge at the discovery of the lifeless bodies of two of their mates, lying where they had fallen near the rear gates of the park. Tigg handed over the medallion he had found to the captain of the company, and informed him of what they suspected was its significance. The sentry turned it over in his leather-gloved hand without recognition.

"A vengeance medallion, is it?" he said at last, squinting in the light of the lamps on *Athena*'s mooring mast. "I shall bring it to Count von Zeppelin's attention as soon as he and the baroness see to the grandchildren."

"Let them know we are all well," Claire said. "I would not want them to suffer a moment's anxiety on our behalf."

But they were not all well. Ian was still missing, and a quick search of *Athena* proved that he had not returned.

"He must be on *Swan*," Alice said at last, her hands on her hips and a frown wrinkling her brow. "But if he isn't, I suppose we'll have to wait for the sentries to make a full search of the grounds. I don't fancy being shot while I'm looking for him, either."

"We'll come with you," Andrew said. "If a chance exists that a fourth man might be on *Swan*, you'll want reinforcements."

This had not occurred to Claire, and she exchanged an anxious glance with Alice. "We shall all go together," she said. "Lizzie, Maggie, arm yourselves with your lightning pistols. I do not wish to be taken by surprise again."

"We'll be putting pockets in our dresses for the pistols after this," Lizzie said, rather too happily, considering the circumstances. "Imagine coming armed to the dinner table."

Not for the first time, as they searched the crew's quarters on *Swan*, Claire wondered with some despair what it would be like to be that imaginary *hausfrau*, living a quiet life quite unconcerned by the evils that dwelt in the world. Then her good sense caught up with her.

Someone had to manage the evil, and it was her own good fortune that around her had gathered men and women suited to that task. Or, if not precisely suited, then certainly with the capacity to grow into it. Not for the first time, her thoughts turned to Gloria, who seemed to have been this second kind of person.

Perhaps that was why they had become friends after their meeting in the Canadas. Perhaps each had recognized in the other that capacity to rise to a challenge, and thereby change the course of events. Perhaps even the course of history.

Gloria, where are you? What has happened to alter your course? And what are you doing about it at this very moment?

But if there were answers to those questions, they had to be put aside. For Jake called out from the catwalk traversing *Swan's* cargo bay, the alarm in his voice startling them all.

A fourth villain!

"Lady!" he called when Claire dashed out behind him, rifle at the ready. "It's the captain—I think he's dead!"

Claire's lungs constricted as she flung herself against the iron railing, her gaze straining to see below in the dim light of the operating lamps. "Where? Alice, can you see?"

And then Alice pointed. "There, behind those boxes of supplies. Get lamps. He might still be alive. You three, we still need the ship secured."

Tigg, Lizzie, and Maggie scattered along the catwalks and gangways. Agile as a cat, Jake swung down to the cargo deck while Claire and Alice hiked up their skirts and negotiated the ladder. Andrew, carrying a lantern, met them a few moments later, holding it up to illuminate Ian's shivering form.

Shivering...?

"He's alive," Claire breathed, bending down. "Ian, are you hurt? Can you hear me? Ian!"

A high, wavering sound was her only reply, muffled by the hands pressed to his face.

"Ian!" Alice touched his shoulder. "Come on, man, what has hap—"

He jumped violently and struck her hand away. In the light of the lamp, his eyes, normally so sharp and commanding, were distended and wide, darting hither and yon as though expecting an attack. His face was so pale that even in the golden light it looked positively gray, and a sheen of sweat stood out on it.

"Cor, Lady," Jake breathed over her shoulder. "I hate to say it, but I think his time in the prison's done for him. The captain's gone completely mad."

A GENTLEMAN OF MEANS

4

Gloria was no stranger to the undersea dirigible. Of her five voyages across the Atlantic, one had been entirely under the water ... an experience whose novelty had faded once they had left the continental shelf behind and the only scenery consisted of darkness, punctuated occasionally by whales and fish. The fact that her father had used the interminable hours to school her in the workings of his business had not helped the situation, but rather made her feel as though flinging herself out the hatch with the daily load of refuse might be an appealing alternative.

The Mediterranean was much more interesting, being shallow and showing the evidence of long human habitation, even on its submerged shores. But even the archaeological delights of the sunken city of Atlantis and the ancient volcanic ruins of Thera, to which Captain Hayes made a point of detouring to give her some relief from rocks and coral, began to pall after the second week.

She had used every trick and weapon in her considerable arsenal of female wiles to get Captain Hayes to divulge who he was and where they were going— *England* being rather a general term. Even a hint as to *why* she was being taken would have been helpful. But to every blandishment, every subterfuge, he and his crew remained immune.

She had even resorted to burglary and theft, only to find that no papers existed other than those relating to the muster in the Adriatic and earlier orders for shipping in the Mediterranean. No messages had been received by the vessel during its periodic surface expeditions for supplies—unless they had been destroyed promptly after they had been read. The only thing concerning her current situation that she had been able to find was a receipt for the feminine underthings that had been discreetly left in her cabin, when they had surfaced at Sicily.

She supposed she ought to be grateful for such a consideration, for she had nothing to wear but what she stood up in. One thing was certain: When they reached their destination, she was tearing off this particular walking suit and leaving it, for she never wanted to see it again.

Captain Hayes's courtesy never failed him, no matter how cross or how cold she was. If he hadn't been kidnapping her, she might have enjoyed his company.

A GENTLEMAN OF MEANS

Each evening—or what passed for evening in the perpetual gloom of fathoms of seawater—she dined with him and his officers in the canteen set aside for their exclusive use. The small library in his cabin was made available to her in its entirety. She had now read the complete works of Miss Austen and Mr. Thackeray twice through, and had recently begun to plow through *A Mariner's Guide to Land Forms and Navigation.* Next up was *Astronomy and Exploration,* and after that, *The Fall of the Roman Empire.*

She was leaving that one for last. If she survived that long and did not go completely mad.

The only facts she currently possessed were that their heading was westerly, and aside from the detours, they were traveling at the upper limits of the engines' capabilities. Why the crew had not staged an airship somewhere so that this interminable journey could be made in three or four days instead of weeks, was a question she had not bothered to ask, for she already knew the answer. Stealth was the most urgent necessity, and airships could be spotted and pursued. Airships were subject to sovereign air space and identification and the filing of flight plans. Undersea dirigibles, being a new technology not yet in use on the Continent, had no such restrictions. And not even her father could track one until it surfaced and a pigeon could locate its magnetic code.

No one knew where she was. And somehow the utter loneliness embodied in that fact was the most horrifying thing of all.

She, who had tasted the delights of friendship, of conversation with active minds and warm hearts, had developed a taste for it that had spoiled her for her previous life. Before she had met Claire, she'd thought she had friends, but now she knew differently. The girls from school understood friendship to be mutual society—and mutual use of one another's connections and talents. But friendship was not that at all. Friendship was being understood. Being esteemed for one's talents, yes, but even if one had none, one could still be appreciated for one's other qualities. The ability to laugh at a joke. The need for solitude on occasion—but not too much. The appreciation of a piece of music or a line of poetry. And most important of all, the ability to offer a hand when a hand was needed—and being able to instantly recognize such a need when words could not be spoken.

After two weeks under the sea, Gloria missed Claire and Alice and the girls and even that outspoken rascal Jake with an intensity that was almost becoming a pain in her middle. And she had had just about enough of moping about and trying to distract herself by reading of other women who had friends and family while she did not.

"We're a flock," Maggie had told her once, as though it were the most obvious thing in the world.

Gloria wanted a flock. She wanted to be reunited with her friends, not putting mile after mile of bubbles and water between herself and people whom she was quite sure actually cared about her.

In fact, she realized now, she was quite put out that she had been removed from them against her will under circumstances that would paint her in the blackest of lights, and her days of being complaisant and polite were over. She swung her feet over the side of her bunk, and as she stood, her ears popped.

A GENTLEMAN OF MEANS

She gripped the iron rails of the bunk. That meant only one thing—they were surfacing.

A horn blew and feet began to pound along the corridors, in exactly the same manner as they had on the three previous occasions.

But on those occasions she had not yet had enough. Now the Meriwether-Astor temper, which she had thought utterly cowed over the years and groomed into more acceptable forms such as *spirit* and *determination*, and occasionally, *bull-headedness*, flooded her system with a tingling need to act.

Under the bunk was a sea-chest belonging to the cabin's real occupant, a middy of some fourteen years. She had already rifled it, but now she jerked it from its place with more purpose. Swiftly, she put on the linen pants, blouse, and jacket that identified her as a member of the crew. She flung her hair up and pinned the tail in such a way that it fell all about her face, as shaggy as that of a boy who hasn't seen a pair of scissors in six months, and jammed the middy's cap on top. Stuffing the contents of her slender purse—ten pounds in coins, her identity papers, and two rings—into the pockets, she rolled up her skirt and petticoat and stuffed them under the bedclothes, then pulled the covers up.

It might pass for her recumbent form, and it might not. But she no longer cared.

Opening the door, she jogged along the corridor and joined a stream of men heading to the upper deck. As she reached the hatch, it opened, letting in the first sunlight she had seen in weeks. Choking back a groan of anticipation, she went up the ladder like a monkey, took a deep breath, and jumped over the chasm between streaming deck and sturdy wooden dock with as little hesitation as the other middies. Immediately she busied herself with ropes and boxes.

Little by little, she moved down the dock. She had perfected the art of looking productively occupied years ago, and it stood her in good stead now. Only a gangway stood between her and the shore, so she hefted a small barrel to her shoulder and walked down it in as unstudied a manner as she could.

"You there!" someone shouted. "You're going the wrong way!"

A glance over her shoulder showed her a longshoreman as big as a house, with his greasy hands on his hips. "It's empty, sir!" she called. "Won't pass muster wiv our cap'n, so I'm going to fill it."

"Drink it yourself, more like," the man grumbled, clearly too busy to bother himself any more.

Her stomach jumping with nerves, Gloria lost herself in the crowd on the dock, dumping the barrel in a pile the moment she was out of sight. The air smelled of rotting fish and tar and overheated steam engines, and she dragged great, satisfying breaths of it into her lungs.

A woman selling fried kraken tentacles, cut crossways and rammed on a stick, looked up as Gloria stopped at her brazier. "Can I interest you in a kraken stick, young sir?" she asked.

"Not at this time, mum, but p'raps you might tell me the name of this port?"

The woman's eyebrows rose under the kerchief tied about her head. "First voyage, aye? Silly trout. Look up."

Gloria did so, and saw nothing but a great cliff of

rock that seemed familiar, though she was quite sure she had never been here in her life. "What...?"

The woman frowned at her ignorance. "Ye git, it's the Rock of Gibraltar. How long you been at sea?"

"First time," Gloria said faintly. Gibraltar! An English colony, one of the largest trading ports in the entire Mediterranean ... and the last stop before skirting the Royal Kingdom of Spain and entering the Channel. "My thanks, mum."

"Sure you don't want kraken? Plenty tasty, mine is."

Gloria's nerves were stretched to the point that any food, never mind the greasy, fried remains of a species that had likely meant the end of her friends, would have come up again immediately. "No thanks, mum. But maybe you might know where a man could send a pigeon?"

"Lawful correspondence here is sent by tube, lad, as anybody knows."

Gloria eyed her. "And is there another kind?"

"No, but if there was, a man could inquire at the Barnacle."

"My thanks." Gloria dug a sixpence out of her pocket and gave it to the woman, waved off a stick of tentacle with a sickly smile, and jogged off down the waterfront in the direction she'd indicated.

In the public house, the pandemonium seemed less the result of drunken merriment than a deliberate screen for the sundry illegal activities going on. Thankful for her male disguise, Gloria inquired and then pushed her way back to a cage where a boy sat sucking a peppermint. "I need to send a pigeon."

He moved the peppermint from one cheek to the other. "Be a pound."

A pound! Highway robbery! But she was in no position to quibble. She handed it over, and he pushed a piece of paper and a pencil under the grate.

Alice, or to whomever this note may come,

I have been abducted by Captain Barnaby Hayes on Neptune's Fancy. He is taking me against my will to England. I don't know why, or where. Please believe I did not leave Claire and Andrew willingly. Sending this from Gibraltar. Will try to escape and reach Munich.

Gloria

A note was one thing, but as desperately as she tried, she could not recall the delivery code for *Athena*, nor for Alice's ship, provided the latter had recovered it. She did not even know if either of them was alive— and if they were not, whether whoever received the note would give a flying fig that she was being kidnapped. But she had no choice. She must try.

In despair, she looked up. "Have you a directory of some kind?"

"Do I look like someone who has a directory? You want one of those, go to the post office and send a tube."

She cursed—one of the saltier versions she'd picked up in the Americas.

"Where you sending it?"

"To Count von Zeppelin in Munich." It was the only address she could think of that had any hope of reaching ... anyone.

A GENTLEMAN OF MEANS

The boy straightened on his stool. "I know that one. Lot of air traffic here. Give it."

Gloria pushed the message under the grate and he stuffed it into what she had mistakenly believed to be a lantern hanging from the ceiling. Seeing her surprise, he said, "What, you think we have 'em out in the open for the postal authority to pinch?" He spun the numbers, opened a hatch behind him, and shoved the pigeon out into the sunlight, where it rose into the sky and disappeared to the northeast.

She must do the same, somehow. And quickly.

"Where is the airfield?" she asked the boy.

"Out on the point, past the docks, between the Rock and the sea. Can't miss it."

In her fear, she'd already managed to miss the Rock of Gibraltar once, so this didn't mean much. All the same, Gloria thanked him and pushed her way back out of the taproom, keeping her head down and her posture crablike and subservient.

The moment she stepped out on the cobblestones, she heard the hue and cry. It could have been a boiler explosion. It could have been an escaped horse causing the running, shouting, and relaying of information. But she couldn't take the chance.

She ran along the waterfront, dodging carts and steam drays and even the swinging cargo on a walking crane, which might have decapitated her had she not ducked in time. But the sounds of a chase did not dissipate with distance. Looking over her shoulder, she saw one of the officers from *Neptune's Fancy* running, his face red and sweating, followed by a cluster of middies and bathynauts in Meriwether-Astor colors.

Blast! No, she would not be taken!

Abandoning caution, she began to run in earnest, feeling her leg muscles stretch and her lungs clutch in a way that told her she might not be as fleet of foot at twenty-three as she'd been at fifteen.

She was no match for the middies, used to haring up and down decks and loading supplies. In moments they surrounded her like a pack of hounds, baying and shouting and closing around her long enough for the officer in charge of the search party to catch up and seize her by the arm.

"Miss Meriwether-Astor, you have led us a merry chase," he said between breaths as heavy as those of a blown horse. "Enough of this nonsense. You are coming with us."

"I am not!" She kicked the nearest knee, threw an elbow, and would have broken the circle of her captors, too, if it had not been for the middy whose clothes she was presently wearing, who grabbed her about the waist and swung her around.

He had arms like iron, the wretch.

Cursing like a bathynaut herself, Gloria was soon dragged onto the *Fancy* and shown to the bridge, where Captain Hayes waited, his hands clasped behind his back and an expression in his eyes that was almost hurt.

"I am sorry to see that you prefer the dangers of the waterfront to the safety of our vessel," he said. "I very much regret the action I must take, Miss Meriwether-Astor, but we cannot allow you the freedoms you have heretofore enjoyed if you cannot be trusted. I am afraid you are confined to quarters for the remainder of the voyage."

He seemed rather taken aback at her language.

She hoped he had learned something.

A GENTLEMAN OF MEANS

5

Claire's official title at the Zeppelin Airship Works was Junior Engineer, Flight Development Department. But she had been occupying space here for two weeks now, and had not yet had a chance to develop so much as a turnscrew, never mind anything approaching flight, despite her excellent credentials. She and Alice had, after all, invented the automaton intelligence system that Zeppelin was currently installing in all of his airships. It stood to reason that she should have begun the illustrious career she had been expecting in that hangar, but no.

Instead, she had been walked over to the Flight Development Department and informed by the person in charge that she would start at the bottom, as did every engineer who crossed the threshold.

"Can't have the count accused of playing favorites, now, can we?" said the gentleman with every appearance of geniality.

"But the automaton intelligence system—I know it better than any person on earth save one. I should be working there." In her black skirt and protective gray laboratory coat, Claire had tried to be firm and dignified. But all it had netted her in the end was a bare bench and a gleam of spite that, she suspected, revealed the man's true feelings on the subject.

She hesitated to take her grievance to the count, though she was living in his palace and it would have been the work of a moment to visit his study after dinner one evening for a private conversation. But delicacy prevented her—that, and the stubborn conviction that if they wanted her to prove herself, she would do it so spectacularly that they would face reprimand for being so short-sighted as to hold her back.

So for some days now, instead of dusting her bare bench, calibrating Bunsen burners, sweeping floors, and asking Herr Weissmann, the department head, if he would like a cup of tea—oh, yes, they expected her to do all those things—she tinkered. She found gears that did not mesh, and flywheels that needed grease, and came in early in the morning to splice cable so that a signal might be detected in a ship's engine room as well as in its navigation gondola.

In short, the Flight Development Department began to see an improvement in its production. The next stage was to generate memoranda. For every improvement, she documented what she had done, with drawings, and laid it on the department head's desk. This went on for some days, until the morning she completed the cable project. When she took in her memorandum, she was so early that she discovered the previous day's report still in the rubbish bin.

Pressing her lips together, she took it out, enclosed it with the completed report on the cable, and popped it in a tube addressed to the managing director's office.

Not surprisingly, she was summoned thither at the end of the week.

She stood quietly in front of Herr Brucker's desk, where a series of her reports was fanned out in front of him. "What is the meaning of this, Fraulein Junior Engineer?" he asked without preamble. "Why am I honored with so much information regarding the progress of your labors?"

"Because Herr Weissmann merely tossed them in the rubbish bin," she said calmly. "I felt that the improvements to the process here ought to be documented so that others might change the procedures."

His monocle fell out as his eyes widened, and he hastened to screw it back in. "Young lady, do you know the meaning of the word *insubordination?*"

"Of course," Claire replied. "But I hardly see the relevance."

"If the head of the Flight Development Department does not believe your reports are significant and chooses to disregard them, and yet you go over his head to bring yourself to the attention of his superiors—this does not strike you as relevant?"

For a moment, Claire was transported back in time to the Chemistry of the Home laboratory at St. Cecilia's Academy for Young Ladies. Professor Grünwald's tone had been very much like this, his underlying fear that she might be more intelligent than he becoming more apparent the more he spoke—and the more he attempted to discipline her.

But she was no longer the cowed seventeen-year-old she had been.

"I do not call it insubordination," she replied. "I call it common sense. Count von Zeppelin is the last man on earth who would accept shoddy workmanship and deliberate stupidity among his employees. I am simply emulating his excellent example."

"Ah, because you are such great friends."

Claire inclined her head. "I consider it a privilege to have earned his esteem."

"And you feel that you are undervalued in your present position, though it is one that has been honorably occupied by every engineer to pass through these doors?"

Here was a sticky wicket to navigate. "I am not averse to working my way up the ladder. I wish to be useful to the count. My only aim in writing these reports is to document ways in which, in the absence of a permanent assignment, I have been able to contribute to that end."

"Do you believe it is useful to him and to this company to point out the faults of others?"

"If they have not been pointed out before now, then that is also something which might be improved."

"Fraulein Junior Engineer, in the noble pursuit of improvement, let me point out a thing or two. We are not in the habit of brooking such arrogance and self-aggrandizement as this. It is one thing to do well in one's assigned duties. It is quite another to believe oneself above them."

Arrogance! Self-aggrandizement! Shades of Lord James Selwyn!

A GENTLEMAN OF MEANS

"I am above them—since I have been employed here nearly three weeks and have not yet been informed as to what exactly my duties are. I have a bench, with no parts or projects upon it. I have a department head who has not yet seen fit to assign me to a ship. I have an engineer's ring and a mind eager to begin work, but I am expected to sweep floors and fetch tea. Tell me, Herr Brucker, would you not do the same in my place?"

He gazed at her for so long that she began to suspect that might have been the wrong question.

"I did do the same in your place," he said at last. "I have swept my share of floors and fetched many a cup of tea."

And here was the crux of the problem. He had accepted being treated like a janitor instead of an engineer, and had risen in the ranks for what appeared to be twenty years, his star finding its zenith in this third-floor office, this leather chair.

Her star was out there in the flight paths of Count Zeppelin's mighty ships, plying the winds and wheeling over time and tide alike.

And therein lay her sin.

"You will return to your bench," Her Brucker said in a tone all the more dangerous for its quietness. "You will fulfill your assigned duties with patience and goodwill, and cease this meddling in levels of operation far above your pretty head. Am I clear, Fraulein Junior Engineer?"

She could defy him. She could go over his head, too, and bring the shortcomings of the Flight Development Department to the attention of the vice president or even the count himself. But what would that net her except a widening circle of resentment, dislike, and quite possibly sabotage?

"Quite clear," she replied, her jaw tight with the need to restrain herself from slapping him. "Shall I take my reports with me?"

"That will not be necessary." With deliberate precision, he picked up each report by the corner and dropped it in the rubbish bin behind his desk. When he was finished, he folded his hands on its glossy surface and regarded her with something akin to triumph. "You are dismissed."

She turned on her heel and left, practically hissing with rage. If ever the thought had crossed her mind that she might show someone besides the count her sketches for the power-generating fuselage skin she was calling the Helios Membrane, she abandoned it now. They should never get her invention.

Then she snorted, a sound of derision in the quiet laboratory. She could leave her engineering notebook on her bench for a month and nothing would happen to it. For it was clear that no one within two hundred feet would recognize what they were looking at.

*

That evening, while the girls were preparing their assignments for the next day, and Alice and Jake had gone back to *Swan* to see whether Ian could be persuaded to take some nourishment, Claire sipped her thimble of port and debated whether or not to approach Count von Zeppelin.

"You are a man," she said at last to Andrew. "If you were in my position, what would you do?"

Andrew laid down his pencil and let the drawing he was working on roll itself up. "That is precisely the difficulty, my dear. I could not be in your position. There is a reason I maintain my own laboratory in Orpington Close, shabby and smelling of fish and mud though it might be. I am the sort of man who must be his own master—even more so now, since James's departure from this world."

She gazed at him. "I have always wondered what brought two men of such differing temperaments together. I could not imagine how you would have found companionship in one another's company."

"I would not call it companionship," he reflected. "Certainly not friendship. I should call it rather a shared goal, with skills complementary to one another that made it possible to attain that goal."

With a sigh, Claire put the tiny glass on the table at her elbow. "It distresses me that I find none of those things at the Zeppelin Airship Works. And I had such high hopes of it—of finding like minds with mutually agreeable goals. What shall I do if I am like you, Andrew, and unable to call men of lesser capability master?"

"There you go, being arrogant and self-aggrandizing again."

"I know," she said sadly. "It is becoming quite a failing in my character. I am glad to find a similar flaw in yours, otherwise I should be in danger of thinking you quite perfect."

At this point the drawings were abandoned altogether and Claire rejoiced in the affections of a man whose attentions gave her as much pleasure as his conversation. She was reminded again that if she did not pay more attention to her wedding plans, she would be married to Andrew in her laboratory coat, and how disappointed Mama would be then!

When she extricated herself from his embrace, she tucked up the strands of her hair that had caught on one of his buttons and become disarrayed. "Andrew, tell me true, as the little ones back at Carrick House might say. Do you think I ought to go to the count?"

"Let me ask you a question in return." He straightened his waistcoat. "If you do not, do you have the endurance to last in the Flight Development Department for as long as you must?"

If he had not told her his own feelings, she might have felt obliged to say yes. But here was another path, forming a third possibility next to the one labeled *Return to London a Failure*. But balanced against it were her obligations to the count: four years of university in exchange for her acceptance of the post. Room and board in the palace while the girls finished school.

"I cannot simply walk away from my obligations," she said at last.

"Then there is your answer," Andrew told her gently. "But I should not abandon a conversation with him altogether. He will still be interested in your feelings and, were I in his place, I should be deeply interested in a department that puts status before innovation."

Andrew was right. She should speak to the count not for her sake, but for his. On Sunday after church, when she saw through her French doors that the count was inspecting the last of his roses in his sunny private garden, she slipped out and along the flagged path to join him.

"Claire!" His voice was warm as he indicated a yellow rose. "Look at this. She has been hiding in the foliage all summer, and now that the other roses have faded, at last she gets her chance to bloom."

Might that not be a fitting epigraph for her own situation? Perhaps she could use it as a way to ease into the conversation she wished to have with him.

"What a pity that with the end of the season, her time in the sun will be so short," he concluded.

Oh, dear. Perhaps not.

"I have not seen you all week." He straightened and offered her his arm. "How is Captain Hollys? My personal physician tells me his health is not all it could be, and recommends that he be removed to England with all possible speed."

Claire nodded, pacing beside him on the walk toward the gazing ball. "He informed us of that last night, as well. Alice is the only one free to take him home, but she is reluctant to leave the safety of friends, to say nothing of your sentries ... despite the excitement lately."

"I have confirmed that the medallions belong to the Famiglia Rosa," he told her, his voice dropping although they were alone. "Those emblems stand for Venice, Naples, and Rome—the three cities ruled by the brothers di Alba. Frankly, I should feel more comfortable if she did go. It was clear that their target was *Swan*— and that the price on her head has not been removed."

Claire could not bear it. To lose both her friends at once?

But of course she must not be selfish. Ian would do better in his own house, with his own physician, and Alice would be far safer in England than she appeared to be here.

"You are quite right," she said. "Now that the repairs to the fuselage are finished, I will speak with her and find out when she can pull up ropes. We cannot risk any further danger to either of them."

"And what of you? You will be sad to lose your friends, but as you say, it will be for the best. And you have much to occupy your mind here."

Claire took a breath and leaped into the metaphorical breach. "Yes, I have been very busy with documenting improvements to the processes and equipment in the Flight Development Department."

"Have you?" His brows rose—and since he had been looking into the gazing ball, his reflection seemed all circles and curves. He straightened to face her. "Are improvements necessary?"

"Oh, yes," she said, rather more bluntly than perhaps she should have. "I am not meant for fetching tea and sweeping floors, I am afraid. So I fill the hours with fixing things and then documenting what I have done. Sadly, though, I have been asked to cease and desist. Apparently the managing director does not appreciate more paper arriving on his desk."

She smiled, hoping he would smile, too, but he merely gazed at her, puzzled.

"And what of the department head?" he asked. "Should not the notice of these improvements be directed to him?"

"They were, but after I found my reports in the rubbish bin, I'm afraid that in a fit of pique I sent them to the managing director."

"Did you?"

He might have sounded a *little* more encouraging. "He called me into his office earlier in the week and, well, I shan't be writing any more reports." She brightened. "But he did not tell me I must stop improving things, so that is some comfort."

"What improvements are we speaking of?"

"The cable that runs between the engine room and the navigation gondola in the A5 model, for instance," she said eagerly. "I spliced in a communications wire so that commands might be given simultaneously, as we do in the newer models. Such a simple adjustment, yet so much more usefulness and efficiency! And then—"

"Claire, let me understand you correctly. You have made engineering changes to parts that are already in production?"

"Yes, because—"

"But this must not be."

She stopped walking, and at the drag on his arm, he stopped as well. "Why not? I have documented everything, despite my so-called superiors' choosing to ignore it."

"Changes such as these must come from the Office of Quality Control on the third floor and be disseminated correctly."

"I sent them to the third floor for that very purpose. And they were tossed in the rubbish bin."

"That is because you are a junior engineer."

"Then they are fools. Had you treated my modifications in such a manner, we should both be dead under a snowdrift in the Canadas."

"That was different."

"How so?"

"Lives were at stake."

"If the A5 plummets to earth because the engineers and the bridge cannot communicate efficiently, lives would be similarly at stake." With an effort, she remembered his many kindnesses, and attempted to rein in her distress at his lack of understanding.

"My ships do not plummet to the earth, and that is because men of talent and skill take care that they should not."

"But sir, what of my talent and skill?"

"It is a raw, untried talent that needs cultivation and discipline," he told her kindly. "It needs to be tended by men of greater knowledge, who have come up through the ranks and learned just as you will learn."

"So Herr Brucker said."

"I am glad to hear it." He gazed at her. "I know how you feel, Claire."

Did he? Could he possibly—a man with a Blood heritage, who managed his own empire without let or hindrance, with the possible exception of the odd command from the Kaiser himself?

"I once burned with ambition, too," he went on, "and fate conspired to place me where that flame would do the most good. There is a reason the hierarchy operates so well at the Zeppelin Airship Works, my dear. You will see. You will rise quickly through the ranks and prove to one and all that you deserve every promotion—and that your improvements ought to be taken seriously."

At last the truth was borne in upon her. "So you can do nothing to change my situation? I cannot work on the automaton intelligence system, as I had expected when I accepted the post?"

"If you were to do so, you would be like that rose there." He pointed to a spindly-looking specimen. "It has not had the benefit of sunlight on all its petals, and is therefore lopsided. We do not want our best engineers to be one-sided, only working on projects that appeal to them. Our best engineers can turn a hand to any project in the hangar. Can manage any ship, any engine. That is what I see for you, Claire, if you can only be patient."

What could she do but nod, smile at him with affection, and squeeze his arm in thanks for his encouragement?

It was consequently a very good thing that he did not see her once she regained her own bedroom, where she flung a cushion at the wall with such energy that it split all along the seam. Feathers drifted gently to the floor.

They had not the means to fly any longer, either.

6

Restless and dissatisfied, and unwilling to take the customary Sunday afternoon nap, Claire walked out to *Swan*. Andrew had gone to call upon a colleague, and the girls were walking along the river with Tigg and Jake. The walk across the park did her good, and she was able to board with something approaching calm, if not good humor.

"Claire," Alice said with some surprise, coming along the gangway from the saloon, having clearly felt the slight dip and recovery in the ship's trim that told her someone had boarded. "I didn't expect to see you—I thought you might go with Lizzie and Maggie."

"And provide an unwelcome fifth wheel to that merry gig? I think not."

"I hardly think you'd be unwelcome."

"I'd rather spend a little time with you. How is your patient?"

The corners of Alice's blue eyes pinched a little, and Claire felt a dart of anxiety. "Come and see for yourself."

Ian, while dressed in trousers, clean shirt, and waistcoat, was sitting on the edge of his bunk, gazing at something invisible on the floor beyond the hands that hung between his knees. He looked up almost with relief when Claire peered in.

"Claire. You look like an English garden."

Surprised, she smoothed her green walking skirt with its wide band of floral embroidery at the hem. Perhaps her color was a little high, both from emotion and from exercise. "Thank you, Ian. I have come to ask Alice to take a turn around the park with me, but perhaps you are pining for gardens yourself and would like to join us?"

"Around the park?" The expression of gallant politeness he wore cracked so suddenly that Claire saw it for the sham it was. "You ladies must go. A gentleman can only be an intruder in such a party."

"Not likely," Alice said. "You need to get outside, Ian. You're beginning to frighten me."

"I do not wish to go," he said stiffly. "I have—things to take care of here."

Alice's chin firmed in a way that almost made Claire feel sorry for the poor man. "Nothing will happen to you in broad daylight. If two ladies can walk around the park, then you can, too."

"I do not fear something happening to me." He almost sounded like the old Ian.

But he was not.

Claire knelt next to him—for he had not risen on her

entrance—and laid a hand on his knee. "Please, Ian. I have a matter to discuss with Alice, and I would value your opinion also. It is a lovely day—and who knows how much longer this weather will hold?"

In his eyes, she observed that his fear had a death grip on all the rules of gentlemanly behavior. Valiantly he struggled, silent and still, until generations of good breeding won out. "Very well. Give me a moment to locate my jacket and I will join you in the saloon."

Alice gripped her hand silently as they retreated down the corridor. "Thank you," she breathed when they reached the main saloon, which would have comfortable chairs and possibly even a dining table some day. "He hasn't been off the ship since that night. I'm at my wits' end."

"My dear friend, I am so sorry." Claire stood with her in a warm beam of sunlight falling through the viewing port ... which had the unfortunate effect of showing her just how little sleep Alice must have had. "I've left him entirely to your care and have been so wrapped up in my own concerns that I've hardly spared a thought for anyone else's. I am ashamed."

"You have nothing to be ashamed of. He's a grown man. I'm just so worried." Her voice dropped. "It isn't natural. He's not the same person he used to be, and I don't know how to bring him back."

"Perhaps time is the only thing that will heal him?"

Alice shook her head, and a curl fell out of today's attempt at a chignon. "Jake is worried, too. He says there was a man in that prison who went stark raving mad, and it began in just this way."

"But Ian is far from the prison, and he was incarcerated less than a week."

A GENTLEMAN OF MEANS

"For some men, I think, even a day of being treated as less than an animal, of being starved and beaten and expected to work for hours and hours in a situation where one false move could mean death, would be too much." Alice's lips trembled before she swallowed and regained control. "He is a baronet, Claire. A man of renown, given respect across the skies. Such treatment as he received would have been inconceivable until he was faced with the reality of it. I am very much afraid that being witness to the cruelty this world is capable of has damaged his soul."

Claire gazed at her, at the grief in her eyes, at the ravages of a sleepless night—perhaps more than one— on her face. At the softness of her mouth as she spoke of him.

And suddenly every suspicion she had ever had on the subject of Alice and Captain Hollys formed a conviction.

"Alice ... can it be ... do you have feelings for Ian? Finer feelings that those of a colleague or even of a friend, companion, and nurse?"

Alice's face turned bleak. "Am I so transparent?"

"No. I only this moment realized it, and we have been together for weeks."

"You mustn't tell anyone," she said urgently. "Especially him. You mustn't tell him."

"Whyever not?" Alice loved Captain Hollys. Why, this was wonderful. If ever two brave, capable, stubborn, impossible people were meant for one another, it was they.

"Because—because—oh, you know why, Claire!"

"I do not. Enlighten me at once." Claire barely restrained herself from waltzing her friend about the saloon.

"Because—"

"I do apologize, ladies, for making you wait so long," the subject of their conversation said, stepping over the raised sill of the doorway. "I could not find a hat to save my life, so Alice, I have appropriated one of yours. I hope that is all right?"

"Of course," Alice said so breathlessly that Claire was sure she had no idea what she was agreeing to. "Shall we be off?"

Alice would have gone on ahead had not Claire had the foresight to tuck an arm into both of theirs, which placed her companionably between them and gave neither the opportunity to escape. They set a leisurely pace down the linden walk, which led away from the fountain and the airfield, and would branch into two directions about half a mile farther on. She fully intended to make them walk the entire perimeter—or as long as it took to put some color in their cheeks and find at least a little relief from the fears that beset them both.

After some one hundred yards of remarking upon foliage and several species of birds, Alice became restless and pulled away. But at least she did not leave them.

"What was it you wanted to talk about, Claire?"

Propriety dictated that she should release Ian's arm, as well, which she did, but that did not prevent her from bending to look at a leaf, and then resuming her pace with Alice now in the middle. What a good thing these gravel walks were wide enough to accommodate a carriage ... or a threesome.

"I hope you will give me your counsel," she said, "and then I hope you will allow me to give you mine."

"That seems a fair bargain," Ian said. "How may we help?"

A GENTLEMAN OF MEANS

So Claire told them—of her reports, the rubbish bins, being called upstairs into the managing director's office, and finally, of her conversation with the count earlier in the rose garden. "I am finding it very difficult to resign myself to a career so different from what I expected," she concluded on a sigh. "I hoped you might tell me either that my expectations were wildly exaggerated and I should fit in as others have done before me, or that I ought to tender my resignation at once so that someone more fit for the post might have it."

"Well, there isn't anyone more fit for the post that I can see," Alice remarked. "There are probably many more less fit."

"I speak more of a fitness of the mind and temperament, I suppose," Claire said. "Certainly there are many junior engineers graduating from the university who are perfectly capable of sweeping floors and making tea, and have most of the skills I possess."

"I doubt that last point." Alice's grin seemed to encompass their like-mindedness, and reminded Claire that the two of them had perfected the automaton intelligence system together without assistance of any kind from managing directors or memoranda.

"So now you are on the horns of a dilemma," Ian mused. "You have arranged your life, and that of the girls and Mr. Malvern, to support a career with Zeppelin, and now you wonder if you have made a monumental mistake."

The man did not mince words, even in his emotional extremity. "In a nutshell, yes," Claire said with a fair approximation of grace. "Have I? What do you think? I value your opinions."

"What does Andrew say?" Alice asked. "For of

course you must have discussed this with him."

"I have, yes. And he told me that to be in my situation would be insupportable. He has not the temperament to be happy in a hierarchy, preferring to be the master of his own ship."

"I cannot blame him there," Ian put in.

"What do you mean?" Alice demanded. "You work in a hierarchy yourself. More than one—first, the Royal Aeronautic Corps, and second, your own family and way of life."

For a moment, he seemed taken aback at being thus contradicted, but then Claire realized he was acknowledging the truth. "You are quite right," he said. "It is strange I never thought of it in those terms before. Perhaps I am comfortable in the Corps because I am used to categorizing people according to rank—and therefore it is no hardship to categorize myself."

"But I come from the same background, and I do not," Claire said. "So that is no indication of suitability."

"But how can there be only two choices?" Alice said. "One's life isn't like that path up there, with either a right turn or a left. Which will we take, by the way?"

"Let us go to the right, through the copse," Claire suggested.

She was half afraid that Ian would turn back, but he was still grappling with the question Alice had posed, and passed under the branches without difficulty. "Of course there are not merely two choices for you," he agreed. "To return to London or to stay and be unhappy—such cannot be your only options."

"Let me tell you what I thought, but did not want to consider further," Claire told them. "I could do as

Andrew does, and strike out on my own. Metaphorically speaking. Of course I would not leave my friends and my home."

"What's wrong with that?" Alice said. "It seems sensible. Look at me. I would die in that place, even though it fascinates me in an odd way—rather like watching an enormous difference engine and wondering how on earth all those moving parts produce an answer in the end. But the problem with being on your own is that you tend not to know where your next meal is coming from. Just ask Jake."

"I could always fall back on cowboy poker if I were an utter failure."

"Let us hope it would not come to that," Ian said. "So are you resolved, then?"

"How can I be?" Claire asked in despair as they paced under the maples, red and orange leaves burning as they fell through the dappled, low afternoon light. "How can I renege on the bargain I made with Count von Zeppelin? How can I face his disappointment in me?"

"How can you pay back four years' worth of tuition?" Alice asked a nearby fir.

"The family would be happy to make you a loan to do so," Ian said at once. "It would be an honor to assist you."

"Thank you, Ian, but I have resources that would be up to the task if the count were willing. But somehow I feel that our friendship and camaraderie would end were I to treat his gift in such a manner. He believed—still believes—that he is helping me to make my dream come true."

"But what if it turns out to be a nightmare?"

Alice had just voiced Claire's secret fear. "A very good question. I wonder if I have the fortitude to find out the answer."

Ian bent to pick up a fallen stick, and swished at a pile of leaves. "We have not been very successful in counseling you, have we? Perhaps you will be better at counseling us."

Claire took the cue, though she and Alice ran the risk of walking back alone. "I understand that the count's physician recommended you return to England, Ian."

The stick whistled through the air and thwacked the leaves. "He did."

"And shall you take this recommendation in the spirit in which it was given?"

"I shall not."

"Might one ask why, when there is nothing holding you here, and there might be many benefits to being at home, with familiar things around you and all the care that others can give?"

"I do not need to be cared for." *Thwack.* "I am not ill."

"You are not entirely well, either," Alice pointed out. "You and I have had this conversation."

"And I say now what I said then—I am on temporary leave, and when that is ended, I shall return to my command. When *Lady Lucy* goes to Scotland, I expect."

"When is that?" This was the first Claire had heard of it, though she had wondered more than once when the Corps would demand that its captain return to its service.

"Next week."

Alice made a derisive sound rather like the air rushing out of a balloon. "That's far too soon. You're not fit for duty—and I'm speaking as a fellow captain, not as your blasted nursemaid, so don't give me that face."

"I have never asked you to be my nursemaid."

"Your friend, then, who comes in the night when you scream, and who picks you up when your knees buckle."

Ian, whom Claire had never heard use vulgar language, used it now, with relish and some variety. "Must you say such things in front of Claire?"

"I have stood with you and been shot at for my pains," Claire pointed out calmly, choosing to ignore the outburst and stick to the point. "I do not think either of us is easily shocked or dismayed by simple human responses to dreadful events. You must not be ashamed. We are your friends, and you deserve our loyalty and respect."

"You would not say so if you knew the weakness— this *wretched* weakness that overwhelms me." He threw the stick away with such force it broke against the corrugated bark of an oak.

"My point exactly," Claire said, taking his arm now. "You must allow your mind and heart to heal. Some wounds of that kind need as much time as a broken bone. Even more, perhaps, since one cannot observe their physical improvement."

"But the Dunsmuirs need me. And Tigg. What of him? He has his career to think of."

"There is nothing preventing his return to his duties," Claire said. "But I strongly advise you to listen to the doctor and return to Hollys Park until you have recovered."

"In solitude. What an appealing prospect."

"Certainly not," Alice said immediately. "Jake and I might have repaired the bullet holes in *Swan*'s fuselage, but her general refit has yet to be finished. It's not going to happen overnight—or even by Christmas, I suspect. If you have a field handy, we can fly you home and then you can keep helping us to put the old girl back together, just as we've been doing here."

Oh, bless Alice! What an excellent plan! Claire flung her arms about her and hugged her hard. "What a friend you are, to be sure." For of course nothing would then stand in the way of Ian's seeing her excellent qualities. Her maternal side would come out, her softness and vulnerability, and he couldn't help but fall in love with her.

Ian gazed at Alice as she walked beside him, Claire on her other side. "You would do that, Alice? It seems quite above and beyond. Why, it would mean leaving Claire and Andrew and your other friends here—though I believe I can safely promise that no one will be shooting at you at Hollys Park."

"With those villains dead, and no one to tell the Doge I've pulled up ropes, maybe I won't need to look over my shoulder any longer," Alice said. "Anyway, pigeons fly just as fast between here and England as they do anywhere else. We'll all be in London for the wedding, if nothing else, and that's only five weeks away."

Five weeks! Good heavens. And what had Claire managed to accomplish thus far? Deciding that she must really order her wedding dress was a far cry from actually having it in hand, which any other bride-to-be would have done by now. Being married in a laboratory coat would become a certainty if she did not set plans in motion immediately.

"That is true," Ian admitted.

Claire could smell success in the offing. "And you are all invited down to Gwynn Place for Twelfth Night, so we might be together again there. The girls are anxious to see their families, and Claude is coming from Paris."

"That's quite a long honeymoon, Claire," Alice pointed out.

"What do you mean?"

"Won't you have to be back here to work?"

Claire stared at her, trying to puzzle this out. "I'm sorry, Alice, I feel rather stupid. I don't understand."

"Will you be able to get so many weeks' holiday from Zeppelin, is what I mean—for a honeymoon that includes a trip to Cornwall?"

It had never once occurred to Claire that this might be necessary. "I must ask permission?"

"I expect so. Isn't that how these things work?"

"I have no idea. Is it like requesting land leave from the Corps?"

"That is simply a matter of clearing it with one's superiors and sending in a form," Ian said "I expect it's much the same here. One just cannot cast off and leave others to do one's duty."

"Oh, dear." What a depressing prospect this was. How could one's freedom be constrained to such a degree? How was one to bear it? Why, she might as well call herself a servant, paid for her skill but at the beck and call of anyone in the hierarchy above her, no matter whether they had earned her respect or not.

How, she wondered as the path took a turning and they could once again see the palace dreaming in the distance, seeming to float upon a mist of smoke from burning leaves, had the Lady of Devices been reduced to this?

And by her own hand, too.

7

They had nearly crossed the park and were close enough
to the lake that the swans had begun to swim toward
them, when Alice pointed to a figure running across the
airfield. "There's Benny Stringfellow."

"Oh dear," Claire said. "I do hope nothing has happened at home. Is that a message in his hand?"

Young Mr. Stringfellow ran up, a bit of lined paper
crumpled in his fist, and panted, "Lady, a pigeon. It
come to the palace addressed to 'is lordship, but it's got
Alice's name on it so one of the footmen brought it out
to *Swan*."

"Thank you, Mr. Stringfellow. It was kind of you to
bring it to us so promptly."

Alice unfolded the note and scanned its few lines.
The breath rushed from her lungs and she clutched

Claire's shoulder. Wordlessly, she handed it to Ian and both he and Claire bent their heads over it.

"Great Caesar's ghost!" Ian said after a moment. "I cannot believe it!"

"I can believe that our dear friend has been kidnapped much sooner than I could believe she had deliberately left us to die." Claire clasped her hands and lifted her face to the sun. "Oh, I am so happy to know she did not!"

"Claire, you are missing the point." Ian folded the message and handed it back. "Did you not see the word *abducted?*"

"I most certainly did." She turned a sunny smile upon him. "But I see much more than that. Our friend is restored to us, whole and well. We are free to care for her without let or hindrance—without doubt and without anger." She took the paper once more and read again Gloria's desperate appeal for help. "Truly, I am happier than I have been since we stepped off the stone pier in Venice and boarded *Neptune's Fancy.*"

Ian and Alice exchanged a glance. "And the doctor believes *my* mind to be touched," he muttered.

Genuine happiness welled up in Alice's heart, not because of the first real news of Gloria—she had been abducted, yes, but at least she was alive and had not deliberately left Claire and Andrew, Ian and Jake under the sea to die—but because Ian had made a joke.

A *joke.* Perhaps there was hope for his recovery after all.

One step at a time. That was how you crossed a desert. And lately Alice had felt as though she were crossing a vast, inhospitable expanse since they had made their escape from Venice. These days working with Ian on *Swan* had been the finest kind of torture. She had treasured his confidences, despaired at his depression, and day after day, been the one to wake him from his nightmares and soothe him when he wept.

She had never before considered herself the kind of woman who might soothe a fevered brow. You didn't find many fevered brows in engine rooms and honky-tonks, and the only kind of fever she had run into in Resolution had usually been brought on by the morning after the night before.

And yet, with Ian it had seemed natural. Or maybe caring for him had been the natural part, and dipping the rag in cold water had merely been the outward expression of it.

Whatever the case, it was nice to be needed. To be the one he looked for when he woke, confused and sweating, as though the sight of her face was all he had to anchor himself to reality.

When the doctor had told her that in his opinion, Ian should be returned home to England at once, she had nearly lost control of her emotions and begun to cry. Because if that happened, she was pretty certain she'd never see him again. They might cross flight paths once in a while, since she was still contracted with the Dunsmuirs, but other than that, what reason would a baronet have to keep up a friendship with a pirate's daughter?

Bless Claire for backing her up when Alice had broached the solution she'd hardly dared hope for. Especially when it sounded as though her life wasn't exactly going like a penny clockwork, either.

They had almost reached *Swan* and *Athena*, their steps quickening with urgency even though the afternoon slumbered its way toward evening.

"What do you know of Gibraltar, Ian?" Claire asked. "I have never been there, never seen it, other than illustrations in magazines."

Ian seemed to have been considering his facts already, if his thoughtful expression was any indication. "It is the largest airfield in the Mediterranean," he said, "and is also a dockyard of enormous proportions. Practically all traffic coming from the Colonies into the Mediterranean, the Levant, and Africa puts in there for supplies and clearances. For that reason, there is a lot of wealth floating about—and consequently, the criminal element thrives as well."

"Imagine Gloria being taken against her will and traveling under the sea all these weeks," Alice said. "I can't think of any fate more awful."

"I can," Ian whispered, then turned his head away and cleared his throat.

Alice could have kicked herself.

After a moment, Ian went on, "If by some means she managed to escape long enough to send this message, and was not recaptured and returned to *Neptune's Fancy* or another vessel, I have grave doubts about her safety. The docks and airfield are not a place where a gently bred young lady may go about alone. I would even advise Tigg and Jake to go together, were they to visit."

Alice would think twice about wandering around there alone as well; Gloria was a resourceful young lady, but even the most resourceful could be set upon, injured, or even killed in less time than it took to think about it.

"We must send a message to her father immediately," Ian said. "If anyone has the resources to find a young woman in a shipping port, it is he."

"He probably has the authorities there in the palm of his hand anyway," Alice agreed. "If you grease enough palms, no one is going to notice how many unregistered undersea dirigibles you have swimming about."

"But ..." Claire's forehead creased a little in a frown. "Does it not strike you as odd that she should write to Alice—since she did not know I was alive—in her desperation, and not to her father? I never thought of it before this moment, but why should she do so?"

"Because I'm her friend?" Alice suggested. "It's clear that her forced desertion of you and Ian in Venice was weighing heavily on her mind If she only had a moment to send a message, sending it to me would kill two birds with one stone. She could reassure me as to her motives, and ask for help all at once."

"Of course she would have meant for us to notify her father as well," Ian said. "That stands to reason."

"Does it?" Claire asked. Alice could practically see the wheels turning behind that thoughtful brow. "Unless she feared her father was somehow involved."

"Nonsense," Ian said. "You have shared his letters with us. They do not have the tone of a man who has engineered the kidnapping of his own daughter. To what end?"

"To get her out of Venice secretly?" Alice ventured. "What if the Famiglia Rosa was blackmailing Meriwether-Astor and he had her spirited away so they couldn't get their hands on her?"

"But why not tell her, then?" Claire asked. "Though the matter of leaving us to manage our own escape from the lagoon must still be accounted for."

"I should say so," Alice said. "If the *Fancy*'s captain had orders to get Gloria away, though, he wouldn't stand upon too much ceremony in his departure. I wouldn't, if I were he."

"But then why agree to take a pleasure party at all?" Claire asked. "Why not tell us it was not convenient, see Gloria aboard, and then quit the country? No, I am convinced there must be some deeper motive afoot here. It would seem almost as though Gloria does not trust her own father enough to reveal her whereabouts to him."

"I do not believe it," Ian said. "We saw no sign of that in Venice—they seemed civil enough. When you write to tell him about Gibraltar, I am sure that it will all become clear. And now I believe we must change for dinner. The sun has quite gone and the lamps have been lit."

Claire bade them farewell and walked off toward *Athena* instead of to her suite in the palace, her head bent in thought.

And watch as carefully as she might through the viewing ports, Alice saw no sign of a pigeon's departure.

She wasn't sure what worried her most—that Claire was going to tell Meriwether-Astor his daughter had been kidnapped … or that she had no intention of doing so at all.

*

Rather abruptly, Claire realized she had boarded *Athena* while hardly being aware she had done so. She was nearly perfectly certain that she had intended to return to the palace to change for dinner, and yet here she was, wandering into the comforting embrace of her own ship and climbing the stairs into the saloon.

Andrew looked up from the disarray he had created on the dining table, which he was using as a temporary office until they found a suitable house for their first home. "Is it time to dress for dinner?"

In order to have a home together, one must be married first. And to do that, one must plan a wedding. Oh, why could they not simply take a steambus down to the city registry office and be married there? Or why had she not delegated the wedding preparations to her mother and Sir Richard, who had offered Gwynn Place as the natural location for the upcoming nuptials as soon as she and Andrew had become engaged?

Because she enjoyed her own way too much, that was why.

In her joy to see her only daughter married—even if it was to a man with neither title nor property—Mama would make a spectacle of the entire affair. Twelve bridesmaids from the neighboring families, enough flowers to keep an airship on the ground without benefit of ropes, and a wedding breakfast that would pay off every social obligation she had managed to acquire in the five years since she had returned to Cornwall a widow.

Claire realized belatedly that Andrew had spoken, but before she could formulate a reply, he said, "Dearest, what is the reason for such a sigh, and such a downcast expression?" He let his drawing roll up and crossed the saloon to take her in his arms. "Something has happened, hasn't it?"

She laid her forehead on his shoulder. "Several things—one of them being the fact that there are five weeks between now and our wedding, and I do not have a dress, to say nothing of a church, flowers, or so much as a biscuit for the wedding breakfast."

By his stillness, she sensed that she had surprised him. "I had no idea that this was presenting a difficulty."

"We should have let Mama take everything in hand when she offered. I fear I have been rash—and arrogant—and self-aggrandizing, Andrew."

"Nonsense. Rashness I will grant you, but not the others. Is it so necessary to have a dress, flowers, and a wedding breakfast?"

"Well, unless we propose to elope to Gretna Green, one usually observes the social niceties. We have not even inquired of Reverend Peabody if the Belgrave Square church is available on Christmas Eve morning. If we were to be married at Gwynn Place, we could have used the chapel on the estate and not even had to ask."

"We still can, if that would remove one worry from your mind."

"But what of our London friends?"

"What of them? Load them all into *Athena*'s cargo bay and take them down to Cornwall."

"Andrew, be serious." Between the uncertainty of Gloria's situation and her own failings as a bride, Claire felt very close to tears.

And Andrew saw it. "My darling," he said softly, "I cannot believe that our wedding is causing you such distress. Nor can I allow it. We will be married in the registry office here in Munich, and people may throw us as many parties as they like when we return to London as man and wife—as long as you do not have to arrange them."

She raised her head. "Do you mean it? Not have a church wedding?" Then she collapsed against him once more. "Mama would never live it down. The gossip in London would be dreadful. We must have that at the very least."

"Then we will, if that will make you happy. At Gwynn Place?"

"No," she said slowly. "What do you think of the mermaid's chapel in Baie des Sirenes? The one where Maggie was baptized as a baby?"

He paused for a moment, as though his thoughts had been taking a different path entirely. "It is very small."

"Intimate."

"We could not invite many people."

"Your mother and mine. Snouts, of course, and the children from Carrick House. The Polgarths. And Alice, Jake, and Ian."

"Ian?" Now he did more than merely pause. He set her away from him just enough to gaze into her face. "Is that not rather unkind, since he once cherished hopes along that line?"

"Not at all." She lowered her voice to a whisper, in case Jake and Tigg had returned to the ship. "Alice is in love with him, and I believe he is half in love with her. He just does not know it yet."

Had Andrew been in the dreadful habit of wearing a monocle, it would have fallen out in his surprise. "Are you sure?"

"She has confided in me—but you must not let on that I have broken her confidence. I have never been a matchmaker, but weddings, you know, are an excellent environment for experiments of that kind."

"My word." He took her hand. "I believe that when

we are eighty, you will still continue to surprise me."

"It keeps life interesting," she said, feeling rather better, and kissing him in thanks. "Speaking of interesting—and appalling—this came to the palace and was delivered to Alice just now." She produced Gloria's note from her pocket and handed it to him.

When he had read it, his hazel eyes met hers with concern and a measure of shock. "Abducted?"

Rapidly, she told him of her discussions with Ian and Alice, and the conclusion she herself had reached. "Do you think I am completely mad? Do you think it possible that the reason she wrote to Alice rather than her father is because she does not trust him?"

He fell into his chair rather suddenly, and she pulled up another next to him. "I feel we must certainly entertain the possibility," he said at last. "But Claire, Ian may be right. The letters we have received from Meriwether-Astor are the letters of a father frantic with worry for his daughter. We have no right to interfere— or to hesitate in sending him news of her."

"But what if that is not her wish?"

"Then she would certainly have said so in her note."

"What if she had no time? One doesn't always, you know, in the midst of an escape."

"You would certainly be the authority on that subject. But dearest, think how you would feel if it were Maggie or Lizzie—if those in Cornwall or the Baie des Sirenes had known of their whereabouts and deliberately not told you."

"I would have been beside myself. More than I was at the time."

"Then ...?" He set the note on his pencil box and took her hands. "There comes a point at which you must realize you cannot save everyone, my darling. You are the most loyal and brave of friends, but this is not your fight. It is Gerald Meriwether-Astor's."

"But—"

"He is her father, and regardless of what we might read into or out of this note, he has a right to know of her situation. And goodness knows he has the resources to find her and return her to safety."

"But—"

"Claire." He squeezed her hands with gentleness, and she raised her gaze to his. "Promise me you will write to him tonight. It is the right thing to do, and in your heart you know it."

Logic and every familial expectation told her his counsel was sound. But what if logic was wrong? What if there was some missing bit of information that would make everything clear—and in its absence any such action would endanger Gloria?

The grip upon her fingers became yet firmer. "Claire? Tell me you are not thinking of doing something rash."

"I am not." And she was not.

Yet.

"Family ties aside, you are in no position to act in any case. We have been through this before, when Jake was in danger."

"That turned out well," she pointed out. "It was manifestly the right thing to do."

"Because Jake had no one to help him. The cases are different. Gloria does—in spades. Besides, think of your career, if nothing else. The count might have acceded to the last sudden departure, but I would not lay a silver *schilling* on his being willing to do so a second time, not a month later."

At this, she released his hands and stood. Crossing to the viewing port—which showed her nothing but her own shape in the reflected lamplight—she said, "Perhaps that would not be such a bad thing."

"I beg your pardon?"

"If I were to pull up ropes and go in search of Gloria, and he did sack me. Perhaps that would not be such a calamity."

"Good heavens." He rose, too. "Certainly it would be—not least because all my efforts on your behalf would have gone for nothing."

"What do you mean?"

He unrolled the drawing on which he had been working for days now, and weighted its corners with paperweights—two bolts, the pencil box, and a whiskey glass—that sat on the table for just such a purpose. Wordlessly, she gazed at it.

"Andrew," she breathed at last. "It is the Helios Membrane for *Athena*'s fuselage."

"Precisely."

"Have you been stealing glimpses at my engineering notebook?"

"I have," he said brazenly. "Do you approve?"

What a relief it was to leave her troubled thoughts for a moment and concentrate upon something purely theoretical. She pointed to a cluster of lines. "I believe this collector ought to go on the top of the fuselage, not in the bow."

"In the bow, it will be closer to the controls of the navigation gondola."

"But it will be less exposed to the sun."

He considered it, then nodded. "You are quite right.

This posed some difficulty in the case of the steam locomotive, but of course the vessels are quite different. I will make the adjustment. At this rate I must remember to buy stock in pencils."

She turned and hugged him about the ribs, pressing her face to his shoulder once more. "You are lovely to do these drawings for me. Thank you."

"I look forward to the day when you can present them to the count. To see his face will be worth the price of admission."

Instead of replying, she hugged him again.

For she had grave doubts that the future she contemplated held any such day.

8

"Miss Meriwether-Astor," Captain Hayes said on the other side of her prison door, "you will be relieved to know that we are leaving *Neptune's Fancy* here and taking to the air. Gather your things, please, and be ready to depart in ten minutes."

The air? Ten minutes?

The air!

Gloria had been locked in this noisome cabin for only twenty-four hours, but there was an enormous difference between sleeping in it and being able to open the door, and attempting to sleep with the knowledge that no matter how hard you banged upon it or how loud a fuss you made, no one would unlock it until the times appointed. She had been allowed out to make use of the privy and to eat with Captain Hayes and the officers, as before, but that was all. Afterward, she was marched back in and endured once more the sound of the bolt crashing home.

It had only been twenty-four hours, and yet she had been reduced to utter gratitude at the prospect of another prison, as long as it wasn't this one.

How pathetic. Claire would never behave like this. She would have picked the lock with a hairpin and swum to safety ... or at the very least have secreted a paring knife about her person to be used at the first opportunity. Gloria had tried both, and succeeded with neither.

Accordingly, ten minutes later, she stood ready, the hated walking suit and blouse donned once more, her hair neatly coiled in its customary braided coronet, her hat pinned upon it. This time she had taken the precaution of stashing her money and few valuables inside her corset, so she need carry nothing in case the opportunity presented itself once more to escape.

Four bathynauts escorted her to the chamber under the bow where one of the *Fancy's chaloupes* bobbed, its top open to receive passengers. Captain Hayes was already within, handing her down into the round body of the vessel as though she actually had a choice as to whether or not to place her hand in his.

"Am I permitted to ask why the change in prison?" she inquired with icy politeness.

"Certainly," he said. "Do sit down on this side, with me. As you know, these little vessels will not trim unless the passengers' weight is distributed evenly."

"Yes, I know. I assume we are going ashore in a location inhospitable to the *Fancy*?"

"You assume correctly." The remaining bathynauts

boarded, and then the one with an officer's bars on his collar ignited the *chaloupe*'s steam system and minutes later, it submerged. Instantly they were bathed in a wavering green light that told Gloria the water was shallow and the seabed sandy. Her knowledge of geography was greater now than it ever had been in school, but she could not imagine what coastline in the Mediterranean might match this description.

Except one.

"Have we not left Gibraltar?" In the time she had been locked in, they might have gained the west side of the Iberian Peninsula, at least.

Captain Hayes gazed at her with admiration. "In fact we have not. We had rather a little excitement with the port, you see, upon the *Fancy*'s being recognized. As you know, your father's ships are not permitted in any English port, and Gibraltar being a territory, the authorities were anxious to uphold Her Majesty's will in this matter. So we are forced to come in through the back door, as it were, and approach the airfield with rather more subtlety."

"You are going to beach us in the *chaloupe*, then, and hope that you can withdraw before you are discovered." She nodded, as if this were business as usual.

Inside, hope was bubbling like a cauldron. If she could only escape and smuggle herself aboard a ship bound for the Kingdom of Prussia, she could bring herself that much closer to her friends. Surely there would be a vessel flying the Iron Cross here. It was almost impossible that there should not be. Oh, this was good news indeed!

"We are," the captain said. "An airship is waiting to take us to England, where you will be accommodated with every comfort."

"What part of England?"

But he only smiled that charming, self-deprecating, maddening smile that conveyed nothing but regret at his inability to answer.

Gloria gritted her teeth and pinned her hopes on the next few minutes.

But to her dismay, the phalanx of bathynauts disembarked with her once the *chaloupe* had trundled its way up the beach. And there, on the extreme edge of the airfield closest to them, was moored the most unremarkable, plain, innocuous airship she had ever seen. It flew the dragon of St. George, however, which meant an unremarkable exit and an easy arrival in England.

The bathynauts had grips of iron as they took her arms and escorted her up the gangway. Not even a second's opportunity did she have to run—or to scream, for that matter, because the stiff offshore wind blew any sounds other than the flap of canvas and the singing of ropes out to sea.

She was shown into a cabin, cheerfully informed by Captain Hayes that dinner was at eight o'clock, and before she could even judge the width of the porthole and whether she would have to disrobe before worming her way out of it and dropping the considerable distance to the ground, she felt the floor pressing up against the soles of her feet.

"Blast!" The very word choked in her throat with disappointment as she pressed her nose to the isinglass. Gibraltar and the dozens of possibilities for escape moored in her airfield dropped away at a dizzying rate and soon all she could see were empty expanses of sky.

It was, she supposed, better than empty expanses of

water, but not by much.

A polite knock came at the door.

"Yes? I am still here, unfortunately."

To her surprise, Captain Hayes leaned in. "Are you comfortable, Miss Meriwether-Astor? May we provide anything for you?"

"The porthole is too small," she remarked, rather snappishly. "What are you doing aboard? Have you abandoned your undersea command so easily?"

He laid a hand upon his chest. "You dishonor me. But no, my remit is to see you safely to England. My first officer now has command of *Neptune's Fancy*."

"I wonder what he will have to say to my father when he returns to the fleet. One is usually allowed last words before one is shot."

"Oh, as to that, *Neptune's Fancy* will not be returning to the fleet. As you so rightly point out, that would be dangerous for the crew."

"So you are stealing the undersea dirigible as well as the daughter? What a callous lot you are."

"I should prefer the word *practical*. The *Fancy* has her uses and she will serve honorably in the execution of them."

"What does that mean? Are you going to use her to sink the other vessels?"

But he had done humoring her. "We expect to moor tomorrow evening, so we have only tonight to enjoy each other's company at dinner. Remember, eight o'clock."

She turned her back on him. If she had hoped the cut direct would cause him to withdraw, she was again disappointed.

"And since an airship, unlike an undersea vessel, offers no opportunity for an escape while under way," he said, "your cabin will not be locked unless you choose to lock it yourself. Good afternoon, Miss Meriwether-Astor."

The door closed behind him and she waited, but he was as good as his word. No lock turned from outside.

She turned back to the viewing port where, far below, she could see the sere, wrinkled outline of the Iberian coast. Her stomach seemed to hollow out with grief. There went her last chance of regaining control of her life, of returning to the people she had come to regard as her friends—or at least, whom she desperately wished might regard her as a friend.

Where were they going? And once they got there, what would happen to her? Had Alice Chalmers ever received her message? Oh, why had she written that nonsense about trying to reach Munich? How many days would they waste searching the miles between Gibraltar and the Kingdom of Prussia before they concluded they must turn their attention to England?

Would she even be alive by then?

For whoever was behind this abduction would have sent a ransom demand to her father, would they not? The fact that she had not been informed of the answer that should have met them when they surfaced at Gibraltar meant nothing. It only confirmed what Gloria had always suspected—her father would not pay a ransom because he did not value her life, and Barnaby Hayes was too kind to tell her so.

Oh, Dad had said often enough that he wanted her to helm the company after he was gone, but that had only been civility. And a means to keep her busy when she was not fluttering about spending his money in

Paris and entertaining her erstwhile friends in London.

Sending her plea for help to him would have been a waste of paper and a pound sterling. At least Alice might make an attempt—and if even she did not, Gloria had the cold comfort of having told her she had not meant to leave her friends to die in the Venetian lagoon.

No, the most sensible thing for her father to do was to cut his losses and move on—to marry again and spend the next several years trying for a boy. Perhaps he would erect a memorial to her in one of the squares in Philadelphia.

IN MEMORIAM
GLORIA DIANA MERIWETHER-ASTOR
AN ORNAMENT TO SOCIETY

Hmph.

The gong sounded and Gloria realized she had been standing here woolgathering for an hour, at least. Not that it mattered. She had nothing to change into, and no inclination to regret it. She straightened her spine and prepared herself to spend yet another dinner sparring with Captain Hayes.

And wondering how on earth a man so amusing and charming and unfailingly kind could be such an utter villain.

*

The nameless, featureless airship dropped out of the clouds as it circled closer to its destination, fighting a headwind that swept toward it from the east. At the large viewing port in the main saloon—which, being furnished only with the bare necessities, had not much more than a spectacular view to recommend it—Gloria gazed down at the ground. A hawk stooping upon its prey could not have concentrated with more energy as she attempted to spot even one recognizable landmark.

They had definitely arrived in England—that much was obvious.

The rolling hills patchworked by harvested fields and stone walls had a calm, provincial beauty that she had never fully appreciated before. Roads meandered like threads across the countryside, punctuated by jewel-like towns, church spires, and dark folds of forest whose autumn colors were nearly finished. Far to the north lay a sheet of silver, turning slightly pink in the setting sun.

The sea. In the north.

That could not be. In her mind's eye, Gloria examined one of the charts pinned to the wall of her father's office in Philadelphia. The country spooling out below the ship was far too well-behaved to be northern Scotland. No, this was definitely England, so to the right would be—

—Bristol. With a sigh of satisfaction, Gloria felt the world slip into its proper place as the heavy vapor from the city's steam engines created a smudge below them like a second cloud. The map in her memory superimposed itself upon the landscape. That was no sea, but the Bristol Channel. If that were so, and they held their course, within ten minutes they would fly directly over Bath.

When her prediction proved correct, Gloria fought down a whoop of triumph at the sight of the Royal Crescent and the Roman steam baths as they passed below, and schooled her face to impassivity. It was fortunate she did, for a lightness in her body told her they were losing altitude, which meant the ship was coming in for a landing slightly to the east of Bath.

She must not be caught parsing out their location, tempting as it was to observe every detail. It was enough for her to know in which direction Bath lay. Bath, and the possibility of losing herself in the busy town until she could buy a ticket on the steam train to London and thence to Claire's house.

She gained the privacy of her own cabin moments before a knock came at the door. As the ship settled onto its mooring ropes, she glanced out the porthole and saw a thick stand of maples and elms close by, the last of the red and yellow leaves even now being whisked from their bare branches by the November wind.

It had been months since she'd seen a proper tree. There were none in Venice.

She opened the door to find Captain Hayes in the corridor. "Miss Meriwether-Astor, I am pleased to inform you that we have arrived."

"And where might that be?"

"I am not at liberty to say." He offered her his arm and, having no choice, she took it.

She felt rather clever to be in possession of forbidden knowledge, and was consequently quite pleasant as they disembarked and he escorted her across a wet field to a path through the trees. "Am I to be housed in a prison?" she inquired. "Is this wilderness Dartmoor?"

"No, and yes," he said.

A lie! The wretch, did he think her so simple? This pretty country in no way resembled the inhospitable moors surrounding the prison. Clearly he intended that she believe herself to be some hundred miles to the south and west, in case she took it into her head to send a message or attempt an escape.

"Goodness. I had not suspected it to look so ... civilized. The pictures in magazines are quite different."

"Never believe half of what you read," he said easily.

Or a quarter of what you tell me henceforth.

They passed into a wide clearing, and then a view opened up before them that, had she been here as an invited guest, might have taken her breath away.

A house sat nestled in a fold of the hills, the golden light of electricks gleaming on the wet gravel sweep in front and the tall pediments before the door. Below it ran a small river, the laughing sound of which Gloria could hear from where she stood. Spreading oaks and the pointed tapers of Italian cypress were visible in the last of the fading light.

To someone, this was a much beloved and cared-for home. To her, it was yet another series of locks and bars.

"What a lovely house, and such an appealing prospect, so close to one of the most dreaded prisons in England," she said.

For a moment, he hesitated, and then he seemed to catch himself. "Yes, it is, isn't it? We post a watch for just that reason."

She clenched her teeth, and forced a smile. "Am I to be similarly incarcerated here?"

"I would rather you thought of yourself as a much anticipated guest, worthy of every comfort and attention. Miss Meriwether-Astor, may I be the first to welcome you to Haybourne House."

"Thank you, sir. Is it the property of friends of yours?" *Or of whomever has engineered my abduction?*

"No." His smile was that of a man looking on a much beloved face after many years away. "It is my home."

A GENTLEMAN OF MEANS

9

As she clocked in, feeding her *Stempelkarte* into the mouth of the difference engine that ran the administrative operations of the Zeppelin Airship Works, Claire still struggled with the decision that had kept her awake half the preceding night. Should she tender her resignation today, come what would?

The prospect of spending so much as a month catering to the whims of Messrs. Weissmann & Co., never mind ten or twenty years, was such an appalling one that it threatened to overwhelm even her sense of obligation to the count. She would have to pay back four years of tuition, and move her things and those of the girls onto *Athena*. Would he accept a scheme of monthly payments—which would include moorage fees—until the girls completed their schooling in June?

Or would he wash his hands of all of them and ask her to pull up ropes at once?

When she arrived in her laboratory, feeling rather ill, she was astonished to find Herr Weissmann standing next to her bench, clearly waiting for her.

"Ah, Fraulein Junior Engineer. Would you come with me, please? We are expected in the offices of the managing director without delay."

"Why? Has something gone amiss?"

"I assume he will tell both of us when we arrive. Hurry, now."

Mystified, Claire snatched her gray laboratory coat from its hook and fastened its horizontal clasps as they walked briskly to the telescoping ironwork of the elevator. What could Herr Brucker want with both of them? Unless …

Oh, dear. Perhaps someone had discovered her bit of spliced cable and, in the absence of a memorandum documenting the change, had demanded an explanation. She was rehearsing what she might say when she and Herr Weissmann were ushered into the august presence.

The managing director laid down his fountain pen and regarded her unhappily. "Herr Weissmann, do have a seat." When Claire looked about her, she observed that the other wooden chair had been removed from the office, leaving her no choice but to stand. "Fraulein Junior Engineer, thank you for coming so promptly."

She inclined her head, stiffened her spine, and folded her hands before her. This did not seem to be the moment to insist on a lady's prerogative to be seated first. Perhaps they were unaware such a prerogative existed.

"I will waste as little of Herr Weissmann's time as possible, and come to the point directly. This morning upon my arrival I found der Landgraf von Zeppelin himself waiting in my office, with no fanfare and no notice."

Claire's lashes fluttered with surprise, but otherwise she made no movement. However, a measure of triumph warmed her heart. The count had changed his mind and come to her rescue, obviously having come to the conclusion that she was wasted here. She settled her feet more comfortably in anticipation.

Herr Brucker regarded her coldly. "He informed me that you had gone over the heads of several levels of management and approached him directly with your dissatisfactions concerning your employment here."

She frowned at his impugning her motives for speaking up. "I live in the palace, and in the course of a walk through the rose garden, met him there. Naturally he inquired as to how I was enjoying my work. I did not complain. I merely told him the same things I told you." She stopped herself before saying, *clearly to greater effect.*

"And what was his response to your remarks?"

"What one might expect. He referred me back to your ... leadership and advised me to be patient."

Once more his gimlet glare reminded her of poor Herr Grunwald back at school. "He has also advised me to be patient, but I find it increasingly difficult in the face of so obstinate a young lady."

Arrogant, self-aggrandizing, and now *obstinate.* It was fortunate that the people closest to her did not agree with his estimation; otherwise, she might find herself taking these criticisms to heart.

"I am afraid that I must put the interests of the Zeppelin Airship Works before those of patronage and obligation. Der Landgraf has given me a free hand with the engagement of new engineers; he also gives me a free hand with their dismissal. Fraulein Junior Engineer, please collect your things. As of this morning, you are no longer employeed with this company."

Claire stared at him. "No longer employed? You cannot sack someone whom the count has appointed. Does he know of this?" It was one thing to be impaled upon the horns of a dilemma. It was another thing entirely to have one horn—and one's choice of it—taken away entirely.

"No, but he will. It is within my authority to let a man or woman go if I determine they are disruptive to the work and safety of others. That, I am afraid, is what my report to him will say."

The rage that had been tamped down these last weeks while she tried to balance ambition with obligation flared wildly into life and Claire lost her temper.

"Then I suggest you include something a little more truthful in your report," she snapped, enunciating with the icy clarity learned at the silken knee of Lady St. Ives. "I came here this morning with the intention of handing in my resignation. Never in my life have I seen a business so mismanaged, so dependent on *patronage* and *obligation* as this one. If I put together every brain in the entire Flight Development Department, I still would not find the intelligence of one of my automatons."

His eyes bulged, and he glanced past her, as if about to call one of the uniformed men who acted as security at the main doors.

"I shall be glad to shake the dust of your laboratory off my feet—and I shall have to, since cleanliness is a foreign concept and no innovations have been made in weeks that might stir up the dust in any case." She laid a hand on the doorknob, shaking with anger. "I shall inform the count of your actions, of course, when he asks me at dinner this evening. If I were you, I should *dust* off my curriculum vitae."

With that, she swung open the door, swept through it, and slammed it so hard behind her that the secretary sitting just outside jumped practically out of her dirndl.

Within ten minutes, Claire had returned her laboratory coat to its hook, removed the brass plate bearing her name on her bench, and marched out of the hangar to her steam landau. She could barely sit still long enough to wait for the boiler to heat, but when it did, she piloted it out of the gates at a far greater speed than she had coming in.

And if a few tears were whisked out of her eyes as she bowled along the Talkirchnerstrasse, it was only due to the wind, nothing more.

*

"Sacked?" Andrew gaped at her, eyes wide with astonishment. "They let you go? Are they mad?"

"They are the equivalent of a horse and carriage, mired in the mud of tradition and hierarchy." Claire collapsed onto the sofa aboard *Athena* and pulled the driving goggles from her hair. "I would never have expected this from a company so far ahead of the rest of the world in technology and vision. It is heartbreaking, Andrew. I do not understand how the greatest innovations of the modern age could come from minds as small as those."

Andrew got up from his drawings to sit beside her and take her hand. "Clearly there are other minds better occupied in other hangars," he pointed out. "I wonder what these men believe the charter of flight development to be?"

"Whatever their belief, they no longer have my assistance in bringing it about. I will make it clear to the count that, despite what they say, I have resigned my post. I do not wish it known among the Royal Society of Engineers that I have been sacked. That would be intolerable."

"Quite so," Andrew agreed. "What now? For I do not for a moment suppose you have left without a plan in mind."

For the first time that morning, Claire smiled, and turned her hand so that it clasped his, palm to palm. "I shall form a partnership with you, if you will have me. I have come to believe that I, too, am the sort that must captain her own ship."

The smile that broke upon his face warmed her heart the way the sun will warm the coldest dawn. "I confess that when I saw your indecision, I was hard put not to attempt to convince you to do that very thing. We shall be partners in life and in work, and I will be the happiest man on earth."

He leaned in to seal this prediction with a kiss.

"I am likely to be homeless shortly," she reminded him.

"You have two homes in England."

"But the girls' education—I cannot pull them from the *lycee* when they are mere months away from matriculation. We cannot leave Munich until afterward."

"Then we will find that farm posthaste, for until we

are married, I must continue to live aboard *Athena*. A landing field must take priority over a laboratory for the time being."

Athena. The resolution she had formed on the drive home rose up inside her, and Andrew must have seen her face change, for he sat up, his keen gaze unwavering.

"Have I said something? Have you changed your mind about a farm?"

"Andrew—now that I am free—I must—oh, you will not like it." He looked positively alarmed now, but the words must be said. "I must find out what has happened to Gloria."

Those beloved eyes gazed into her own in a moment of disbelief before his face slowly darkened.

She hurried on before he could contradict her. "I know that you said her father must be informed about the note—"

"And was he?"

"No."

"Claire!"

"Andrew, listen, please. She sent that letter to Alice—to us—in her extremity. To *us*, not her father. I cannot avoid the conclusion that she did not want him to know her whereabouts. And the only reason for that must be because she does not trust him."

"Ridiculous."

"Perhaps with the threat from the Famiglia Rosa, he had her removed for her own safety—but that does not seem right. Why not tell her? So I must conclude that either they are behind it, or some other nameless party is using her as a pawn in a larger game."

"You are boxing with mist—and moreover, it is none of your affair. Claire, for the love of heaven, tell the girl's father and be done with it so that we can get on with the planning of our own lives."

Her lower lip trembled at his tone. She had seen him angry with her before, but that had been motivated by fear for her safety. What was his motivation now?

"I cannot," she whispered. "My friend is in danger and she has no one to help."

"If she is, then she has asked for help in the wrong quarter. Whether or not she trusts her father is immaterial. It is his duty to rescue her, not yours. He is a man of enormous resolution and nearly limitless resources. You are a young lady with responsibilities and prospects of your own that have nothing to do with Gloria Meriwether-Astor."

"She is my friend."

"She is my friend also, and Alice's, and Ian's ... and you do not see us haring off to fetch her when others are better equipped to do so."

"Andrew, you do not mean that." He could not be so heedless of the plea for help that Gloria's letter had contained.

"I do mean it!" As if unable to sit still for another moment, he leaped to his feet and began to pace. "Claire, I do not understand you. Time after time you have put aside your own welfare and that of those who love you to fly off into danger. Time after time we are left behind wondering when it will ever be our turn to enjoy your full attention. Time after time we wonder if indeed you love the adventure and the risk more than you care for those whose hearts you hold."

She stared at him, her cheeks prickling as the color drained from them. "Of whom do you speak?" she managed at last.

"Of Maggie, of Lizzie, of Alice ... and of me."

"I do not fly off without you. We go together, if we go at all."

"Perhaps I speak metaphorically. For if we do not go physically, we run the risk of never seeing you again."

"That is not true."

"Perhaps it has not been. But that is no guarantee of the future."

"The future is never guaranteed."

"Do not split hairs with me. The point is that your life is being left behind while you dash off to save someone else's. I do wonder if you do it on purpose. I do not want to, because that would make you unnatural and unwomanly ... but I do wonder."

How could he say these things to her? How could he be so cruel? "On purpose? What on earth are you talking about?"

He stopped and turned, his face as colorless as her own—and his eyes—

"Do you really want to marry me, Claire?"

"Of course I do! How can you say that after all we have been through together—after all the plans we have made?"

"Then prove it." He took a breath and pressed a fist to his heart, as though it pained him. "Abandon this plan of going to Gloria's rescue and let her father handle it, as I advised you. Then turn your attention to our wedding with a heart undivided and free—just the way you were when you accepted my proposal that day on the cliffs."

That day on the cliffs, she had had no inkling of the dangers that awaited—dangers brought on almost exclusively by and encapsulated in the person of Gerald

Meriwether-Astor.

In one blinding sweep, Claire saw the truth behind all the events that Maggie and Lizzie referred to as their *adventures*. In the Canadas, he had attempted to start a war by assassinating Count von Zeppelin. He had sold Lizzie's father the massive telescoping cannon with which the latter had planned to assassinate the heir to the throne. He had cozened the Bourbon pretender into an invasion of England, selling him his guns, his underwater dirigibles, and his war machines. And he had bargained with the Famiglia Rosa for the lives of English men and women—no matter that they were convicts—and condemned them to a short life and a watery grave.

Claire had not brought their adventures on herself out of a mad need to dance on the edge of danger. Gerald Meriwether-Astor was the architect of them all—the reason she could not lead the kind of life she wanted with Andrew. And he was undoubtedly the man who had prevented his daughter—her friend—from living the life she was capable of and deserved as a woman of resources and potential.

If she, Claire, could find Gloria, perhaps together they could put an end to his machinations and his maniacal desire to rule—women, convicts, countries, kings—it did not seem to matter. Gerald Meriwether-Astor was out to rule the world, and he did not seem to care that his daughter and her friends had been drawn again and again into the massive gearworks of his ambition.

The end result, unless they extricated themselves once and for all, was that they would be ground to powder.

Unless someone became the spanner in his works.

Andrew was waiting for her answer, his face solemn, his eyes filled with pain. "I cannot abandon her," she said simply, her distress causing tears to start in her own eyes. "It is only for a few weeks. Not forever."

"And if something happens to you? Will that not be forever?"

"Nothing will happen to me. I am well armed and have—"

He made a pushing gesture with one hand and turned away so that she could not see his face. "Claire, I cannot bear it."

"Then come with me."

"That is not the point." He dragged in a shuddering breath.

"Then what is the point? Andrew, surely you must see—"

"No. All I see is that once again you choose someone else over me and a life with me."

"I do not! I gave you a promise and I intend to keep it."

"You say that. But Claire, my darling, your actions put the lie to your words every time." Slowly, he turned to face her. "Who will it be next time to delay our wedding, our happiness, our prospects of a family? Willie Dunsmuir? Young Mr. Stringfellow? No, I cannot put myself through this." He choked, then gained control of himself once again.

Cold water was running through her veins, loosening her limbs with fear. No. He could not mean it. Not Andrew.

"I release you from your engagement," he said at last, when he had mastered himself. "I wish you every success in your venture, but I cannot be a part of it. My heart will not survive, and so I must cut it out entirely and attempt to make a life without it."

"Andrew—please, you do not mean it—you cannot mean it."

He crossed the room to the dining table, and rolled up the drawings for the Helios Membrane—what was to have been their first project together as husband and wife.

"I mean every word. Good-bye, Claire. I will move over to the crew's quarters on *Swan* and bunk there until Alice is ready to leave. I am sure she will not object to an extra passenger as far as London."

"Andrew ... please ..."

But he merely put the drawings under his arm and collected his coat from the back of the chair. And then he walked out of the saloon, leaving her standing there wondering how it was possible to lose nearly everything she valued in the course of a single day.

A GENTLEMAN OF MEANS

10

Lizzie and Maggie settled themselves opposite Claire at the little glass-topped table where they were accustomed to take breadfast. With a pang, Claire was reminded again how very quickly they were growing up, and how soon it would be before they were making wedding plans themselves.

And until then, what kind of life would she be able to provide for them, after her disastrous conversations with the two most important men in her life? A wave of grief rose in her chest, towering and threatening to fall like the massive combers on the coast at home, which could throw a person up on the beach and knock the breath from her as easily as if she were an empty seashell.

"Lady, what is it?" Maggie said, her amber gaze becoming concerned as she examined Claire's face. "Have you—have you been crying? And you are so pale. Have we had bad news?"

She had a number of very hard things to tell them. She may as well begin with that. "Mr. Malvern and I have decided that … we will not be married after all."

There. That was the bald, horrible truth of it. And the words tasted like bile in her mouth.

Lizzie gasped, and Maggie's eyes filled with tears. "Lady, how can that be? Why, only yesterday—"

"Yesterday belonged to a different world," Claire said with uncharacteristic harshness.

"But how—"

"Girls, if you do not wish me to sink altogether under the crushing pain of this experience, you will not question me. Suffice it to say that we have parted, and he will be going with Alice and Captain Hollys to England tomorrow."

"Oh, Lady," Lizzie whispered, a single tear escaping despite obvious efforts to control it, and tracking down her cheek. "You were so happy."

Claire could not prevent the sob that clutched her chest and caught her by surprise. "I cannot speak of it," she gasped. "Do not make me."

Wordlessly, Lizzie and Maggie rose and wrapped their arms around her. Claire could not help it—her body shook with the force of her sobs, their loving embraces taking her grief into themselves and offering only warmth and comfort in return … just as she had done many a time in the old days at Toll Cottage.

When at length the storm passed, they did not take their seats at the table, but instead curled up together on the sofa. Claire tucked her sodden handkerchief into her sleeve and sniffled.

"There is another, less personal matter I must discuss with you both, and it must be done without delay," she said. "As if today could be any worse, I have also resigned my post at the Zeppelin Airship Works."

"Because your superiors are dolts?" Lizzie asked, the sympathy of her tone marred somewhat by interest in the answer.

Claire would have remonstrated with her for using such a disrespectful term, but frankly— "Yes. Because they are dolts, and because the count and I do not see eye to eye on how exactly my career is to begin."

"Does he know you have resigned?" Maggie asked. "Because if he does not, he will be dreadfully upset when you tell him."

"I am afraid he was informed by tube before I even arrived home at the palace this morning. He sent for me, and he was dreadfully upset. He feels I have betrayed him."

"How can refusing to work for a dolt be a betrayal?" Lizzie wanted to know. "I should do the same myself."

"Because he has paid my tuition on the condition that I should spend at least the first part of my career with him," Claire told her. "When I offered to pay it back, I merely added insult to injury. Today, it seems, I am doomed to make everyone I see angry with me."

"You shan't make us angry," Maggie told her, leaning comfortably against her shoulder.

"I would not hold my breath, my dear one. For we must come to some decisions about your educations rather more quickly than I had anticipated. You see—" She hesitated. Perhaps she might keep this part to herself. But no, she had never lied to them, no matter how difficult it had been to give them facts rather than comforting fancies. "You are young women now, and able to withstand the truth, so I will not insult you by attempting to protect you. The count is very angry with me. So angry that he has asked us to leave his house."

Maggie gasped. "I do not believe it! Uncle Ferdinand would never be so cruel."

But Lizzie's keen gaze had already penetrated the shock and seen right to the difficulty. "He is hurt, and is striking out at the source of his pain. Is he not, Lady?"

Claire nodded. "Perhaps at some time in the future we might be able to be friends again—some very distant time—but for the moment, we must pack up our things and take them out to *Athena*."

"Will he continue to allow us to moor in the park?" Lizzie asked.

"I hope so, or we shall have to remove to the Theresienwiese and pay a fortune to rent a mast," Claire said. "The question is, do you wish to finish out the term at the *lycee* and return to London with me over Christmas—" Oh, how was she to face London at Christmas with no wedding? How was she to endure Christmas next year, or the year after, or any year after that for the rest of her life? Claire struggled to get a grip on her emotions. "—and take your final term at St. Cecelia's? Or remain in Munich to finish sixth form entirely and matriculate?"

"Return to London with you ... or stay and matriculate?" Maggie's gaze was puzzled. "Would you not be coming back after Christmas and staying as well?"

"Here is the part where you will be angry with me," Claire told her. "I have resolved to do my best to find Gloria. This resolve, in fact, is what finally caused Mr.

Malvern to—" *Never mind.* "He does not agree. But I cannot leave it to her father when she wrote to us looking for aid."

"We will come with you, of course," Lizzie said promptly. "We can help you find her."

"It is not so easy as that, darling," Claire said. "If you do not finish sixth form, you will not matriculate and be eligible to attend university, should you choose to do so."

"I don't care."

"But I care, deeply. We have made any number of sacrifices and accepted the count's help without reserve so that you and Maggie might have this opportunity. I would not like to see you throw it away for the sake of a task that may be completed in as little as a week or two."

"As you have thrown away your engagement to Mr. Malvern?" Lizzie asked.

"Lizzie!" Maggie exclaimed, shocked. "How can you be so unkind?"

"I can see how he feels, if she is going to fly off without him," Lizzie said defensively.

Claire sighed. "I told you that you would be angry with me."

"We are not angry, Lady," Maggie said. Then, with a glance at her cousin, "At least, I am not. So what you propose is that we board at the *lycee*, like Katrina Grünwald and some of the others do, until you find Gloria and return to bring us home for Christmas."

"Precisely."

"And then we will return for our final term and entrance examinations while you do ... what?"

Claire touched Maggie's cheek, and brushed a tendril

of her dark hair behind her ear. "How very like you to settle upon the very question I have been unwilling to face myself. For I do not think I am well suited to being a lady of leisure, making calls and taking tea with people I do not particularly like."

"You could go down to Gwynn Place."

"And face my mother's wrath at being once more unattached and on her hands? I think not."

"You could go and visit Lady Selwyn."

"I could, and I may yet ... but one cannot haunt one's friends indefinitely."

"You could go into business with Alice and Jake," Lizzie said. "Sign on *Athena* with the Royal Aeronautics Corps and request Tigg as your first engineer."

For the first time, the ghost of a smile came to Claire's lips. "That is a capital plan—the best I have heard all day."

"A first engineer is going to need a wife with an education," Maggie said to no one in particular. "A wife who doesn't quit, who sees something through in order to achieve larger things."

Lizzie's eyes narrowed. "Are you trying to tell me something?"

"I am simply pointing out the obvious," Maggie said airily. "How will you hold your own at all those dreadful Admiralty teas and balls if you quit? Lady So-and-so will say, *Oh my, I hear you were educated in Europe,* and you will have to say, *Well, I was, partly, but I couldn't stick it out and so I abandoned it.* And she will say, *Dear me, what does this say about Lieutenant Terwilliger's ability to choose a proper wife,* and you will say—"

"None of your bloody business," Lizzie said crossly.

"What do you know of Tigg's career?"

"I know that were I you, I would want to be a woman he can be proud to take into that ballroom on his arm. A woman of conversation, and taste, and accomplishment, like the Lady. Like the woman you were so determined to become once upon a time. Have you lost sight of her, Liz?"

Lizzie glared at her, but even so, she was the first to admit she could see through a grindstone when there was a hole in it. "No, I have not, and you know it. You think we ought to abandon our posts, and stay here safe and warm while the Lady flies off into danger?"

"I think that if Jake and Alice have anything to say about it, she will not be alone. I think that we have a job to do, and we should not grieve the Lady further in our hurry to abandon it."

Lizzie's lower lip took on a mutinous cast.

Claire knew when to speak, and when to remain silent. She had been speaking all day, and had received nothing but blow after blow for her trouble. If Maggie could not convince her cousin to do the right thing, then nothing Claire could say would help the situation—and might even hinder it.

Lizzie might be stubborn, and headstrong, and even heedless sometimes, but she was not stupid. They had cut it rather fine with their headmistress over the Venetian adventure. There would be no second chances along the same line. Why should she risk years of work for a voyage that might not even end in success?

Claire saw the moment when Lizzie answered this question for herself, and raised her eyes to meet Claire's gaze. "Is this really what you want us to do, Lady?" she asked softly. "To stay here while you do this alone?"

"I will not be alone," Claire said softly, taking her hand and drawing lines upon it. Forming letters. *I love you.* "I will have our friends with me. But mostly I will have peace in my heart knowing that my resolution has not harmed *your* prospects."

Lizzie's lip trembled. "We have not been separated so long before."

"Then we will keep the pigeons very busy."

"We will have to be careful about them if we are to be boarding students," Maggie put in. "Remember, it is illegal to send them to fixed addresses."

This prospect seemed to cheer Lizzie to no end. "And you will be careful," she said to Claire.

"Exceedingly. I will have the lightning rifle to hand, and when I do not, the pistol will be in my pocket."

"And may we write to Mr. Malvern?" Maggie asked. "I hope he does not mean to end his friendship with us as well."

"I think he would be glad and honored to write to you," Claire assured her over the sinking in her stomach at his name. "He and Tigg are fast friends, and I should not like you to be estranged simply because he and I are not—not—"

"Do not cry, Lady." Lizzie hugged her, and Claire gulped back her tears. "If our staying here will ease your pain even a little, then of course we will. I am sorry to have been stubborn. You are right, and we will do all we can to make you proud of us."

As she kissed them both, tears of gratitude coming now instead of grief, Claire thanked God—not for the first time—for that night outside Aldgate Station when her life had so irrevocably changed.

She could only hope that after today's events, her

life would make a difference in someone else's, too. She must find Gloria, or all the losses she had suffered today would have been for nothing.

11

During times such as this, Claire could find it in her heart to be grateful for her mother's training in the social graces. She had hated every moment of it when she had lived under Lady St. Ives's critical eye, but now, as *Athena* descended gracefully to her moorage at the Carrick Airfield on the south bank of the Thames, she clung to it as she clung to her own principles. How else was she to face Andrew for the last time without breaking down?

"There's Snouts!" Tigg waved as the ground crew jogged out to the mooring mast, and the lanky, foreshortened figure gave an answering wave. "Seven, cut engines, and Eight, vanes full vertical, please. How did they know we were coming? I expected we'd have to tie off our own ropes."

A GENTLEMAN OF MEANS

"I sent a pigeon last night, silly." For Snouts had
above all to be informed about the change in her marriage plans, so that neither he nor Lewis or any of the
other children would let slip a remark in public that
would increase her pain or that of Andrew. "He is most
anxious to see you."

"And I him." His attention on the landing, Tigg said
almost offhandedly, "Could be Lewis can put out the
word about our Gloria and see what turns up at the
Gaius Club, and I can do the same among the aeronauts' haunts in town."

"An excellent plan. Since we have hardly any information to begin with, even a hint to a possible direction
would be helpful."

"And speaking of direction ... here we are."

Athena shivered as her ropes were secured, and in a
moment Claire and Tigg were surrounded by a joyful
crowd as Snouts, Lewis, and several of the Carrick
House orphans stormed the gangway to welcome them
home. In the joy of their reunion, it would have been
easy to allow Andrew to slip away as he disembarked
from *Swan*, but when had Claire ever allowed any of the
children to choose what was easy over what was right?
She could do nothing herself but what she required of
them.

And so, as he shouldered his rucksack after making
arrangements at Toll Cottage to have himself and his
trunk delivered to Orpington Close, she laid a hand on
his arm as he was about to board the ramshackle landau in which they conveyed passengers into town.

"Claire," he said, his eyes in shadow under the goggles he had already pulled on. "I trust you had a good
journey?"

"I did. Will you come to Carrick House for dinner? Alice, Jake, and Ian have all accepted, and our party would not be complete without you."

My life will not be complete without you. Oh, Andrew—

"I think not. I have been gone so long that I will likely have to spend the evening battling the rat population for my bed. Best to get that over with sooner rather than later."

"Gaseous capsaicin is very effective in such cases."

Oh, why are we talking about rats, of all things?

"I still have your recipe. Well ... good-bye, Claire. I expect I shall see you at a meeting of the Royal Society of Engineers one of these evenings."

"Perhaps," she said faintly. *To shake your hand and politely discuss the latest developments in steam-driven automata? I think not.* "Good-bye. I will let you know when we locate Gloria."

He muttered something about perdition, and then without another word, climbed into the landau and commanded the driver to be off.

Claire was still standing there watching the plume of steam dissipate on the breeze when Tigg came to stand at her shoulder. "All right, Lady?"

"No, dearest. I do not think it will be all right ever again."

"Chin up. Mr. Malvern loves you. He'll come round."

"Dear Tigg." She touched his face, the tears so close to the surface that her lips trembled. "I hope you will never have to experience this."

He shook his head, and offered her his arm, clad in khaki since any flying time meant he was on duty. "I've known Liz most of her life. I know her faults, and she knows mine. I know we won't pass through life without a quarrel, but all the same, I can't imagine living without her."

Neither could she imagine a life without Andrew. But she supposed she would have to bring herself to do so. Even the thought of not loving him was so painful that her heart contracted with it. How did one bring oneself to set out on the road to such a state on purpose?

"Lady—I know this might not be the right time—but—" He stopped their leisurely amble toward *Athena*, his face flushing. "Never mind. Of course it isn't."

"If there is something on your mind, then you must tell me. We have a minute yet before we must join the others."

"It's terrible to ask this when you and Mr. Andrew—forgive me—"

"Tigg." She stopped, the skirts of her raiding rig swinging against her ankles. "Spit it out, as Snouts would say."

"Very well. Do you think that the day after she matriculates is too soon to ask Lizzie to marry me?"

The surprise of it nearly caused a huff of laughter. Hastily, she schooled her face to the solemnity appropriate to the occasion. "I think that you will know the right moment when it comes. But certainly you are wise to wait until after she has finished this stage of her education. But Tigg ... if she writes the entrance examinations, she may choose to go on to university. What of your plans then?"

"I've already thought of that. At the end of four years I'll almost certainly have a first engineer's bars, and will be able to afford a home for her. In any case, we will have to wait until then, and she has already told me she is willing."

"Then it sounds as though my advice is hardly necessary."

"It will always be necessary, Lady. I wouldn't think of taking any step of which you didn't approve."

"You already have my blessing, darling. Lizzie will be seventeen in March, and quite able to make up her own mind about her future. If you marry when she is twenty-one, then all will be as it should."

Snouts had already unloaded her landau from *Athena*, and was beckoning for them to hurry.

"Thank you, Lady. I'll go fire up the old girl, shall I? And Alice and the captain can ride with you. I'll go with Snouts to make sure he doesn't overturn and do in all the kids. He hasn't been piloting as long as we have."

Smiling, she watched him lope away.

Still smiling, she saw her friends loaded into the landau along with as much luggage as could be tucked in, and headed off along the familiar roads to their home in Wilton Crescent.

And under the smile, her heart cracked, her life as formless and directionless as the steam left behind after Andrew's departure.

*

The children under Claire's care had proven time and again to be a balm to her spirits, and tonight's homecoming was no exception. Charlie had gone to extra effort with the orange cake, knowing it was her favorite, even somehow managing to write *Welcome Back Lady Claire* in wavering letters of drizzled honey on the top. Kitty, who at the age of eight had come to them when her seamstress mother had drowned, had proven to be skilled in that art. She gave Claire a handkerchief whose stitching, in Claire's opinion, rivaled anything a professional modiste could have done. Benny Stringfellow lorded his employment as a middy over Robbie and Dickie, who, at only ten, were feeling cast down in any case at not having a gift ready for the Lady's unexpected return.

"But you have gathered eggs for my breakfast, for which I am every bit as grateful," she said, gathering them close for a hug, and pretending not to notice their subsequent stealthy departure for the walking coop to collect the eggs from Holly and Ivy and the other hens before anyone else did.

When the little ones went upstairs to bed, chivvied thither by Alice, who could not resist the novelty of seeing them bathed and tucked in for the night, Claire went to the sideboard and poured sherry for those who remained.

"Thank you all for making this such a lovely homecoming," she said, offering the tray of tiny glasses to Ian, Jake, Tigg, Snouts, and Lewis. When Alice came in a moment later, flushed and smiling, Claire was not the only one to notice that it was Ian who made certain she had a glass from the tray.

"Thank you for offering us a kip for the night," Captain Hollys said. "My, this vintage is excellent."

"That would be Lewis's doing," she said with a smile at that individual, who flushed with pleasure. "He has developed quite an acquaintance among the merchants who supply the Gaius Club, I understand."

The captain toasted him and turned his attention back to Claire. "So you are resolved on finding Gloria, then?"

She nodded, and set her glass aside. "I am. Tigg has already told me that he and Snouts will put the word out among their wide acquaintance—"

"Meaning they'll tip the street sparrows and flash-men, then?" Jake translated with a laugh. "If the Famiglia Rosa are in London, they won't have been able to keep a low profile. A proud, saucy lot, they are, and inclined to be above their company."

"Just so," Claire agreed. "Lewis, I depend upon you to keep an ear open at the club. One never knows what gems may drop from inebriated lips."

"Of course, Lady," he said. "Though I've heard no whispers lately of Miss Meriwether-Astor. Mostly it's been betting on the sex of Princess Alexandra's next baby, and whether young Lord Mount-Batting will lose again at the balloon races."

"Is there any way we might see that he does?" Claire asked, whimsically.

Lewis gazed at her, one eyebrow raised. "Of course, Lady, if you wish it."

When she realized he was quite serious, she shook her head. "No, no. I was merely joking. Please do not, or I shall have yet more upon my conscience."

A little silence fell, until Ian said, "Claire, I have been thinking. We know so little—only where Gloria has been, not where she is going. Even that young scamp at the Barnacle in Gibraltar could only say she had been there, and was subsequently recaptured. I suppose I am relieved that we did not have to scan every valley between Munich and the Rock, but all levity aside, how do you propose to find her?"

With relief, Claire turned to wrestle with a problem she might actually have a hope of solving. "We know one or two things, other than that she is certainly in the hands of Captain Barnaby Hayes once again. And that they cannot mean to return *Neptune's Fancy* to Mr. Meriwether-Astor without risking being put to the rack to tell him where she is. Therefore, it seems that they will have to come ashore somewhere—likely along the Cornish or Devonshire coasts. And if they do, they will be seen."

"That seems a vague proposition, with too many variables," Alice said. "We'd do better to start with a known factor. What do we know of this Captain Hayes?"

"A good question," Snouts said. "What are his habits? His weaknesses? What does he value and where is his home?"

They looked at one another. "You are quite right. These are questions that I suppose we must answer," Claire said slowly.

"I can assist there," Captain Hollys said. "If he is English, and a captain in the colonial fleet—undersea or not—then there will be a record of him at the Admiralty. He *is* English, is he not?"

"He is," Claire confirmed. "An Englishman serving in the colonial fleet. I wonder how he came to be there?"

"I only hope he is a gentleman, and treating her well," Alice said. "I can't bear to think of her going hungry, or being cold wherever they're holding her."

"I shall make it my business to find out what I can

of him." Already there seemed to be more liveliness in Ian's face. "If it is humanly possible to bring Gloria home to her friends, then we will do it."

As the light came into his face, it faded from Alice's, and she looked away, ostensibly to pick up her glass. Claire moved to fill it, with a smile. "So we may have your company for a few days longer, then?" she asked. "You will not fly to Hollys Park before Sunday?" It was Thursday. Surely they would see at least a few straws to indicate which way the wind blew by then.

"If there is anything to be found at the Admiralty, I will have it by tea-time tomorrow," Ian assured her.

"While you are doing that, perhaps Alice and I might make some calls in town," Claire suggested, thinking aloud. "My former schoolmates have not proven as useful as I had hoped, so I will widen my net. I wonder if Peony Churchill is in London? We could call in Chelsea."

"You don't need me for that," Alice said. "I would rather go with Ian to the Admiralty."

Claire paused, rather taken aback. "You wouldn't have to dress up," she said at last. That was usually what kept Alice from many forms of social interaction. "These would merely be polite social calls."

"It's not that. I have an errand there, and now is as good a time as any to do it."

"An errand?" Ian repeated. "At the Admiralty? What business could you have there?"

"As a mere colonial?"

"Alice, forgive me," he said. "Of course I did not mean that. I only meant that—well, it seems strange, that is all."

"It might seem strange to you," she said with a lift

of her chin, "but it's my business. If I get the answers I'm looking for, I'll share it with you all, but until then, it's my nevermind and no one else's."

Goodness. She was in a fair way to becoming offended. What had upset her so suddenly that she was willing to pick a fight rather than allow anyone to see it? Claire nodded in encouragement. "You must do as you see fit, Alice, of course. I shall take Kitty with me as a kind of shield. Everyone will be so astonished at the sight of me with a child that I will be able to ask impertinent questions quite unmolested."

Snouts had leaned forward as if to add something to this, when Mr. Stringfellow came in bearing a folded piece of paper. "Lieutenant Terwilliger, sir, a boy come from the airfield with this for you. Says it came to *Athena*."

"For me?" He exchanged a glance with his captain. "Perhaps the Dunsmuirs are in a greater hurry for our services than we thought."

"They are in the habit of sending a tube," Ian pointed out. "Though since I informed them we were to leave Prussia, *Athena* would be the logical choice."

Tigg unfolded the note and scanned it. His mouth dropped open and so much color faded from his face that he looked positively gray.

Claire's stomach plunged in sudden fear, and she started from her seat. "Tigg—Lizzie—?"

He looked up from the note, staring at her as though he had never seen her before. Then, slowly, recognition of her—the room—his company—seemed to filter into his stunned gaze.

"No. Not Lizzie. It's—he—" He swallowed. "It's from someone who says he's my dad."

12

Dear Tommy,

You'll be surprised to hear from me after these many years. Truth be told, I thought you were dead. You probably thought I was, too. I was enjoying a tankard in the Barnacle in Gibraltar when in walks a fine young man in Her Majesty's uniform whom his captain called Lieutenant Terwilliger. Could only be one such with skin like mine and eyes like his mum's, so I made a few inquiries. I'd like to meet you proper. I'll be in the Sea Horse in Southwark Saturday night should you be inclined.

Sincerely,
Tom Terwilliger senior

A GENTLEMAN OF MEANS

"Of course you must not go," Alice said as they walked briskly down the Mall toward the Admiralty. Tigg thought she looked rather nice in her dark-blue skirt and matching jacket with the kind of puffy sleeves that Lizzie favored, but she'd certainly kicked up a fuss at having to put them on for the occasion.

"How would you feel if, when we went to meet your dad in the Canadas, he'd refused?" Tigg asked her. "I don't mind meeting a man I haven't seen since I was a little tyke of four. He means nothing to me. He's a stranger—and he might have information we could use."

"How do you reckon that?" The mention of her dad, coupled with having to put on a skirt, seemed to have made Alice as cross as two sticks. Even Ian had not offered her his arm. Perhaps he felt that treating her like a woman instead of a fellow captain would only be poking the tiger's already sore spot.

"Think about it, Alice," Tigg said, happy to direct the conversation along difficult but at least not incendiary lines. "He seems to treat Gibraltar as though it's nothing special. Perhaps he spends some time there. Though he's an aeronaut and not a bathynaut, perhaps he might know some of the *Fancy*'s crew and can give us a tidbit to add to the rest of this puzzle."

"And maybe he's an impostor who wants to cosh you on the skull."

The captain said, "He would hardly go to the trouble of making inquiries about the ship Tigg serves on if that were his aim."

Tigg almost thought she was going to cosh the captain, but at the last moment, she recollected herself.

"I'm just saying, he might not have Tigg's best interests at heart. Perhaps he's down at heel and looking for a handout."

"If he was, I'd give him what I had and wish him well," Tigg said, though as the words passed his lips, he wondered if he would. What was the man's business with him? It made no sense to disappear, leaving your wife and son with nothing but a one-room flat and her skill with feathers and furbelows, and then just as suddenly reappear wanting to get acquainted. Had he even wasted a thought on them in the fifteen years since he'd vanished?

Tigg hardly cared. He had long ago set aside any resentment he might have had at being abandoned, once he'd seen what fathers could do to other children. Snouts and Jake had given him quite the education on that score.

His mother had died before he was seven, the hard life she had fallen into having taken its toll. The madam of the brothel had had no patience with the all-too-common results of the trade, and had booted him and another boy out onto the street. If he hadn't fallen in with Snouts and the gang, Tigg was quite sure he'd have been dead by now, his father blissfully plying the skies without a single clue as to what might have happened to the family he'd so cavalierly left behind.

All told, Tigg would be more likely to cosh the blighter himself ... but that wouldn't be becoming to a man in his position, with his prospects. And the Lady wouldn't like it.

She was the first person besides Snouts and Lizzie to whom he'd given his complete trust. He'd come to love her like a mother—or an older sister, really, since she wasn't so very much older than he was. Her opinion mattered more to him even than the captain's, his actions guided by an internal question: *Would the Lady like it?*

Somehow, coshing this unknown Nubian aeronaut would probably fall on the negative side of that ledger. But that was not until tomorrow. Today, they had other fish to entice into their net.

Tigg had thought they might have to inquire at a counter of some kind—to consult ledgers and perhaps even cross someone's palm with a bit of blunt. But he hadn't reckoned on Captain Hollys ... and his rank.

"Come this way, Sir Ian, Lieutenant, madam," the clerk said, leading them through a warren of offices and audience rooms to an upper floor, where they were shown into a room resembling a library—except the shelves were lined in small, neat metal boxes, not books. "I am the Clerk of Records, at your service. If you will make yourselves comfortable, I will consult the records for you."

As Tigg sank into a navy-blue plush chair, the man slid back a section of the wall to reveal a cavernous space beyond—several floors of it—entirely filled with movement. Gears, grates, arms—the mighty difference engine that recorded every movement of Her Majesty's vessels, their flight plans, their crews. Suddenly Tigg realized that deep within that glimmering, busy brass edifice were bits and pieces of his own life. His enlistment, his promotions, his examination results ... his marriage to Lizzie would even be recorded there, some day.

Perhaps he'd best not mention that to her.

With a happy whirring of cables and tapping of arms resembling the insides of a piano, a number of long cards fell into a slot. The clerk carried them over and presented them to the captain with a flourish.

"Allow me to interpret our rather cryptic shorthand, Sir Ian," he said. "The officer you inquired about, Barnaby Aloysius Hayes, joined Her Majesty's service at the age of fourteen aboard the *Galaxy*, a ship of the line, serving the route between London and St. Petersburg. He rose through the ranks, becoming a midshipman and then lieutenant at twenty-two, when he purchased his commission and was assigned to the colonial route at twenty-six. We have no official record of his career following his departure from the service three years ago, of course."

"A moment, sir," the captain said. "You say he purchased a commission?"

"I did. Or rather, it was purchased for him. By old Lord Mount-Batting—the current duke's father—before he died. This enabled him to take the lieutenant's examinations, and upon passing them, to take up his new post as an officer."

The captain snapped his fingers. "I knew I had heard his name before. Captain Hayes is the old duke's—" He glanced at Tigg and Alice.

"His illegitimate offspring, sir." The clerk was obviously a man who dealt in facts, not the sensibilities of unmarried young men and women. "That is correct. He was born in 1864, when the old duke was nearly sixty years of age."

The captain had gone rather red over the pristine white of his cravat. "Er, quite so. There was a scandal, if I remember. Something to do with ... oh, what was it? My mother always hustled me from the room when it came up among her friends."

"If you are referring to the property transferred into his name, sir, that is also here, in the record." He shuffled the card to point to it, but Tigg could not see it from where he sat. "The scandal you refer to occurred when the old duke conveyed one of the family estates into his bastard's name. The heir—the current Lord Mount-Batting—raised quite a fuss, but since it had come into the family through the old duke's first wife, it was all quite legal."

Tigg found his voice. "And where is this estate located, sir?"

The clerk perused the card, his spectacles low on his nose. "It was formerly known as Aldercroft Court, eight miles east of Bath, but it was renamed in 1891 as Haybourne House, no doubt in remembrance of the family who raised him. Hayes, of course, is their name. He is not entitled to any of the old duke's titles and honorifics, naturally."

"Naturally," the captain murmured, his mind clearly sailing well before the wind. "Thank you, sir, for your assistance."

He began to rise, but Tigg took his fate in both hands and gave the tiller a metaphorical push. "Sir, if I might be so bold, could you make one more inquiry of the—the difference engine?"

"Certainly. You wish to know the name of a man who served?"

"I do. One Thomas Terwilliger. Not I," Tigg added hastily. "My father. I know nothing about him and should appreciate as many facts as the records might supply."

The man smiled kindly. Perhaps he was not the automaton he seemed to be—perhaps he was just more used to engines, as Alice was sometimes. "It would be an honor, Lieutenant. Facts are my bread and butter."

Once again the gears whirred, two storeys of little arms clattered up and down, and a series of cards spilled into the tray.

Once again they were politely presented; once again the clerk was obliged to interpret.

"Terwilliger, Thomas John, born 1861. Entered Her Majesty's service as an airman—a ropemaker, to be specific—and rose to the rank of sailswain, whereupon he left service in 1880."

"Left service?" His father had left the family in the same year. The two events had to have been connected. "Why, I wonder?"

"The records do not indicate the reason, only the fact."

"Quite so," the captain said. "Is there any further information?"

The clerk shook his head, his attention upon the cards as intently as any fortune-teller Tigg had ever seen separating fools from their money at fairs. "Only the date of his marriage to one Nancy Drake in 1874."

"They were married?" Tigg said in some surprise. He had no memory of his mother wearing a ring, or of speaking of his father in such terms. "Then that means I have a right to my name?"

He remembered Lizzie's and Maggie's pain over the question of their surnames—and of their legitimacy. Tigg had never given it much thought. He had known his surname, but when the boys couldn't get their tongues round it, he had simply become Tigg—and since being nicknamed was a mark of acceptance in the gang, he had preferred that by far.

"Certainly, if you are Thomas Drake Terwilliger, born in 1875."

"Drake?" Tigg exclaimed. "I never knew I had a second name. Drake. Well, burst your balloon and dance a jig upon it."

"Tigg!" Alice said. "Mind your manners."

"I beg your pardon." He directed the apology to the room at large. He hadn't meant to blurt that out—but sometimes surprise made the jaws flap whether the brain wanted them to or not.

But it seemed the captain had taken no offence. "Are you satisfied with this information?" he asked. "May we return this gentleman to his duty?"

With a nod, Tigg offered his hand to the clerk, who shook it heartily. "May I be so bold as to make these corrections to your enlistment records, Lieutenant? We strive to be as thorough as possible."

"Why, yes, I suppose you ought to." He would then be linked for eternity with Thomas John, in the mind of the difference engine, at least. It remained to be seen what other links existed in the world.

He was still turning over in his own mind what he had learned, half in a daze, when he became aware as they paced down a different corridor that the captain and Alice were in the midst of a quarrel.

"Dadburn it, Ian, mind your own business. I can ask a question of these folks without you poking your nose into it, thank you very much."

"But you will get answers much more quickly if I am with you."

"So you can pull rank again and make them scurry about to do the baronet's bidding? What if I don't want you to know my business?"

Tigg had to admire the captain for keeping calm under high winds. "Alice, my friend, you know all there is to know of *my* business. I had hoped that in this matter, at least, you would allow me to help you, and repay in small coin what you have done for me."

That put a hole in her gasbag, for true. Alice looked as though he had struck her. "You don't owe me anything."

"Perhaps not, in monetary terms." The captain dropped his voice so that it might not be heard in the busy offices they passed. "But if friendship has a value, then I must repay you in that coin. Please let me do so."

For a moment, pride and independence struggled with something deeper. Tigg was no fool. Maggie and Lizzie had briefed him thoroughly on the subject of the two captains—one commissioned by Her Majesty (and blind where women were concerned) and one commissioned by her own intelligence and survival skills (and shy about revealing her feelings). He waited to see which way the wind would veer.

"Very well," Alice said at last. "But only because we are short on time and Claire is waiting for us." Another moment's struggle. "Thank you, Ian."

The captain's face reminded Tigg of someone who has received a gift he hadn't been looking for. "It is my pleasure. Come. The Registry is this way."

At the Registry, where all airships—commercial, private, or military—were commissioned into Her Majesty's service, and staffed with trained aeronauts, any difficulties they might have encountered were magically made to evaporate in the brilliance of the captain's name and family connections. They were shown into the office of the registrar himself, and offered tea, which they declined.

"In what way may I assist you, Captain Hollys?" he asked, the gold on his epaulettes winking as brightly as his teeth.

"My colleague, Captain Chalmers, has a number of questions, sir," the captain replied. "She will take the helm from here."

If the registrar was surprised, he only showed it by a rapid blink. "Certainly. Captain Chalmers?"

Alice was sitting very straight, her spine not even touching the ladder back of her chair. "I wanted to inquire about the commission procedure for an unregistered vessel," she said.

"Unregistered, Captain?"

"As yet unregistered," she amended. "I have a decision to make. I am a citizen of the Texican Territory, yet I contract my ship to Lord and Lady Dunsmuir—"

"Ah!" The registrar seemed to relax. "Yes?"

"My ship, Swan, is of Prussian origin, one of the original B2 cruising vessels. Its ownership was transferred to me and my navigator, Jake Fletcher McTavish, last month by Count von Zeppelin."

She had the registrar's complete attention now. "The B2? The military vessel constructed for speed over long distances?"

"Yes."

"Transferred to you ... by the count himself? How very singular."

"We have had several business dealings, and I have the honor to call him friend."

"It is an honor not vouchsafed to many, I understand."

"So you see my difficulty," Alice said, inclining her head. "I can choose to register it here, or in Prussia, or in the Fifteen Colonies."

The man looked as though he could barely wait for her to finish speaking. "Might I presume for a moment upon your kindness, madam, and urge you to register this vessel in Her Majesty's fleet. For I can tell you now that any captain worth his salt would be honored to serve aboard her."

It was not possible for Alice to straighten further, but Captain Hollys did. Tension filled the air between them, blowing up as suddenly as any tropical gale.

"I am sorry, I do not understand you," Alice said at last. "If I were to register *Swan* in England, I would captain her."

"You?" The registrar's gaze took her in from hem to lacy jabot. "But a woman cannot serve in the Corps. Surely you see that."

"I do not. Why shouldn't she?"

"Because—well, think of the crew's quarters, for one. And the disruption and distraction among the men. No, no. It is impossible—to say nothing of the vagaries of the female mind, which is simply not designed for the mathematics of flight."

Tigg waited for her to snatch up an ink pot and throw it at his head, but she merely took a breath as if preparing to plunge into a pool.

Then she leaned forward, as if to make sure he clearly understood. "I've been flying for most of my life. Captain Hollys can tell you I'm as conversant with the Daimler and Mercedes steam engines as I am with the Crockett—more so, since I wouldn't fly a Crockett if you paid me—and in fact I codeveloped the automaton intelligence system that Zeppelin is installing in all his ships. So I have already proven that nonsensical prejudice you hold to be false—as has my co-engineer, Lady Claire Trevelyan, of whom you may have heard."

From his blank look, this was clearly not the case.

"I congratulate you on these achievements," he said at last. "But regulations do not permit females in the Corps."

"Then perhaps regulations should be changed."

"I am afraid it would take more than the wishes of you or I to do so. But, madam, this does not prevent you from registering the B2 as its owner. Most of the private entities do. It is the rare military man who both owns and captains his ship."

"This woman does both." She straightened once again. "And until I am permitted both to own it and to fly it in Her Majesty's service, then I suppose I shall have to register it elsewhere."

The loss of the B2 was clearly a greater catastrophe than Tigg had imagined, for as Alice rose, the registrar came around his desk to take her hand.

"Please, madam—"

"Captain. Captain Chalmers, as I believe Captain Hollys said when he introduced me."

"A colonial captain, excellent," he said, babbling now. "Please allow me to make an appointment for you with the Registry, so that we might welcome the B2 into—"

"Sir, I believe I made the conditions of my registration clear."

Tigg resisted the urge to cheer. Good for her for not backing down. He couldn't wait to tell Lizzie about this in his next letter.

"But we simply cannot—"

Alice pulled her hand from his and strode to the

door. "Good afternoon, sir. Thank you for your time. It has been most instructive."

"Captain Chalmers, please—"

But Alice did not wait.

Captain Hollys bowed to the registrar and Tigg did the same. And then they both practically scampered out the door.

Alice had already reached the end of the corridor, bearing down on the exterior door like a ship with vanes set full horizontal. They didn't catch up with her until she was halfway across St. James's Park.

13

Alice was closeted with the Lady for a very long time that afternoon, and even Robbie and Dickie looked nervous at the sound of raised voices not quite muffled by the office door.

"She's in a proper temper, she is," Jake murmured to Tigg that evening as Charlie brought in the tea and Kitty helped everyone to a cup and a slice of fruitcake. "I haven't seen the captain like this since the Famiglia Rosa told her the *Stalwart Lass* was to be impounded at the Venice airfield. That were a proper Donnybrook, it were."

Quickly, Tigg filled him in on the details of their visit to the Registry. If he had thought Jake would be surprised, he was in for a letdown, for he only laughed instead. "I have to give her credit for trying. Our Alice ent afraid of nothing—I never seen her back down from man nor beast. And some of the folks we met have been both."

"I hope it doesn't make her fly off to the Fifteen Colonies in a temper," Tigg said. "Not with Captain Hollys still on land leave and Christmas coming."

"If it does, I'll spike the automatons so they don't do as she says, and ground us." Jake grinned. "I picked up a trick or two in my travels." Then he sobered, and held Tigg's gaze. "Which is why you ent going to the Sea Horse alone tomorrow night."

Instead of taking offense, Tigg nodded. He'd already planned to ask for help, but it was nice to have it offered without asking. "I'm not that stupid. Without Liz and Maggie for scouts, I suppose I'll have to make do with your ugly mug."

"And mine," Snouts spoke up from the corner of the sofa, where he'd been totting up a column of figures on the back of an envelope. "You don't suppose we'd let you go off to meet a stranger in the Cudgel's territory, do you?"

"Is he still alive?"

"Alive, though after that incident with the Lady, of course, there'll be no one to carry on his illustrious name after he's dead. Alive or dead, his temper hasn't improved one bit."

"Do you think he'd recognize us after all this time?"

"I think he knows exactly what we look like. There's a reason I've posted a permanent guard at all the Lady's properties, you know."

That was Snouts—prepared for anything. "Then I'd be happy for your company, too. It will be like old times."

"I hope not." Snouts stroked a velvet waistcoat of particular magnificence that Tigg had not seen before. "I'm fond of the new times, myself."

All in all, Tigg had to agree. His prospects had never been brighter. Once the captain was better, he looked forward to returning to duty with fresh determination to have his first engineer's bars in four years. He and Lizzie had talked about it before he'd left Munich, and settled on a plan. It wasn't quite like being engaged, for he had been mindful of his promise to the Lady, but planning for a mutual future had made him *feel* engaged. And Lizzie's kiss good-bye had been everything a man could wish for in the woman he wanted to make his wife.

The Lady and Kitty concluded their calls the next day, which according to her account that evening at dinner, proved as mind-numbing and dull as could be expected, except for two tidbits: Peony Churchill was in Paris but expected back before Christmas, and the scandal surrounding old Mount-Batting's gift of property to his baseborn son had not died away among the drawing-rooms of London.

"I am undecided whether this is because of the general opinion of society on the subject of that family which Julia and her husband have done nothing to improve," the Lady remarked, passing the potatoes to Alice, "or because property is always a subject that excites conversation among the Bloods."

Alice had been down at the warehouses with Captain Hollys all day buying parts and fittings and rope for *Swan*, and consequently looked much more cheerful and like their Alice than she had the day before. "But it does confirm what Ian and the clerk told us about the family. I just wish there was information more recent than four or five years old."

"It doesn't help us much to know he has a house when no one has seen him on this side of the Channel since then," Tigg agreed, tucking into his slice of pork and baked apples with gusto. "My offer to take *Athena* and patrol the coast for a sign of *Neptune's Fancy* is still open."

"I'm afraid you would have more success finding a hook in a pile of rigging," Captain Hollys said. "It is frustrating to have amassed a number of facts—only to find that they are no help whatsoever."

"We did agree that to paint a picture of the only person we know to have been involved was the best course open to us," the Lady pointed out. "I only wish we had another." She turned to Tigg, lowering her fork to her plate. "You will be careful tonight."

He took it as it was meant—both as an order and as a bid for reassurance. "I will, Lady. I have my lightning pistol, and Jake has a pocketful of Mr. Andrew's walnuts."

The moment that name passed his lips in connection with the tiny Short Range Dazzling Incendiaries he had invented, Tigg wished he could have just shut up. But the Lady bore up under it bravely.

"And Snouts?" She gazed at him down the length of the table, where he occupied the chair opposite her, as the *de facto* man of the house. The chair he had been prepared to abdicate in favor of Mr. Andrew—and now had had to re-occupy. "You will take all proper precautions as well, won't you? It has been some time since you've run a raid."

"Claire, really," Captain Hollys murmured.

"We have no secrets in this house, Ian," she reminded him crisply. "And you are as aware of the manner in which we had to live in the past as anyone here."

Snouts interjected smoothly, "I've kept my hand in, Lady, and will be wearing my pistol in a holster under my coat."

She nodded, satisfied, and her gray gaze met Tigg's once more. "We do not know what may come of your meeting tonight, Tigg, but no matter what it might be, you can count on all of us to back you up."

Nothing he says will change my opinion of you.

Tigg understood her meaning as clearly as though she had said it aloud. "Thank you, Lady," he said quietly. Then he pushed back his chair. "No pudding for me tonight. I'd like to get down there in time to reconnoiter a little."

Jake and Snouts shrugged on their coats, checked their pockets, and the three of them set off. They took an underground train to Tower Bridge and then crossed it on foot, arriving in the neighborhood of the Sea Horse about ninety minutes after their departure from Belgravia. They might as well have crossed the ocean.

In a way, they had—a wide gulf made of the time that existed between their past lives and their present prospects.

They'd reconnoitered many a tavern, and their old skills did not fail them. Jake melted into the darkness in the alley behind while Tigg and Snouts determined that the place had only two doors—the one on the street and one out to the kitchen yard, an unappealing square of brick full of refuse and rats.

"Don't think I'd trust their grog as far as I could spit it," Snouts murmured when Jake joined them once more, one street over. "They probably cut it with rat piss."

"They've got a watch posted on the stairs to the second floor," Jake reported. "I had a peek through a window from the roof. No watch up there."

"I'm not interested in whatever is going on upstairs," Tigg told them. "Just in whether or not this is an ambush."

"Looks fair for now," Snouts concluded. "You go in alone. We'll follow in a moment, see if anyone follows you in who doesn't look thirsty."

Tigg had believed himself to be unaffected by the prospect of meeting the stranger calling himself Terwilliger, but as he crossed the greasy threshold, he took in the faces at the tables with far more intensity than usual.

How often did a man get to meet the father who was no father? One thing was certain—he and Lizzie would have even more in common now.

His gaze settled on a dark corner, where a man sat at a table clearly meant for private conversation. When he raised his tankard in salute, Tigg drew in a slow breath—of an atmosphere flavored with rum and onions and urine—and walked over.

"Buy you a drink, Lieutenant?" The man's skin was so dark that he blended into the shadows in a way that was positively eerie. Until he leaned into the light of the old-fashioned wax candle on the table, all Tigg could see of him in the light of the electrick lantern that hung a few feet away was the glimmer of light along a cheekbone, the white of his teeth, and the gleam of polished skin upon his bald pate. He was not old, but shaven smooth in the way of pugilists or swimmers.

A GENTLEMAN OF MEANS

This had to be he, if he knew Tigg's rank—for Tigg was not in uniform, but in raiding rig: dark trousers, vest, flying goggles, and leather belt studded with pockets and hooks for bombs and weapons. His lightning pistol lay concealed in his pants pocket, and while there were two vials of gaseous capsaicin in the loops in his belt, the vials had been made to look like tiny rum bottles, as befitted an aeronaut.

"No, thank you." He waved the barmaid away, and got a dirty look for his pains.

"So," his companion said, looking him over. Did he expect to see some hint of himself in Tigg's face and form? "You've got her forehead, too. Nancy's. And her way of frowning, with the two lines, just here." He touched his own forehead. "Would you like to see her?"

For a moment, Tigg wondered whether, if his father had come back from the dead, his mother might not as well. But no. That couldn't be right. The night-hens had wrapped her body right there in the kitchen before she'd gone to the potter's field to be buried. "What do you mean?"

In answer, the man fished a chain out from under his shirt, from which hung a round brass locket, plain and unadorned. He pressed the screw and it opened to reveal a daguerrotype portrait. He handed it over. "Do you remember her?"

"Not like this." For the face in the portrait was young and smiling, with a cloud of golden hair. "Before she died, she was thinner, and the pox was coming on, and she'd sold her hair to the wig maker for money to eat."

Something flickered over the man's face, and he took back the locket. "I didn't want to leave you," he said.

"Take that for what it's worth."

"It's worth nothing to me," Tigg said evenly. "I don't know you. What you want now or didn't want then makes no nevermind to me. I got on with the life I was handed, and as you see, made something of it with the help of others."

"You sound like you've been in the Colonies."

"Perhaps."

"The wind. It's in our blood. I've been on every continent on this earth, and most of its islands."

"I came by my profession by my own will, not because of you."

The man regarded him more intently now, not looking for himself in Tigg's face any longer. "So you say. Well, perhaps you did. How do you like being in Her Majesty's service? Suit you?"

The more he spoke, the more Tigg tried to place his accent. Not English. Not from the Fifteen Colonies. Was he French? With a name like Terwilliger?

"It does. Where do you hail from? You don't speak like an Englishman."

"I was born in England, true enough, but grew up on the Moorish coast. My pa was from Yorkshire. He was an aeronaut, too. I learned my trade in Rome, and hired on as a ropemaker in the Royal Air Corps. They needed men, and I needed work. That's when I met your mother, when we were based at Hampstead Heath. I was married and you were on the way before I knew it."

"Why did you leave? You left the Corps at the same time. Seems fishy to me."

His eyebrow lifted, cocked at a diagonal, and Tigg felt a shock of recognition. That eyebrow—his mother's finger, drawing a line along it—her laughter—

The door opened and Tigg glanced over his shoulder to see Snouts and Jake come in. They sat four feet away, their backs to them, their faces toward the door as they chatted in low voices, and ordered drinks.

Tigg settled his flight jacket on his shoulders, feeling the truth settle upon him at the same time.

"Something wrong, boy?" Terwilliger asked.

"No. I just recognized something about you, that's all. I hadn't expected to, and it surprised me."

"Ah. Didn't trust me, did you?"

"I still don't. Why did you want to meet me, after all this time?"

"Can't a man want to be acquainted with his son?"

"Depends on whether he ever wanted to, I suppose."

Terwilliger leaned toward him on one elbow, his eyes somber, his pupils dilated in the dim light. "I did want to. You want to know why I left the service?" When Tigg shrugged, he went on. "I had to. I got into bad company—made some poor decisions. It was either desert and face court martial if I ever set foot on English soil again, or be killed on the spot. I chose the long-term plan, if you will."

"So if you're discovered here, you'll be shot? Why would you take the risk?"

"Because I saw you at Gibraltar, and I realized I'd missed my chance. We won't see one another again, my boy—not on this side of the ocean, or of eternity, probably. I have debts to pay, and a harsh master to serve."

"Who? Old Scratch?"

Amusement twitched at the corners of his lips. "I'd choose him in a moment. No. The Doge of Venice."

Tigg felt his face go slack, and struggled for control. "You fly for the Famiglia Rosa?"

His father grabbed his wrist and yanked him toward himself across the table. "Keep your voice down!"

"Are you mad?" Tigg tugged his wrist out of his grasp—not without difficulty, for the man was as wiry as a fighting cock, with muscles ropy and honed from years of scrambling up and down fuselages. "Do you have a death wish, to work for them and yet return to England with nothing to look forward to but being seized to the rigging?"

For aeronauts were not hung, or shot, if they received the death penalty. They were tied in the rigging of the fuselage on the ship they had wronged, and left there until the elements and the cold of the clouds caused them to perish.

The man shrugged. "It was worth the risk to see you."

Tigg could not imagine someone who valued his life so little that he was willing to take that risk. If he only had one last chance to see Lizzie, would he take it, come what may? Somehow he thought that he would. But in her case, love lay in the scale, heavy as gold and twice as fine. This man could have no such counterweight.

But he had told the Lady he would try to find out what he could of the comings and goings in Gibraltar. New information of the Famiglia Rosa could only be to their advantage.

"What do you do for the Doge?" he asked, more quietly still.

"Anything he asks of me. At the moment, the family has the wind up about convict labor in Venice. A deal gone bad or some such. So my being here is self-serving, I suppose, while their eyes are turned to the Adriatic and not to the north."

Tigg nodded. "I heard. Something to do with Meriwether-Astor, wasn't it?"

His father's eyes gleamed. "That's the last name I'd expect to hear on your lips."

"I was just in Venice—third engineer on a ship taking a party to the art exhibition. Heard about the fuss."

"Rich folks, must be."

Tigg shrugged. "A job's a job."

"What do you know of the convicts, then?"

"Nothing. Just that they work under the water, cleaning the gearworks. Nasty custom, if you ask me."

"The family lost a couple of them. Big stink about it. Some young lady broke them out and got away with one of the impounded ships. Stupid gambit on her part—the family are like dragons. You touch even one coin and they'll burn you to hell and back for it."

Alice. It had to be. "There's a price on her head?"

He tilted one shoulder up in a half shrug. "Death medallions come at a pretty high price."

Tigg's stomach did a slow swoop that made him feel a little ill. "Does everyone in the Levant know about the sentence, then? A man wouldn't have much of a chance—a young lady even less."

"No. There was a price of a hundred gold guineas on her head, but that's been lifted. When the family give a medallion, it's to a trusted man. And he doesn't come back until the job is done or he dies trying."

Medallions. Tigg's mind flashed to that night in the park at Schloss Schwanenburg. Three men had not come back. Did the Famiglia Rosa think they were still looking, or did they know the men were dead? It had only been a couple of weeks. Surely that was not enough time to send out another squad?

He dared not ask further. But it seemed clear as day that a medallion meant a man was charged to deliver the death sentence to a victim. Best to change the subject before a word slipped loose that would give Alice away.

"So," he said with an air of a man who has another appointment, "you spotted me at Gibraltar. Do you moor there often?"

"It's the gateway to the Mediterranean and the family have business interests there," his father said, clearly equally willing to change the subject. "But I was on two days' land leave, soaking up the sun—and the excellent grog at the Barnacle. You might be interested in this— ever seen an underwater dirigible?"

Tigg schooled his face into polite but slightly disbelieving interest. "No. Sounds impossible."

"There you'd be wrong. Talking of Meriwether-Astor, he's got a fleet of them in that part of the world, and no one the wiser. Just between you and me and the wall here, I think the family would be wise to throw in with him. But that's none of my affair. I'd never seen one, or the little bubble they use to come ashore."

"You saw one come ashore?" *Chaloupes*, Lizzie had called them. But he could betray no knowledge of that.

His father nodded. "I was too far away to see much, just saw the dirigible surface and send out a little bubble of a thing. Rolled up to a ship and rolled back into the sea in about ten minutes, neat as you please."

Tigg's heart felt as though it would beat so hard the man would be able to see it right through his jacket.

"Seems impossible—like they'd be swamped. Does it roll onto the beach like a ball?"

"No, it has wheels. Brilliant, the mind what came up with that."

He couldn't ask about the airship. Bad enough he was asking questions about the undersea dirigible. But those might be asked by anyone with an interest in engineering marvels—anyone who had never seen what he had described.

"I can't say the Sea Horse's grog measures up to the Barnacle's," he finally said. "Or anywhere but the bottom of a rat's nest."

The man smiled. "You see I'm only drinking enough to be polite." He tilted the mug until its noxious contents lapped at the rim. "Those gents are doing the same. Smart coves. Obviously been here before." He nodded toward Snouts and Jake. "Not me, I'm here on business."

"For the family?"

"Aye."

"Rocks and hard places come to mind."

His father nodded, and pushed the tankard away. "I want you to have this." He reached into his pocket and pulled out what looked like a coin. "Nope. Not that." He laid the locket on the table. "It's all I have."

The locket with his mother's picture. Tigg's heart pounded, and he felt as though his next breath might choke him. "I can't take that. It's yours."

"She had her portrait made and gave it to me on one of my first voyages after we were married. She would want you to have it. I have no ties here now save this one. It should be with you."

"No ties?" Tigg couldn't help it—he challenged him

with the implication, though his mind was churning like the funnel clouds he'd seen in the West Indies. How could this man say *no ties* when the biggest one of all was sitting right across from him?

"Aye, I've hurt your feelings, haven't I, when that was the last thing I wanted." His gaze faltered at last. "Like I said, once my business here is concluded, I'll be gone far away. You and that picture are the only evidence that Tom Terwilliger ever visited this corner of the world and left anything good behind. You take it with my blessing, and I'll die content."

Tigg couldn't wait to escape this place—this man—this moment. He scooped up the locket and tucked it into one of the pouches on his belt. "All right. Fair winds, then." He stood, and his father stood with him.

He offered his hand, and Tigg felt his stomach roll. He couldn't shake it. He couldn't. And yet, there was no reason anyone could see that he should not.

So for the first time in his memory, he put his hand into that of his father.

"Good-bye, Tommy. I wish you well."

He couldn't even return the wish. But he must say something. "Perhaps we may meet again."

"We won't. But it's good of you to say so. Fair winds to you, too."

Tigg's throat closed and he turned away, stumbling blindly toward the door and knocking into Snouts's chair on the way past. Once outside and well away down the street, he gasped and pressed one hand to his mouth. When his mates caught up to him a few minutes later at the meeting point on the south end of the bridge, he was ashamed to have to dash tears from his cheek.

Jake put an arm about his shoulder—Jake, who was not a demonstrative individual and would as soon punch someone as offer him comfort. "Laddie, it's all right. It's done now and no harm."

"No harm?" Tigg croaked. "No harm? Did you see what he carried?"

"No. He pulled that necklace out and gave it to you. Is there something wrong with it?"

"Not the necklace. The other."

"What other? What are you going on about, man?" Snouts demanded. "What's wrong?"

"The medallion. In his pocket. Like the ones we found in Munich. They're given to men commissioned to carry out the death sentence."

Jake dragged in a breath, understanding breaking over his face in the light of the electrick lamp on its post. "Alice."

"There's a death warrant for her. He told me." Tigg gasped for air and choked on it. "And my father is the one who's been sent to carry it out."

14

Lady Claire gazed at Tigg in horror, at the pinched expression of pain around his eyes, and knew the truth even before she had to ask. "Are you sure?"

He nodded. "How many men can there be in England in the Famiglia Rosa's employ, carrying a death medallion, and with such specific knowledge of Alice's actions in Venice?"

"But he seems to have mixed up the actions of two or even three women—Alice, myself, and Gloria." She glanced at Alice, sitting white-faced on the sofa with Jake while Ian paced in front of the fire like a caged lion.

"He saw Gloria loaded onto an airship and said nothing to make me believe he even knew her, or her connection with breaking out their missing convicts."

Granted, it had been from a great distance.

"Goodness," she said a little shakily. "In that case, there is as good a chance that he meant me and not Alice at all." Tigg reached out, and she took his hand with gratitude for its comfort.

"But Claire, you did not have a hundred-guinea price on your head," Alice pointed out, her voice a whisper as dry as sand. "I did. He meant me, sure as rain means flash floods."

Claire gave Tigg's hand a squeeze. "But you, Tigg. What are your feelings after tonight's events? What kind of a man did you find your father to be?"

"Besides the kind who can be hired to kill my friends?" Claire's heart broke afresh at the bitterness in his tone. "I hardly know. Anything I might have thought before that medallion came out of his pocket by mistake was completely wiped away afterward. It was all I could do not to shoot him on the spot."

"At the Sea Horse, you might have got away with it," Jake put in helpfully. "I was waiting for something—but not that."

"I thought the worst we'd have to deal with was the Cudgel," Snouts agreed. "I'd never have expected this."

"One never does expect a Venetian assassin," Claire said in despair. "Well, so much is clear—Alice must leave London immediately."

"Hey!" Alice objected.

"You were planning to anyway," Jake reminded her. "Tomorrow, if I'm not mistaken."

"But what about Gloria?" Alice asked. "I'm not going to abandon her—for all we know, her situation is as bad as mine. We ought to find her first and then run off and hide later."

"It is not a matter of hiding," Ian said. "It is a matter of keeping you safe until—" He broke off with a glance at Tigg.

Her dear boy's jaw firmed in a way that told Claire he was a boy no longer—and likely never would be again. She just wished his final step into maturity and the knowledge of the betrayals life could hold did not have to be like this. Not cutting so close to the heart.

But then, was that not the case with betrayals, by definition?

Tigg looked his captain in the eye. "Are you saying that my father must be killed before he can kill Alice?"

"I am not saying that at all. But he must be brought to justice if he should make the attempt. We will do our best to make certain he does not—but if he should do so, we must be prepared. I must inform the Admiralty that there is a deserter back in the country, in any case. If Her Majesty's men can apprehend him, then Alice will be able to breathe easily."

Something told Claire that a man who had slipped into England with such insouciance that he could order a tankard in full view of a tavern's company would present more of a challenge to the Admiralty than Ian gave him credit for. But that was not her affair.

Her friends were her affair.

All I see is that once again you choose someone else over me and a life with me.

Sick at heart at the memory of Andrew's words, she grasped at something Ian had said to turn the course of her thoughts. "This airship, Ian, that lifted with Gloria aboard—while you are at the Admiralty, is there a way you might find out its course? At least we might be able to narrow down Alice's present location."

"That was days ago, Claire. She could be in the Hebrides by now—or the Antipodes, for that matter."

"But surely we could ask. It is the only clue we have."

"But without identifying numbers or even a flag, how should we know what to ask for?"

"He—Terwilliger—said that the *chaloupe* rolled up the beach, rolled back, and they lifted, all within ten minutes," Tigg said. "But we saw that beach. It was rocky at high tide. They had to have come ashore at low tide, when the sand was exposed. If we consult the tide table, we could know approximately when they lifted. And any ship departing for England on that day at that time has a good chance of being our quarry."

For the first time since they had come in and she had seen Tigg's face, as drawn and ill as that of a prisoner, Claire felt a little bubble of hope. "Your logic is sound, Tigg. Ian, can you accomplish this on Monday?"

"I can," he said. "And once I do, what then?"

"We go to wherever that ship was bound, of course," Alice said a little tartly.

"No, we go to Hollys Park, as planned. With all due respect, Captain," Jake added hastily to Alice. "We've got to get you someplace safe, where the average assassin wouldn't think to look for you. To say nothing of the problem we have with *Swan* being unregistered."

"That is an advantage," Ian told him. "As long as we are discreet and stay out of the passenger and shipping lanes, we can slip out of London to Somerset with no one the wiser."

"The fewer wise, the better," Alice said cautiously, "and I can see the benefit of stashing *Swan* at your house for the time being. But we can be of more use to

Gloria if we ship out on *Athena* after that."

"A moving target," Jake suggested.

"I must agree," Claire said thoughtfully. "And within England's borders one might fall a little behind on filing one's flight plans without incurring too much official interest."

And so it was settled. Alice would not attend church with them the next day, but instead lie low at Carrick House. Needless to say, this did not sit very well with her, but Claire had a brain wave and detailed Captain Hollys as her companion. On Sunday afternoon her foresight was rewarded, for Alice had to be restrained practically by main force from going out to *Swan*.

"I've got the fidgets and no mistake," she snapped at Claire. "Wouldn't you? I have to do something."

"It's only for one more day, dearest," Claire said soothingly. "*Swan* is safe enough at our airfield. No one shall harm her—or board her without your leave."

"She's too recognizable," Alice said. "I need to replace her fuselage—the silver and blue marks her for a Zeppelin ship, and she was the only B2 in that cursed impound yard on the Lido. Anyone with half an eye will know her—and from what Tigg says, Terwilliger was in full possession of both his eyes."

Replacing an airship's fuselage was no casual operation. It took days and a full crew to deflate the gas bags, disconnect all the rigging and lay it out on the ground, remove the old fuselage and then put in the new. The beauty of it was that it would be the perfect project for Alice and Ian to do together at Hollys Park. Perhaps when they were reunited with Gloria once more, they might all repair there and spend Christmas with him.

In a location utterly unlike the Christmas she had planned with Andrew.

As if she had heard Claire's thoughts, Alice said almost wistfully, "What a shame we don't have the Helios Membrane you and Andrew were designing, Claire. It would be just the thing."

"It would be." The hollow around her heart had become a physical pain with this additional reminder. She must not think of it. "When we have Gloria safe and sound, I will make the return of those drawings my first priority. After all, we still have our living to make, don't we?"

Alice was wise enough to drop the subject.

On Monday their patience was rewarded when Ian returned from the Admiralty. They all crowded into the drawing room to hear what information he had been able to gather.

"First of all, the Admiralty has been alerted to your—to Terwilliger's presence in England," he told Tigg. "If it is possible to apprehend him, Her Majesty's finest will do it."

"And if it is not?" Claire asked when Tigg could not speak.

"Then we must be prepared, and keep Alice safe, as we discussed. Now, as to this ship he mentioned at Gibraltar, thanks to our bespectacled friend and his difference engine, we now have an identity and a flight plan."

"Excellent," Claire breathed. "What and where?"

"She was not even given the dignity of a name, only a set of numbers. She is an older model cargo ship, meant for short-range flights between port and city, and she was leased by some run-of-the-mill concern." He consulted a bit of paper. "Amalgamated Division."

"That's a contradiction in terms," Alice observed from the sofa, where she was poring over a two-year-old edition of a supply catalogue.

"Never mind that," Claire said impatiently. "Where was she going?"

"Where we suspected—hoped—she might," Ian said. "Bath."

"I knew it!" Claire exclaimed as the pieces snapped into place in her mind. "He is taking her to his house, the wretch. Did he not imagine that he would be found out?"

"They went to some lengths to prevent that," Alice said. "It's only because we have the right people here in the drawing room asking the right questions that we know anything at all."

"For which we can all be grateful." Claire gave her an exuberant hug, which did nothing for the state of her hair, but which left both feeling much better for it. "We depart for Somerset at dawn tomorrow, leave *Swan* at Hollys Park, and reconnoiter the few miles to Haybourne House in *Athena*."

"Claire, it would behoove us to think this over a little more—" Ian began.

"I am tired of thinking," Claire informed him. "I am equally tired of people stealing my friends and treating them badly. We are going to put an end to it once and for all."

*

"Great snakes, Claire," Alice breathed as they carried their bags from the private landing field to the gravel walk that led to the house in the distance. "He tells me he owns all this—and you turned him down?"

Ian had pointed out landmarks as they circled the field prior to mooring—the house, golden even in the cold light of November, with its elegant Georgian façade, its gardens laid out behind ("The roses and other flowers are finished for the year, of course," he said, "but the shrubbery and the maze are evergreen") and the extensive park with its gravel walks and long drive that terminated in a circle at the front door.

Maybe she'd spoken out of turn, for Claire only bit her lip and glanced behind, where Tigg and Jake were piloting the landau down the ramp out of *Athena*'s cargo bay. Ian was tying the last of the mooring ropes, which gave them a few moments of privacy.

"Of all this I might have been mistress? Is that what you mean?" Claire said at last. "I'm afraid there is more to a man than his property. Ian will make a wonderful husband for the right woman—but I am afraid that I am not she."

Some twist of anxiety that had been winding tighter and tighter in Alice's chest since Andrew and Claire had ended their engagement loosened, and she took a deep breath.

"Were you worried?" Claire asked with a sidelong glance.

"I have no right to be anything at all," Alice said bluntly. "We are comrades in arms, no more."

"But he kissed you, in Venice, did he not?"

"A moment of madness, I suppose. It hasn't been repeated—not since he became ill. And I don't suppose it ever will be."

"Do not give up hope, Alice. I believe you are just the woman to make a different kind of man of him."

"He's already the best of men."

Alice's spirits lightened as a mischievous smile spread across Claire's face. "Even when he is arguing with you and you are throwing wrenches?"

"I didn't hit him—or intend to. I didn't even hit the bulkhead, and the deck can withstand anything short of a bomb."

"And you have neatly avoided my question."

"If you must know, even then. In fact, sometimes I provoke him just to rile him up and pull him out of the megrims."

"Does it work?"

"Sometimes. And sometimes I just have to drop the wrench and hold him until the fit passes." Alice felt almost guilty telling Claire Ian's darkest secrets, but weren't they all friends and companions? And if not Claire, who else would she tell? She had no other confidante—and Jake, much as she liked and valued him, was not the kind of young man to whom you revealed your vulnerabilities or those of others.

"I am sure you would much rather do that than fling hand tools at the man."

Now Alice had to smile. "I would. But it feels dishonest—as though I'm taking advantage of him."

"I doubt he feels that way when he is in the depths of a nightmare. Are they coming less often?"

"Some. Not much. I hope that with the return to his home the hours between will be greater and the severity less. Distraction helps. If he is focused on finding Gloria, then perhaps he won't have room for the megrims."

She looked away, but not in time. Claire shifted her valise to the other hand, which brought her closer—close enough to see Alice's face. "What is it, dear?"

Alice threw another glance over her shoulder. Ian had finished tying off, and had climbed into the landau with the boys. They would catch up to them in a moment.

"Nothing."

"I do not think *nothing* brings such a bleak expression to a woman's face."

"It's silly. Gloria is much the better choice for him anyway."

Claire seemed to trip on her own hem, which was highly unusual for her. "Gloria?"

"Of course. Don't you see that the thought of her is practically all that is keeping him going right now?"

"Gloria."

"Don't sound so skeptical. You know they'd make a perfect pair, with his breeding and her money."

"The woman who shares his passion for flying and mechanics is not Gloria, of that I can assure you."

Alice sighed. "But marriages aren't based on flying and mechanics. They're based on ... well, you of all people know what they're based on, in this day and age—and money is the foundation of it all."

"I do not agree," Claire began, but a hail from behind closed her lips. "You are wrong," was all she had time to say before the landau puttered up behind them.

"Care for a lift, ladies?" Captain Hollys said, smiling as he got out and handed them in to the rear compartment. It was a tight squeeze, but Jake wasn't a very large individual, and Claire was slender.

Ian directed them down the gravel walk and around the walled garden on the side of the house—the kitchen garden, he had explained, as opposed to the rose garden or the ornamental garden or the water gardens. Which just went to show you, Alice thought, the difference between people who named their houses and gardens, and those who tried to keep a six-foot square of chiles and squash alive. Gloria's house in Philadelphia probably had a name, and gardens with names, too.

But that was just too depressing a thought, so she shook it off and followed the company in through the tall front door.

"Welcome home, sir," said a butler, bowing his master over the threshold.

"And glad I am to see it, Boatwright," Ian said. "Is Mrs. Boatwright well?"

"She is indeed, and the proud grandmother of a baby girl."

"Oh, that is good news. I shall send a gift to young Ian and his wife. The rooms are ready for my guests?"

"Of course, sir. In the west wing, next to your own. I have put the young ladies in the large room on the end, facing the rose garden, and the young gentlemen in your boyhood room opposite."

"Thank you, Boatwright. Lady Claire, does dinner at six suit you?"

"Admirably well. And perhaps Boatwright may know something of the neighborhood about Bath."

"Young Ian is plying his trade there, is he not?" Ian asked his butler.

"He is, sir. The missus and I travel there frequently, by your leave, and she and our daughter-in-law can store up enough news for a year in a single trip."

"Excellent," Claire said with satisfaction.

Alice had been down to Gwynn Place, Claire's family's estate in Cornwall, so she was expecting elegant appointments similar to those in that house. But Hollys

Park was altogether a homier establishment. Where one house might have elaborate cornices and medallions in plaster on the ceilings, painted white to contrast with cool green or blue walls, the rooms here were papered in light florals, the ceilings plain, glossy wood, or at most, carved or made of squares of pierced tin. The ceilings were high, and the windows tall, but with comfortable velvet and damask drapes in rich colors, they merely seemed to open the rooms to the terraces and gardens outside, rather than holding a person in.

Ian had said that the house was not very old, and indeed it had modern water closets and running water. His great-grandfather had had the land and title as a gift from the Prince Regent early in the previous century, and had built the house upon marrying a local girl whose family had made a fortune in shipping china and ceramics from the kingdoms of the Orient.

"Isn't it lovely?" Claire said, dropping her valise on the Turkish rug and throwing the shutters wide to let in the last of the sunset. "It is almost enough to make one reconsider."

Alice's stomach plunged, and Claire turned just in time to see her face change.

"Do not even think what you are thinking," Claire said firmly, looking at her over a pair of imaginary spectacles. "Having cleared the air between us, I think I can safely make a joke. For do you not agree that this house feels different from many in which we have been guests?"

"I'm not in the habit of having lords and ladies invite me to stay." Alice hadn't quite recovered yet from the possibility of Claire reconsidering.

"Then you had best get used to it. Consider this

house an example of what taste and love can do when they are combined in one woman. Lady Hollys must have been quite remarkable."

"I'd rather see *Swan* fitted out."

"I would, too," Claire admitted. "*Swan* needs all the care and attention we can give her—and if the truth be told, *Athena* is due for a refit also. I wonder if Mrs. Boatwright would mind our staying for ... oh, say a year?"

Smiling, Alice shook her head. "Your kids at Carrick House might object to that. You had a pretty fine welcome. They missed you."

"And I missed them. You are quite right. I shall refit *Athena* at my own airfield and be practical. I was simply thinking that you would need a chaperone."

But this was too much, even from Claire. "Now you're talking nonsense. Come. I hope the hominess you spoke of extends to not dressing for dinner, for all I have along is my walking costume and one lace blouse."

"You will look like a jewel in its proper setting," Claire said, shaking out her own skirt.

But Alice very much doubted that. More like putting a potato in a necklace meant for a diamond.

15

"The Lady will kill us," Tigg said, removing his uniform jacket and tossing it on the bed. "And she will never trust us again, which would be worse."

"But if we tell her, she'll say no, that we must wait for Captain Hollys and daylight." Jake was not getting ready for bed—a bad sign.

The dinner had been first rate, a fact that Tigg found himself surprised he was able to appreciate, considering he had found out two days ago that his father was commissioned to murder a woman he considered a friend. For Alice was certainly one of the flock. Aside from her friendship with the Lady, she was a fine shot, and excellent aeronaut, and told jokes that made them all laugh.

But her vulnerability now tugged at something deep

inside Tigg—something he had never admitted to himself.

Alice might be the daughter of an air pirate, but he seemed to be the son of one. She had not let her parentage hold her back. It was just the way things were. And her pragmatic way of looking at it allayed his fear that she and the Lady would look at him differently. As if he were no longer one of them.

As if he were tainted by his father's poor choices.

But the Lady and Alice had made it very clear the night before and on the journey here that their opinions of him had not changed—that in fact they respected him all the more for overcoming his modest beginnings and making something of himself.

He was in no frame of mind to do anything to damage that respect. But taking the Lady's landau without permission and running down to Haybourne House to spy out the lay of the land would do damage with a vengeance.

"Come on, Tigg. Has your stint in the Corps really made you the kind of bloke who has to wait for his orders?"

"Better that than take them from a hothead like you. Besides, we don't know exactly where the house is. There's more than one road between here and Bath."

Jake gave him a look that plainly said, *What kind of noddy do you think I am?* "I spied it out as we passed over. I know exactly where the house is. It's ten miles off. We can be there and back in two hours with no one the wiser."

"And how will you explain your newfound knowledge to the Lady in the morning?"

"Better to ask forgiveness than permission, lad."

Tigg rolled his eyes.

"Lizzie and Maggie would go with me," Jake said slyly. "They know their business, and you'll notice that the Lady always forgives them their disappearances, because they bring back the goods."

"Is that what you plan to do?" Tigg's exasperation rasped in his voice. "Bag Gloria and bring her back, and present her to the company all tied up in a bow instead of a rope?"

"Maybe," Jake said. "She'll be looking for an opportunity to escape, won't she? And like true gentlemen, we'll provide it."

"And get ourselves shot for our pains. You forget she's in the company of an officer of the Corps. Or more than one, for all we know."

Jake shrugged as if this were no great handicap, but if he really believed that, he would have gone alone, wouldn't he?

"We'll just be scouting, Tigg," he said. "Nothing more. She may not even be there—they may have taken her another leg farther in a landau, or put her on a train. Wouldn't it be good to know that before we pretend we're a walking party from Northumbria looking at great houses?"

Personally, Tigg thought the idea Alice had broached at dinner a good one. Why did Jake have to muck it up like this and complicate things?

"Why are you so fired up about doing this?" he asked at last, taking the battle into the opponent's camp. "What's in it for you that's worth the risk?"

In the light of the electricks running on their track around the wainscoting, Tigg saw his friend's cheeks flush.

Oh. "You're sweet on her, aren't you? On Gloria. You want to be the one to save her."

"Don't be stupid. She's ages older than me."

"Five years isn't ages. Many a match has been made with greater."

"I said forget about it. A man can think well of a woman and want to see her safe without being sweet on her. Like Mr. Malvern is with Alice."

"And the captain is with Alice."

"The captain?" Jake looked so shocked that Tigg realized that possibly he and the captain himself were the only ones among their little company who didn't know.

"Of course, you numpty. She's mad about him, and he's mad about her—he just doesn't know it yet. Why do you think they argue all the time?"

"That ent no indication. The Lady and Mr. Malvern weren't the arguing kind, and you couldn't say they weren't mad about one another." He paused, his voice trailing away as he thought it over. "Though Alice *is* the one he calls for in the night when I'm sleeping right across the corridor and she's away down in the captain's cabin."

"There you go."

"The captain and Alice." Jake's tone held discovery. "I'll be dipped."

"I'll be doing something else to you if you go off and do this. Come. Dawn comes early if we're pretending to be walkers."

But Jake, the stubborn blockhead, shook his head. "I'm still going. Come or not, it's nowt to me." He changed quickly into the tough dungaree pants he'd been wearing since his time in the Canadas, and tossed a dark flight jacket over his shirt.

A GENTLEMAN OF MEANS

There were some things, like Gibraltar and Lady Dunsmuir—and Jake, apparently—that were immovable once they were fixed. The only result you'd get from bumping heads with them was ... a sore head.

"Fine," Tigg sighed. "Two hours. I suppose someone has to make sure you don't get yourself killed or caught."

Jake had not merely been boasting- -he really did have an uncanny talent for reading the land and orienting crew and ship, no matter on which continent he found himself. Unerringly, he directed Tigg onto a narrower and more potholed road, and within half an hour, the Lady's landau puttered up to a granite wall overgrown with moss, the last wet leaves of the maples drooping over it and gleaming in the running lamps.

"Would you really have tried to pilot the landau without me?" Tigg asked in a low voice as he doused the lamps and banked the boiler, making it ready for a quick escape if they needed it. "Or have you learned to do that, too, in your travels?"

"No," Jake said, equally low. "I'd probably have raided the stables and gone on horseback, or seen if the captain had a touring balloon. But that would have taken half the night. The landau is much faster, and quieter, too."

It felt quite like old times as they scaled the wall, which was so old and crumbly they didn't need a grappling hook or even a rope. This was lucky, since they had neither. It was a scouting mission, Tigg reminded himself, not a rescue attempt.

The gardens were as different from those at Hollys Park as they could be. They needed pruning, cutting, and general discipline in the worst way, proving the Admiralty's information that no one had been master here in years. Back at Hollys Park, everyone had gone to bed before ten o'clock, so that they would be rested before playing tourist at dawn the next day. But here at Haybourne, the lamps on the lower floors were still lit, and shadows moved to and fro behind the window glass.

The young men got as close as they could before the river—the bourne that bisected the property and for which it was named—stopped them. "How will we get across without being seen?" Jake breathed. "There's a footbridge, but there's no cover. Anyone could look out and see us crossing the lawn."

"There has to be a groundskeeper's track," Tigg muttered. "Out of sight of the house. He has to get across, too, after all."

They found it soon enough, a thick log with steps hacked into it, wide enough for a man to push a barrow or walk comfortably with a sack on his back. The track took them around to the kitchen garden, where Jake motioned to Tigg to press himself up against the house.

"We'll be hidden by the ivy and the ground is hard enough from frost that our footprints won't be noticed in the dirt."

You'd almost think he'd scouted a few manor houses before.

Moving cautiously, Tigg decided on their objective: an open window on the terrace. Jake nodded, and silently, they moved toward it.

It was the window to the drawing room, where it appeared there was quite a company.

"Is she there?" Jake whispered behind him.

"I daren't look in," Tigg whispered back. "Listen."

It took a few moments to separate the voices—four men, possibly five, and at least two women. But the ladies spoke in the accents of the county, not like the Lady, who spoke with the posh accents of Belgravia and Mayfair. Local women, then, who might live here or in the neighborhood. But where was Gloria? Her colonial way of speaking would stand out in this small crowd.

The gentlemen were discussing a pheasant shoot. The ladies, closer to the open window, were talking of painting and singing. Then—

"Miss Aster, dear, do allow us the honor of hearing you play upon the pianoforte."

Miss Aster? Tigg and Jake straightened, and glanced at one another. That wasn't right—but near enough for shadow work, if you had to choose an alias.

"I'm not much of a pianist," Gloria said dully, her voice so close that Tigg realized she must be sitting on the sofa, the edge of whose arm he could just see.

"Please, dear. You are so out of spirits it would do you good—bring you out of yourself."

In the silence that followed, Tigg wondered what could be happening. Was she struggling with reluctance to give these people anything they asked for? Or was she trying to decide whether politeness was the best course? That was likely, since clearly she had been given a false name so as not to alert the neighborhood that a victim of abduction was living among them.

"Very well," Gloria said at last.

There was a rustle of skirts and then the lid of the pianoforte rattled as it was opened. A moment later, the emphatic chords of a march sounded through the room, and out the window, and Tigg was quite sure could be heard all the way across the park to the road.

She had not quite made it through the chorus when a male voice said, "Good heavens, Gloria, you will wake the dead. Can we not have something more ladylike? Some Mozart, perhaps, or Schubert?"

Jake made a choking sound, and with a start Tigg realized he was laughing. He gripped Jake's arm and dragged him back through the shrubbery to the corner of the house, where a whisper would not be heard.

It might not be heard in any case, for Gloria was now playing the "Moonlight Sonata" with all the grace and expression of the Lady's walking coop lumbering across the keys.

Music, evidently, was not among Miss Meriwether-Astor's gifts.

"What's so funny?" he hissed at Jake, who leaned against the house with a hand across his mouth, trying to get a grip on his self-control. "Jake!"

"That s-song," Jake got out. "Don't you know it?"

"I know this one. It's Beethoven. Lady Dunsmuir plays it—though not quite like that."

"No, the first one. Tigg—it was 'The Battle Hymn of the Republic.'" He dissolved into muffled laughter once more.

Tigg's smile bloomed as well. "That's our Gloria," he whispered in delight. "Poking them in the eye with it— no one would play a colonial song like that here, especially loudly enough to attract attention."

"There has to be a way to let her know her friends have got the message." Jake had finally regained control of himself. "Shall we whistle it as we go over the wall?"

"Too far away for them to hear," Tigg said. "It's enough for us to know she's in the house and being masqueraded as 'Miss Aster.' Come on. Let's be off."

For once, Jake acquiesced—probably because even he realized they could not drag Gloria from the drawing room with at least four men there. They retraced their steps, and as they approached the groundskeeper's foot-bridge Tigg looked back. There was Gloria framed in the French doors to the terrace, pounding out the concluding bars of the "Moonlight Sonata"—which he could indeed hear from here.

If she had not been so clearly torturing her abductors, who were too polite to comment on her execution, he would have felt sorry for them.

Tigg had just turned to follow Jake under the trees when from across the river he saw an elongated flash of light.

Crack!

The French door shattered inward, and a woman screamed.

Pandemonium broke out in the drawing room. Someone in a Corps uniform flung himself upon Gloria, knocking her to the floor as he protected her with his own body. Another man dove past the window and re-appeared a moment later with a rifle, which he aimed out at the forest.

Tigg yanked Jake down behind a fallen log and they watched, aghast, as the second man fired several shots into the forest not fifty feet away from them.

They heard a crashing among the trees, and then silence.

Tigg and Jake gaped at one another in the silvery light of the half moon. Then they took to their heels lest they be discovered by the inhabitants of Haybourne House on the wrong side of the wall.

They hadn't a moment to lose. Tigg couldn't wait to

get his hands on the careless poacher who had shot at poor Gloria—for surely even music as badly played as hers did not deserve *that*.

*

"And you saw no one?" Captain Hollys demanded for the second time. "No evidence of a vehicle or any means of conveyance?"

"None, sir," Tigg told him. At the other end of the breakfast table, facing Captain Hollys as the most senior lady present, Lady Claire had still not recovered from the tale of their adventures the previous night. She had not touched her poached egg, and her tea sat cooling next to her plate while her gaze tracked from one speaker to the other.

Or perhaps she had recovered, and was simply gathering steam to lambaste them right into the next county.

"You don't really think it was a poacher in the woods." Alice was tucking away her eggs with the air of one who didn't know where her next meal was coming from. But then, Alice always ate like that—with good reason, Tigg supposed.

"A poacher would have better aim than that, or he'd starve to death," Jake pointed out. "No, he fired only the one shot, straight into the drawing room with Gloria at the piano right opposite the window. Tigg and I talked it over on the way back, and it seems pretty clear she was the target."

"And while you were talking, did you spend any time on the subject of your own safety?" the Lady asked with deceptive calm.

Here it came. Tigg braced himself for heavy winds. "We took every precaution, Lady. No one saw us—even this supposed poacher. We were well away from the house by the time he took his shot."

"And the return fire was fifty feet away in heavy forest," Jake put in. "We'd have stayed to investigate, but odds were the men in the house were sending out a search party even as we ran."

From the look on the Lady's face, this was not proving helpful to their cause.

"I thought I could trust you," she said. "How could you have taken the landau and embarked on such a dangerous task without even the courtesy of telling me?"

"They probably thought you would not have let them go, Claire," the captain put in.

She picked up her spoon and stabbed the egg so that it spurted all over her toast. "This is not a case of *let*, Ian. For heaven's sake, we are talking about a lieutenant in the Royal Air Corps, and a seasoned navigator, not schoolboys in caps." She gazed at them, and Tigg saw that in her gray eyes lay hurt, not censure. "I would not have prevented them. In fact, I should have thought of their mission myself." She looked at her runny egg, blinking fast. "I fear I have lost your confidence, you two, if all you think is that I am a nagging scold without a brain in her head."

Now Tigg saw the depth of their misjudgement of her—she, who had had such pride in them as they became men!

He abandoned his breakfast and knelt next to her chair. "Forgive us, Lady. We did exactly that—and we were wrong to do so. We won't do it again. Will we,

Jake?"

Jake looked as though one of Mr. Malvern's Dazzling Incendiaries had gone off under his nose. "Nay," he said at last. "I was thinking like a boy and not like a man, and I'm sorry for it, Lady."

Tigg could count upon the fingers of one hand the times that Jake had apologized to anyone. Here was a lesson learned by them both—an astonishing one at that. The Lady viewed them not as her wards or as dependents upon her will, but as men. As partners and as people of necessary skill whose help she needed.

With a hug and a silent promise to himself to remember that their relationships with one another had changed—for the better—Tigg returned to his own potatoes and egg. "Now that we know Gloria is there and being paraded in front of the neighbors as the visiting Miss Aster, what should our next step be? To find out the identity of the gunman?"

"I believe we may count upon Captain Hayes, if that is indeed the man you saw attempting to protect her, to do that," Claire said slowly. "But our attempts to free her will become immeasurably more difficult, since the house and grounds will be swarming with men looking for that individual."

"You couldn't ask for a better distraction, though," Alice mused aloud. "How can we make it work to our advantage?"

"And how can we be sure he will not make another attempt?" the captain said. "Were I in Hayes's position, I should remove her posthaste before he did."

"What I cannot fathom is, why poor Gloria?" Claire said. "And why now? She certainly never attracted this kind of attention while we were at school, and in the

Canadas no one would have noticed her had it not been for her throwing in her lot with us. She had been to Paris, to London, and to Venice for some weeks before we saw her, and no one tried to abduct her during all that time. I do not understand it. What has changed that she has been abducted by one party, and fired upon by another?"

"Perhaps if we knew these answers, we might understand all," Captain Hollys agreed. "I wonder if Gloria herself knows them."

"I would very much like to ask her." Claire gazed at her now empty plate as though it were a scrying glass. "She did not seem to be concealing information of this magnitude from us when we were together, but who can know another's thoughts?"

"Maybe there's a medallion out there with her name on it, too," Alice said glumly. "Though I would happily give up the honor of being the only one in the country, I wouldn't wish it on her."

"Could that be possible?" Tigg took up this thread, since the thought of that medallion was weighing on his mind in any case. "Could the Famiglia Rosa have put a contract out on her as a means of blackmailing her father? If he had reneged on a promise—if something has gone wrong with his deal to bring English convicts to Venice to serve out their sentences on the gearworks— they would do such a thing without much guilt."

The captain threw his napkin to the tabletop. "Intolerable," he snapped. "Using helpless females to coerce people into their filthy business."

"She might be helpless, but I'm not," Alice observed.

"I was not speaking of you."

"No, of course not." Alice's voice faded away to

nothing, and when her lower lip trembled just a little, she picked up her cup of tea and took a sip to hide it.

In sympathy, Tigg, who sat opposite her, looked away.

"One thing is clear," Claire said. "While Gloria seems not to have been in very great danger up until now—because if Miss Aster has nothing more dangerous to do than play the pianoforte, she cannot have been— something has occurred recently to change her situation. Therefore, I believe we must respond to that change rather more quickly. The question remains, do we attempt to spirit her out of the house quietly? Or loose a dozen gaseous capsaicin vials upon every window and pull her out by main force?"

"Gaseous capsaicin." Jake looked heartened at the prospect.

"That might be our best bet, Claire," Alice said, apparently now restored to speech. "Any attempt to spirit her out will have to get past the guard they're sure to have posted."

"We will be stretched thin, what with someone watching the road in case she is removed, someone watching for the poacher, and several someones watching out for the guard," Tigg said.

"At that rate, there will be no one left to fetch Gloria," Jake said. "Definitely gaseous capsaicin."

"If only there were a way to get a message to her, so that she could be prepared," Alice said. "It's always helpful when the abductee assists in her own rescue."

Claire's gaze became fixed upon the small brass door that opened on the tube system for the house. "A message," she repeated. "Why should we not send a message? Why should not Ian invite Captain Hayes shooting or some such? Or better yet, to some event requiring ladies in attendance—a ball."

"Because Captain Hayes is no longer a member of our Corps—and in fact might be considered by some to be a traitor to the brotherhood for signing on with a colonial outfit." Captain Hollys raised an eyebrow in her direction.

"Is that so?" she asked in some surprise. "But was he not honorably discharged?"

"Honor on paper is not the same as honor in fact," he said with rather uncharacteristic brevity.

Claire thought for a moment. "I wonder if he knows of the general feeling? More to the point, would a message from you, whom he has never met, be met with skepticism or interest?"

"It doesn't matter, does it, as long as somehow Gloria is able to read it?" Alice asked. "We might even ask him to provide us direction to the young ladies of the county to this imaginary ball. Then he would share it with her for certain, even if he would never parade her around in public."

"It's worth a try," Tigg suggested. "The worst that can happen is that he shakes his head and tosses it in the fire. We can still go in with the capsaicin."

"I agree." Claire set her napkin on the table and pushed back her chair. "Alice, come with me. We will compose as delightful an invitation as ever two women did—and hope that Gloria's wits are still as sharp as we remember them to be."

16

Enough was ruddy dadburned flaming *enough*. Gloria was up to *here* with being dragged halfway across the world and then shot at for good measure, and today she was going to do something about it.

Just as soon as she figured out a plan.

Fuming, her temper at a rolling boil under its lid of civility, Gloria allowed the housekeeper to attend to the bruising she had sustained on arm and hip last night, and then to dab ointment on the cuts on her neck and shoulders where flying glass had struck her. The bullet had not found its mark—if indeed she had been its target—but instead had passed through a portrait of an insipid young woman and plowed a good four inches into the plaster behind it.

Captain Hayes, whose quick action in bearing her to

the floor beneath him might just have saved her life from a second shot, had still not risen one whit in her estimation. For while he had immediately dispatched two of his fellow captors—men who seemed to be posing as visiting friends and who had completely bamboozled Mr. and Mrs. Roberts, the neighbors who had been invited to dinner—he had not himself joined the search. No, he preferred to stick to her side like a burr from the Texican Territories, and muse out loud upon ridiculous theories involving poachers and gypsies.

As if either one would fire directly into a drawing room!

This morning she had taken breakfast on a tray in her room, pleading shock and indisposition, but the housekeeper had informed him that her condition was improved, if not her spirits, which had produced an invitation to luncheon.

If nothing else, she could fortify herself with excellent food and then indulge in a good tongue-lashing over dessert. Her temper worn as thin as her linen skirt, she didn't even last until the soup was taken away.

"I demand to know what is really going on here, Barnaby," she said, deliberately using his Christian name though he had not given her permission to do so. It put them on a more intimate footing—as being shot at tended to do. "I have been abducted, handed about like luggage, and now fired upon, and I will tell you right now that I have had enough. Either you give me the entire picture or I go down the wistaria vines at the first opportunity and take my chances on the road."

"That would be both foolish and dangerous. Remember our proximity to the prison."

He persisted in the fiction that they were somewhere

close to Dartmoor. She had no idea how he had convinced the Robertses to play their parts in the farce last evening—perhaps he had told them she was soft in the head and had to be humored or she would have a fit.

In fact, that nonsense would be the first to go.

"Oh, bother it. We are nowhere near Dartmoor. We are eight miles east of Bath on the post road, and believe me, I am quite capable of walking them if I must."

He dropped his spoon, and beef broth splashed on his immaculate shirt front.

Good. Served him right.

"How long have you known?"

"*Pfft.* Since before we moored here. Contrary to my father's belief, I do have a brain, and I can read a map. The moment we passed over Bristol I oriented myself to the countryside."

He sat back in his chair, half his attention on dabbing at his shirt with his napkin, the other half on her, rather as one watches a dog that might bite. "I see I have underestimated you considerably, and rather than making you the dupe, it seems I have played that part."

"I hope you will correct whatever delusion under which poor Mr. and Mrs. Roberts are laboring."

"That is not their name. But that is quite beside the point."

"What *is* the point? Barnaby, you are going to tell me the truth at once, or there will be more than soup flying in here shortly." Her meat knife was clenched in her fist, and she relaxed her hand with an effort of will.

His eyes widened only slightly before he pushed his soup bowl aside. "Very well."

"What?" She would never have thought it would be this easy. In fact, it only could be so if he were about to hand her another line. "The truth, Barnaby. I do not have the patience to wait while you fabricate another tall tale for my entertainment."

A smile tugged at the corners of his lips. "Will you permit me to call you Gloria, then, before I embark upon it?"

"Since we were in rather intimate contact last evening in full view of your friends and associates, I think that is reasonable."

Now the smile had more substance. "Have you been compromised, do you think? Do you wish me to make an offer for your hand?"

Blast the tiny leap of her heart that had no business doing any such thing! "I should not wager tuppence on any marriage between us, with such a poor beginning. Now, enough distractions. Yes, you may call me Gloria, if only because 'Miss Meriwether-Astor' has so many syllables it will slow the recitation of the tale."

"Very well. I suppose I should begin with what I can prove. My name is indeed Barnaby Hayes, and until I joined your father's service, I was a captain in the Royal Air Corps. But along with that I performed other duties for Her Majesty—duties that could not be recorded in the difference engine at the Admiralty, or admitted to any living soul."

With Goria's recent experience, one sort of duty came immediately to mind. "Were you an assassin?"

He shook his head, and she realized with a tingle of shock that she had been only partly joking—and he had answered in all seriousness.

"My duties with the Royal Air Corps were merely a façade. My true calling is with the Walsingham Office under the direction of the Prime Minister himself."

"The what?"

"We also refer to it as the Secret Service Bureau."

For the second time during her acquaintance with him, she was rendered speechless.

"What I am about to reveal to you is of the utmost importance. No one may know of it but our two selves."

"And your three guests, and the Robertses, and quite possibly the staff."

He shook his head. "The staff know nothing. However, Mr. and Mrs. Roberts are couriers, bringing secret correspondence from London that cannot be entrusted to either pigeon or tube. My three guests, as you have correctly surmised, are junior agents, tasked with keeping you safe."

"They're not very good at it," she could not resist pointing out. "I suggest a transfer to the Royal Mail."

This time he laughed, his whole face alight with humor. "Miss—Gloria, may I just say that one of my greatest regrets throughout this entire enterprise has been that we did not meet under more ... auspicious circumstances."

She willed herself not to blush, so of course failed miserably. "Go on," she managed, to give herself time to recover.

The laughter faded from his face, and he leaned a little toward her. Since she was on his right at one end of the dining table, and the junior agents were nowhere to be seen, it had the effect of enclosing them in a bubble. She could smell the wool of his tweed jacket, and a subtle scent composed of lemon and fresh linen, dried in the sun. "I very much regret to say that the Prime Minister, Mr. Darwin, has tasked the Office with the capture of your father."

The moment broke with an almost audible sound. She reared back in shock. "My father?"

His gaze was filled with sympathy, and regret, and purpose. "We have all deceived you from the moment you stepped aboard *Neptune's Fancy* with your friends in Venice."

"Yes, I know," came out of her mouth before she could decide whether or not it was wise to say so.

"You do?"

"Not that you were an—an agent, but that you were deceiving me. Obviously. Dartmoor was hardly my first clue."

"Then perhaps it is I who will be taking a transfer to the Royal Mail when all this is over."

"When all *what* is over? Specifically. Please."

"I regret the necessity for it, but as they say, needs must when the devil drives. We are out of options, and your father is a very clever man. He is also a very much wanted man, by at least two monarchs, possibly three. There have been meetings at the highest levels of government to formulate plans to apprehend him, all of which have failed. Which efforts brought us, eventually, to you."

Gloria had comprehended it now, in all its dreadful, painful symmetry. *"You are using me as bait to capture him?"*

With a nod, he said, "I have come to appreciate your fine qualities, which makes this all the more difficult. You are in no way at fault in any of this. And I realize that the ties that bind you to your father will be irreparably severed if we are successful. For that I apologize, though of course no words are adequate."

A trap. For her father. This was all she was—bait,

like a bit of meat tied to a snare. She put down her utensils, her appetite utterly gone, and stood a little unsteadily.

"And if you are successful?" she whispered.

"He will face the trial for treason that his actions have merited."

"His actions? You mean with the convicts?"

He gazed at her. "What convicts?"

"In Venice. He planned to waylay the ships transporting the English convicts by sea to the Antipodes, and sell the people to the Doge for labor on the gearworks."

Now she had rendered him speechless. After a moment, he got his mouth working again. "No. I did not mean the convicts. I am not even sure there is a law on the books that covers such a thing. No, my dear, I meant the French invasion this summer past, which he financed and equipped for the Bourbon pretender."

Into her stunned silence, he related the facts— succinctly and yet with a gentleness that told her he enjoyed it as little as she.

After a few minutes, when she had recovered enough to speak, she managed, "How is it possible for him to invade another country and I not know? I was in Paris for that entire month and heard nothing of it—but then, I do not read the French newspapers."

She read fashion magazines. Perhaps she ought to elevate her thinking henceforward.

"I agree wholeheartedly that the whole plan was toplofty and misconceived. If not for several factors that we are still unraveling, the invasion might have succeeded. But that is not all."

"Really. Enlighten me." She was operating in a sort

of cloud now, while part of her mind tried to sort back through the year past to see if what he said could possibly be true, and the other part wondered where on earth her brain had been not to know what the English government seemed to know.

The Secret Service Bureau. Any other woman would have fainted with the shock by now. Perhaps she ought to consider it.

"Mr. Meriwether-Astor was also responsible for supplying a known seditionist with a weapon which he subsequently used to attempt to shoot down the Prince of Wales's airship as it passed overhead."

"Oh, now, that is simply beyond the pale," Gloria snapped. "Dad cannot be responsible for what people do after they buy his weapons. That is strictly upon their own heads."

"The weapon was made to look like a telescope. In reality it was an air cannon, built to specifications for one purpose only. We believe we can prove conspiracy to commit high treason. Set alongside the French invasion, we are faced with two attempts in one summer to bring down the monarchy, both equipped by your father. You must see that it cannot be permitted to go on."

She supposed it couldn't. What was wrong with Dad that he was never satisfied? She had seen it coming, in her own small way. Seen how one company was not enough—he had to be buying up smaller munitions works and looking to the horizon for—

"The maps in his office," she said faintly.

"What about them, dear?"

"I always thought they were for decoration. But they're not. France, the southern half of England, the

Royal Kingdom of Spain and the Californias, the Levant ... these are the locations you speak of. I suppose the Californias were next. He—oh, no, that cannot be possible. He cannot start wars in other places simply to sell munitions, can he?"

Her eyes held a silent plea. When Barnaby remained silent out of respect for her feelings—for of course a reply in the affirmative was the only logical one he could make—she looked away.

She had always felt she had never been good enough for her father. Not a boy, not smart, simply kept on sufferance because she was the only heir he had. But now ...

Who wanted to be good enough for a monster?

Even the thought of carrying his name for another moment burned her, as though it were a brand, marking her as belonging to him. As being like him. As having the same blood in her veins.

She didn't. She couldn't.

But how could she escape her parentage? It would be so difficult that escaping from this house would be child's play in comparison.

"What am I to do?" she whispered. To whom the question was directed, she did not know. God, perhaps? Tears filled her eyes, almost as though she had learned of the death of someone who had once been close to her.

Barnaby was silent for several long moments. Then, "Might I offer a suggestion?"

"For what?" Where was her handkerchief? She checked both sleeves, and before she could use her luncheon napkin, Barnaby had pressed his own handkerchief into her hand.

She would not cry. Her father did not deserve her

tears.

"You asked what you might do," he said gently. "It is time for action, and there is indeed a way in which you might assist us further."

"I am already bait," she said after she had blown her nose. "Do you require me to wriggle on the string?"

His eyes darkened, as though she had hurt him, but his gentle tone did not change. "If you wrote to your father under some pretext—any pretext save the one we were just discussing—it would hasten his journey here."

"Hardly. If he did not bother to provide a ransom, hearing from me will not change his plans."

"Ransom? We demanded none. Your disappearance, we hoped, would be enough to compel him to come to England, especially since we made ourselves rather obvious at Gibraltar."

There had been no ransom demand? Well, no matter. That still didn't erase the French invasion or the prince's airship. In the face of that, any finer feelings she might have cherished on his behalf were dying like a rose under the blast of winter.

"One last thing," she said. "What of my friends in Venice—the ones who boarded the *Fancy* with me? If they had not attempted the rescue, would you have abducted them, too?"

"Of course not. We should have conveyed them to the dock and pretended to obey your father's order to take you out to sea until the floods subsided. That they acted so precipitately ..." He looked away for a moment. "I have many regrets, Gloria, and their fates are numbered among them. I hope you will believe me."

She nodded, and after a moment he cleared a space at the table and provided her with stationery and ink.

Dad,

   I suppose by now you have realized that my disappearance was deliberate. I am writing to tell you that I am going to be married. I am eloping to Gretna Green on Saturday with Captain Hayes, of Haybourne House in Somerset. Yes, the man formerly in command of Neptune's Fancy.

   By the time you receive this, it will be too late, but even if it were not, nothing you could do would stop me. I am in love with Captain Hayes, though he is not a baron, and we are going to be blissfully happy together.

Your daughter,
Gloria

She looked up to see Barnaby reading over her shoulder, his face scarlet. "If—if it makes a difference—which of course it does not—I am the son of a duke, though sadly, on the wrong side of the blanket."

"Do you wish me to add that?"

"No. Dear me, no."

"He will never fall for it, duke or no duke," she told him, folding up the letter and pressing her mother's diamond ring into the wax that sealed it closed—a habit her father was well aware of. The letter could come from no one else.

It took him a moment to reply. "We shall see. I—I did not expect *this* as a pretext, I must say."

"It will bring him on the run, so I have fulfilled my duty to Her Majesty. Shall I send it to the house in

Paris, or to his personal airship?"

"I can procure a pigeon to send to the airship." The color was fading from his cheeks now. "It will perhaps be most efficient."

He went out of the room to give the order, and when he returned, she had risen to her feet.

"Do you think—" But her throat closed and choked off the rest, as if there were words too terrible to be spoken. She walked to the window, staying carefully behind the velvet drape.

"Yes?" he prompted softly.

"Do you think ... the man with the pressure rifle ..."

"We do not know his weapon, only that it was a most peculiar bullet."

"Hollow, with an external propulsion mechanism, and containing acid?"

She had surprised him again. "How could you possibly know that?"

"Because it was fired from an Astor fifty-five caliber pressure rifle. Dual barrel, double trigger, with a range of one hundred yards."

"Good heavens. If you can tell me who fired it, I will commission you into Her Majesty's service myself."

Her lips attempted to flicker into a smile, but she did not have the strength. "It is the only firearm that can accommodate that bullet. My father makes them." She paused, then, "I cannot tell you who fired it. But is there a chance, no matter how small, that my father might have hired someone to perform the deed?"

She didn't know how she got the words out. All she knew was that her voice had dropped to a whisper of misery. Captain Hayes made a single sound of distress and in the next moment, had gathered her into his arms.

How long she stood in that warm embrace, losing her control utterly and sobbing into his lapels, she did not know. But when someone cleared his throat, she sprang away as though she had touched a Tesla coil.

"I beg your pardon, Captain Hayes, Miss Aster," the butler said, gazing at something over their heads, "but several tubes have arrived."

Barnaby's consciousness seemed to come back from a long voyage. "Thank you." He took the curled envelopes from the silver tray and seemed to find them extremely interesting, which suited Gloria just fine.

She had to get out of here. For her own sanity, if nothing else. For only a madwoman would enjoy the embrace of a man who had lied to her from the moment he had laid eyes on her—who had abducted her, locked her up, and was even now using her as bait to capture a wanted criminal.

Only a madwoman would feel cool air on her arms and miss the warmth that, for one brief moment, had seemed to offer safety and respite. Only a madwoman would care for a scoundrel, no matter his patriotic credentials and ideals.

And Gloria Diana Meriwether-Astor was not mad.

"Good heavens," Barnaby exclaimed. "I declare, the world cannot possibly become any stranger than it is— and yet—"

"What now?" she asked, since the butler had departed and someone had to say something.

He handed her a square of creamy stationery with a crest at the top—a raven with a twig of holly in its claws.

A GENTLEMAN OF MEANS

Captain Hayes,

It gives me great pleasure to welcome you to the neighborhood, as I understand we have both served Her Majesty in a similar capacity, and we are a mere ten miles from one another. I trust that you and your household are well.

My housekeeper tells me that a young lady is numbered among your visitors, and suggested that I extend my welcome to her also. I am hosting a ball on Saturday, and would be honored by your company. The occasion for celebration is the safe arrival of friends from Venice, of whose return from the art exhibition we had been in some doubt. I hope that I may soon have the pleasure of introducing them to you. The moon will be full and you and your friends may travel in safety.

I remain your servant, sir,
Ian Hollys, Bart., R.A.C.

"How peculiar," Barnaby said as she turned it over, as if the direction could tell her something more. "Never met the man, and he is inviting me to a ball as cordially as if we had indeed served together."

Gloria gathered her scattered thoughts the way a small child picks up jack-straws—slowly, and with dogged precision. "Perhaps you met at some military function and don't remember."

"Perhaps I did. I've certainly heard of him. I didn't know he lived in these parts. Decidedly peculiar way of expressing himself, don't you think? Very poetic. Perhaps it's all those years of flying in foreign skies with the Dunsmuirs."

"Barnaby, if you will excuse me, I must go lie down," she said desperately.

"Why, of course." He was immediately all solicitude. "The revelations of this morning would lay a fighting man flat, let alone a young lady. Please, allow me to—"

But she evaded his proffered arm and fled, the invitation hidden in the folds of her skirts. She took the stairs to the room she had been given as fast as her flying feet would go.

Captain Hollys.

Claire.

Oh, thank God, thank God.

For she had understood the message perfectly, as soon as she'd laid eyes on Ian's holly crest. She'd seen that crest before, stamped upon his luggage, and upon the pocketbook he carried in his coat. *The safe arrival of friends from Venice.* They had survived. And not only survived, but were even now a mere ten miles away!

Gloria flung herself down next to her bed, clasped the invitation between her hands, and gave thanks to the Almighty that He had kept them safe, and that their deaths would not be laid to her account.

When she rose, it was with renewed spirits and fresh determination. *The moon will be full and you and your friends may travel in safety.*

Peculiar indeed. From her bedside, she could see the southern sky, where the waxing moon would rise. In three days, when it was full, her friends—her flock—would come to set her free.

She would be ready. And waiting.

17

"We simply do not have enough people." Claire clutched her head in both hands, her gaze on the map in her lap, which Ian had sketched on the back of an old menu plan that probably dated from his mother's time. She released her hair with a sigh and looked about her. "I cannot be a member of the walking party, lest Captain Hayes should recognize me. Alice cannot leave Hollys Park lest somehow Terwilliger should find her. Ian must be here to guard Alice—"

"I don't need guarding. I'm probably a better shot than he is." Alice took another sandwich.

"That is emphatically not true!" the captain exclaimed. "I challenge you to some target practice in the orchard."

"Done," Alice said. "After you lead the walking

party to Haybourne House."

"Ian cannot go to Haybourne House," Claire explained for what must be the fourth time. "If Captain Hayes's eyesight is even half as good as Lizzie's, he might have seen Ian and Jake in the diving bell. We cannot risk it, and while Jake may patrol forest and road safely in the dark, Ian is better used here. Oh, why did I leave Lizzie and Maggie behind?" she moaned. "They are so good at providing distractions."

"Because they have a job to do in Munich, and you all three know it," said an unexpected voice from the hall. A voice so familiar that for the space of a moment, Claire's heart stopped.

Impossible.

"Is there any chance of a cup of tea?" said Andrew Malvern, walking into the library where they were all gathered, attempting to come up with a workable plan for Gloria's rescue. "I have been on an airship, a train, and a wagon behind the most recalcitrant nag you ever saw, and I am famished."

Claire could not speak. Her mouth opened, and though she poured him a cup of tea, put milk in it, and handed it to him, still no words came out. Her heart, having resumed its normal operation, now proceeded to speed up to the point that he must be able to see the pulse point in her throat, beating like the wings of a bird.

How ...?

"Thank you, Claire," he said, and scooped up a piece of Mrs. Boatwright's excellent fruitcake, which had been doused in so much whiskey that a spark from the fire would set it alight. "Do not look as though I am a vision from Hades. I received a note from Alice yesterday requesting my assistance. And though I could not imagine how I might be useful, I threw as many of my completed, er, *projects* into a valise as it would hold, and set off."

Alice? Alice was the engineer of this betrayal? How *could* she?

Her questions must have been quite clear on her face, for Alice blushed up to the roots of her hair. "I'm sorry, Claire. But we needed him—both for brains and brawn."

She must recover, and quickly, before everyone began to feel awkward on her behalf and it had a deleterious effect on the task set before them. "On the contrary," she said at last, "I see the logic in it. We were just discussing the deployment of our resources."

"Which we will take up again in a moment," Ian said. "Let the poor man have his tea. Boatwright, will you see that Mr. Malvern's bags are taken up? And we might put him in the Turkish room, in the guest wing."

The butler bowed and withdrew, but not before refreshing Andrew's tea and offering him grapes and sandwiches.

"Capital," Andrew said at last, with a sigh of satisfaction. He took them all in, his gaze passing over Claire with no greater or less cordiality than he showed anyone else. "Now, then. Where are we?"

She passed him the map while Ian briefed him on their situation, including the strange behavior of the mysterious gunman. "So while we deeply appreciate the addition to our numbers," he concluded, "I am afraid you must be content with the position of mastermind. You and Claire are both known to Captain Hayes, so you must not set foot on the Haybourne estate under any circumstances."

Andrew studied the map, where the house and its river were indicated, as well as the two bridges over the water. The post road and the stone wall had been drawn in by Tigg and Jake, along with an *X* that indicated approximately where the gunman had been concealed.

"We must divide into three groups, then," Andrew finally said. "Ian and Alice will stay here, Tigg and Jake will provide a perimeter in case the gunman returns, and Claire and I will perform the rescue."

Claire and I! How easily he said it—as if such a thing would be just as easily accomplished. Claire could imagine nothing so dangerous to her composure—to say nothing of her heart—than to be walking through the forest in the moonlight with Andrew, gunmen nothwithstanding. She had barely begun to keep his face out of her mind's eye for two minutes at a time, and now here he was in the flesh, looking every bit as competent, every bit as warm and kind, as ever he had in the sitting room at Carrick House.

Oh, no. This was too cruel. What had she ever done to Alice to deserve this? How was she ever to endure the finest torture a woman could be subjected to— yearning endlessly for the man she herself had pushed away?

Andrew tapped the penciled image of the house set in its cup of hills. "You say there are three men at least inside, in addition to Captain Hayes?"

Tigg nodded. "There were three in the drawing room before the shot, and the two ladies. It was also clear that they were armed. One of them dove for the side of the window, and came up with a rifle. They expected an attack of some kind. They were prepared."

"Or a rescue, maybe," Alice suggested. "I wonder if they think her father and an army of mercenaries are coming?"

Claire stared at her, grateful to have something to think about besides the shape of Andrew's fingers as they handled the map. "Alice, I wonder if you might be right. They cannot have known about this mysterious gunman—and yet, who stages firearms beside the windows?"

"Ned Mose used to," Alice said. "Behind all the curtains, just in case, and one next to the door."

Of course.

"Tigg, why did you say nothing of this yesterday?" Ian asked him. "This changes the entire light upon the situation."

"I just thought of it," Tigg confessed. "If Gloria doesn't have a price on her head—and we can't imagine that she does—then why else bring in men who have clearly seen action and arm the house?"

"Because they expect to be besieged," Andrew said slowly, nodding. "My money is on Meriwether-Astor."

"But that makes no sense," Claire objected. "The poor man is desperate to know where she is. He isn't going to put up a fight, or risk her being hurt."

But Andrew shook his head, and she felt a twinge of disappointment that even in this they should disagree. "This is all speculation," he said. "Let us stick to the facts we know. Gloria is there against her will. The house is armed to the rafters, so getting her out on the ground will be next to impossible. Therefore, we must consider getting her out by air."

"What—from the roof?" Jake asked. "We'd only

have a few minutes before someone noticed there was a ship hanging about like a ruddy great cloud over the chimneys."

"Do you have another idea?" Andrew was not being rude, it was clear. He was deeply interested. But the sad truth was that the unknown assailant had complicated matters dreadfully.

"What about the rocket rucksacks?" Jake said with an air of one producing the ace of spades, which was understandable since no one had brought it up before.

"Left in Venice, I am afraid," Claire said, "at the bottom of the Grand Canal."

"But that is an idea," Tigg told them. "We need something smaller than an airship, but larger than a rucksack, and capable of flying far enough to get her and the pilot out of the danger zone."

"I have a touring balloon in the carriage house, I think," Ian said with a smile. "But it hasn't been used since before Her Majesty came to the throne, of that I am quite sure."

"Is it a steering model?" Andrew asked.

"Yes, complete with propellers, but no vanes or steam propulsion. My sisters and I used to go up and down in the meadow while my mother begged us to land and not endanger the line of succession."

"Has it a fuselage?"

Ian laughed. "Heavens, no. They were silk then— and long rotted away. I expect the basket has, too."

Claire gazed at the man she had loved for so long, who was now as far out of her reach as any balloon. "Andrew, what is in your mind?"

He cleared his throat, and for a moment, she almost thought he looked ... guilty. "I left a large parcel at the train station in Bath, with orders that it be delivered as soon as possible. I brought it to show you and Alice, but I had no idea—it is quite impossible—and yet—"

"Malvern, old man, stop babbling," the captain said. "What is in this parcel, and how will it help us?"

Andrew looked up, and Claire found time itself slowing under the intensity of his gaze. "I completed a prototype of the Helios Membrane for a small vessel," he said to her, as though they were alone in the room. "If the basket and rigging for Ian's touring balloon are still serviceable, I thought you might take it up on its maiden voyage."

*

Claire thought it odd when Ian and Alice suggested they take her steam landau to Bath in order to hurry the parcel on its way. But she became downright suspicious when Tigg and Jake vanished in the direction of the carriage house to, so they said, unearth whatever was left of the touring balloon and make any necessary repairs to it. Before she could offer her assistance or even a suggestion, she and Andrew had been left in the library with a scattering of maps and drawings ... and the ghost of what they had once been to one another standing in the room like another living being.

Finally, after several agonizing minutes of pretending to be absorbed in the drawings for the Helios Membrane, which he had fetched down from the Turkish room while everyone else was rabbiting off, she decided that the silence must be broken. Heaven forbid that he should think she had engineered everyone's disappearance in order to be alone with him.

"If I had not been in the room myself, I might have believed they had all rehearsed their departure." She straightened and dared to look him in the face. "Do you not agree that it looks suspiciously like they planned to leave us alone?"

The smile she loved broke briefly on his lips, then disappeared, as fitful as the sun on a March day. "It does, though I do not believe we weigh so heavily on their minds as to deserve such a complicated consideration. I am certain it was only coincidence."

Now he must truly think she had engineered it. If she was not to die of mortification, she must change the subject. "These plans are a work of art," she managed, moving the inkwell so it sat exactly in one corner of the drawing on the library table. "How clever of you to adapt my original concept of the ribbing along the fuselage, and weave these small conductive channels into a fabric that is the next best thing to chain mail ... though much lighter, of course."

He nodded, as though he was as eager not to speak of themselves as she. "It works out very well, since the threads themselves absorb the energy, channeling it through your ribbing to the automaton clusters containing the power cells, where it is directed to the engines. It is essentially a combination of your work with the energy cell and mine with the Helian batteries on the locomotive, turned inside out, if you will."

"Have you tested it with something smaller than a touring balloon?"

He nodded, and when he smiled, it was the smile of someone presenting a gift, and hoping that it will be welcome. "Young Willie Dunsmuir told me about your firelamps, so when he came to visit me at the laboratory the other day, we constructed one with a smaller version of the Helios Membrane. And much to my astonishment, it worked."

"I hope you didn't lose it over the rooftops, like the firelamps. I always hated having to sacrifice them for the greater good."

"He warned me about that, and so we knotted a long tether with which to bring it down again."

She smiled, too, at the thought. "I have not seen Willie in weeks. When I return to London, a visit to Hatley House must be the first thing in my diary."

"He misses you."

"Does he? But he must be very much occupied with school and travel. If the Dunsmuirs are in town, they will want Ian soon, I imagine."

"How is he, by the bye?"

She lifted one shoulder in the French manner. "I am not a physician, but I believe he is better. Being at home, here at Hollys Park, seems to have made a difference. And having someone else to think about has made even more. This affair of the death medallion has brought out the protective side of his nature with a vengeance."

Andrew looked completely at sea—a sea with a kraken surfacing in it. "The what?"

With relief at having another subject to discuss that did not involve either of them, she told him what Tigg had discovered, both about his father and his certainty about the man's mission in England. "He does not say much," she concluded, "but it must be dreadful for him. He is as focused on Alice's safety as Ian is, but for different reasons. If Terwilliger is killed during an attempt on her life, how will he feel then? How could someone feel, so recently reunited with a parent—only to find out he has been coerced into being a villain?"

"Slightly better than if Alice were killed, I should imagine," Andrew remarked dryly. "But you are right, it is a dreadful situation, and one not easily solved. Is there any indication that this Terwilliger senior is anywhere in the neighborhood?"

She shook her head. "Aside from one shot aimed at Gloria for reasons we cannot fathom by someone we cannot identify, it has been as quiet as the frost forming on the lawns. We suspect he remains in London. If it were not for the need to extract Gloria from Haybourne House, I should rather enjoy it here."

A pause. "No regrets?"

"You sound like Alice. Of course not. If there is anything positive to be gleaned from her situation, it is that Ian may finally see that she is the woman for him."

"Do not tell me you are still playing matchmaker."

"Not I." At last she was able to smile a little. "But I cannot speak for Jake and Tigg."

"Do you really think they will suit one another? I cannot imagine two people more different."

"On the outside, perhaps. But during his … illness … she has become more motherly, and he has become less arrogant and commanding. Somehow it has brought them closer to the middle, where they can see one another's good qualities without the trappings of family and rank—or the lack thereof—getting in the way."

He gazed at her over the drawings. "You have become very wise in the ways of your friends, I see."

"I wish I were as wise about myself," came out of her mouth before the thought had even formed in her mind. She turned away, lest he should see her blush and think—oh, never mind what he might think. He was perfectly free to think whatever he wanted. She must bring the discussion back to a more practical subject.

"So if we are to perform a rescue from the air, we must come up with a way to get Gloria up to the roof. Do you have any thoughts in that direction?"

He was silent as she walked to the fire, holding out her hands to the flame, though the room was not cold. At last he said, "We could send a message. Dress it up as a telegram for her."

"We cannot guarantee someone would not open it before giving it to her. Or that they would not simply throw it into the fire. Besides, we have already sent a letter with an encoded message that she should be ready for a rescue late tonight."

"Burglary is always an option."

"The risk of discovery is too great. Particularly with firearms propped next to every window."

"You could always slide down a rope from the balloon, open a window, and fetch her out." From the smile in his voice, it was clear he meant it as a joke.

She turned slowly from the fire. "I could," she said slowly.

"Claire, you must not be so literal. Even if I were serious, I would not put you in such a dangerous position."

"I have been in dangerous positions before."

"If anyone is aware of that, it is I, believe me."

"But consider, Andrew. Ropes and windows aside, we have no idea where Gloria's room is. We do know that at least one lady is staying there, and servants come and go. For the fifteen minutes it would take to locate Gloria and spirit her up to the roof, who better than I to play the part of imperious lady and frighten off anyone asking questions?"

"Impossible. They would see through you in a moment."

"Andrew, you are clearly not familiar with the inhabitants of country houses. There is a very good chance that the staff is not familiar with all the guests, having been brought in from elsewhere to handle a large party. I do not know who this other lady is, but I could certainly impersonate a member of the party for the brief moments I would need."

"No, there must be a more practical way. We must wait for Ian and Alice to return and talk it over with them."

"We have been doing nothing *but* talking since yesterday, and have come up with nothing."

"But now I am here, which might spark a different train of thought."

"There is none. My logic is sound, and you know it." She faced him, hands on hips. "Who better to make the attempt than I?"

Something seemed to break in his eyes. "Who better? And here we are again, Claire, exactly where we were in Munich, with you about to dash off to save someone, and I left behind to worry about you!"

His vehemence took her aback, until with a rushing of the blood in her veins, her temper flared. "That is the crux of the matter, is it not? You worry. And you worry because you do not trust me to succeed!"

"I have never known you to do anything *but* succeed! The crux of the matter is that you do not appreciate the feelings of those who love you!"

In the sudden silence, the last two words rang as though a trumpet had sounded in the room.

Andrew lifted his chin. "Yes, love you. I am not ashamed of my feelings, though you have spurned them."

"I haven't—I—"

To her utter horror, the strengthening elixir of anger drained out of her as fast as it had come, and her lips trembled. Tears welled up in her eyes—tears, when she thought she had cried them all out night after night in the comforting embrace of her pillow and the dark. Oh, how could her physical being betray her in this way— now, of all times?

"I haven't spurned them," she managed with a gasp. "You walked away."

"Because if I had not, I should have had my heart broken again and again instead of only once. Every time you left to go and save someone, it would have broken. Every time you put someone else before me—before us—no matter how worthy, it would have broken. How can any man gaze upon such a future and not quail before it?"

He had said these things in Munich, but now it was as though a different woman was hearing them. How could she not have realized—how could she have been so blind to his point of view? Was it because of Tigg, who had had his father restored to him in body and then been brutally torn away in spirit? Was it because of Alice, who had borne up under the threat of death with a toss of her unruly mane and a sure finger on the ever-present pistol at her side—knowing that her chance for love might be snatched from her at any moment?

Or was it because in these last weeks, she, Claire, had drunk the bitter gall of separation from the one man who completed her, who made her better than she was because of his love?

He had walked away, yes. Hurt had driven him from her. But she had inflicted it and then allowed it to do so. She, who could have stopped him, who could have listened, had let him go and thereby wounded herself beyond hope of healing.

Or ... almost beyond hope.

For the trumpet call still rang in her ears—calling her to an adventure even greater than those she had experienced already. She had not been truly prepared for it when they had become engaged, or even as recently as Munich. But his absence from her life had created such a hollow within that she could not bear to live with it any longer.

She unfasted the top two pearl buttons of her lacy blouse, and Andrew's eyes widened in shock at her impropriety. "Claire!"

Slowly, she pulled up the fine gold chain upon which hung her engagement ring with its three pearls. She unfastened the clasp and slid the ring into her palm, then refastened the chain around her neck and did up the buttons over it.

The ruddy color drained from Andrew's face, and he set his jaw. "There is no need to return the ring, Claire. You may keep it in remembrance of happier times."

"I do not wish to return it," she said softly. "I would like you to restore it to its rightful place upon my finger."

His gaze met hers and locked. "If I do, it does not mean that you and I shall never be parted. It will mean that if we must part, we do so in faith and trust."

"It could also mean that we will not part at all—that we will do what must be done together."

"It could," he allowed. "For I must tell you that

parting holds no charms for me. The last weeks have held more misery than I ever believed possible."

"They have for me as well. I do not want to live through such misery ever again, Andrew. I want to live with you, as your wife."

He took a step forward, and so did she. They met in the middle of the rug before the fire, and he took the ring from her palm.

"For as long as we both shall live," he said tenderly, and slid it onto the fourth finger of her left hand.

She went into his arms, and it was like coming home after a very long time away.

18

The air held the kind of cold silence that meant snow was on the way, if Alice knew anything about weather, and so she convinced Ian to put the top up on the landau despite his preference for the wind in his face. "You're on the ground now," she grumbled as she pushed the acceleration bar out as far as the potted road would allow.

"I miss the air," he said simply. "Don't you?"

"Sure, but it's not going anywhere. It will be there when *Swan* and Jake and I are ready for it." She swerved to miss a pothole, and Ian gripped the leather seat to steady himself.

"And when will that be?" he asked.

She slanted a sidelong look at him, then focused her

attention on piloting Claire's pride and joy. "When we get the refit done, I suppose. I'm quite prepared to pay a moorage fee for your airfield, if that's what you're wondering. I don't take something for nothing."

"Certainly not. You are my guests for as long as you care to moor there. Look." He pointed. "There is Haybourne House—or its wall, at least. I just glimpsed the plaque upon the gate."

She didn't dare slow down, in case there were watchful eyes in the woods, but that didn't stop either of them from getting a good gander at the lie of the land. Not that there was much to see—the wall had to be six or eight feet tall, and made of old stone covered in lichen and moss. But it didn't encircle the entire estate; it only seemed to enclose the forest—what the nobs called a *park*.

"Is it meant to keep people out of the woods?" she wondered aloud. "Look, you can just see the house through those trees."

"It seems rather that they are trying to keep the deer in," Ian said, looking while trying to make it appear as though he was not.

A shadow passed over them, and out of habit, Alice looked up. She gasped, and they practically ran up on the bank until she remembered where the braking lever was and hauled on it.

"Great Caesar's ghost, Alice—are you trying to kill us? It's only an airship."

"Sorry," she mumbled. "I thought it was—something else."

He waited until they were bowling along again at their previous pace before he asked, "It is heartening to think that this time it is not I ducking in fear and gibbering upon the floor boards. What did you imagine it was?"

"I don't know—so close to the ground—I thought it might be—"

Realization dawned in his eyes. "You thought it might be the assassin? Terwilliger?"

Miserably, she nodded. "I don't like to think about it, but sometimes—I remember the three in Munich, and how they must have come—"

"I do not blame you. This expedition is foolish. We ought to have stayed at Hollys Park."

"If we're going to fetch Gloria tonight, we have to have the Helios Membrane. It was either me or Tigg, since neither you nor Jake know how to pilot a landau."

"I must remedy that forthwith. It is ridiculous that I have neglected this part of my education. When all this is over, I hope you will teach me."

"You'll have to buy one, first. Unless Andrew manages to convince Claire this afternoon that they belong together, she'll want to leave as soon as we do what we came for."

"It was cruel of you all to desert them."

"Perhaps. But sometimes you have to leave two wild horses in the same paddock until they settle their differences."

Alice could only hope that their accidental stratagem would work. Meanwhile, it felt good to do something other than pacing around the lovely rooms of Hollys Park or pulling down yet another section of *Swan*'s rigging for repair. She ran a risk appearing in public, it was true, but all things considered, it was worth it.

The Bath train station was a chaotic roar of trains, people dashing hither and thither, and piles of baggage waiting for porters. It took nearly an hour to determine from the baggage master that a large parcel bearing Andrew's name had been assigned to a steambus scheduled to leave that afternoon, and twenty minutes after that to convince the driver of said bus that they were not in fact stealing the parcel, but were the bearers of a letter from Mr. Malvern with permission to collect it personally.

The thing weighed as much as two of Alice together, and it was all they could do to stagger to the landau and deposit it in the rear compartment.

"How does he expect a touring balloon to fly under that weight?" she said, gasping, as she leaned on the wing to catch her breath.

"Perhaps there is more in that parcel than he told us." Ian flexed his arms. "I am pleased to see that my shore leave has not— " He stopped.

"Not what?" Alice leaned forward to catch his eye, and his arm caught her on the collarbone, pressing her back against the warm golden wing of the landau. "Hey!"

"Alice, stay behind me."

"Why? What do you see?"

"Dash it all, he is coming this way. Quickly, we must pretend—forgive me— "

"Wha— "

Ian gathered her into his arms, and, trapped between his tall body and the landau, she could not move. And in a moment, she didn't want to, for he dipped his head and kissed her.

Alice forgot how to breathe. Forgot that his heart belonged to Gloria Meriwether-Astor. Forgot that this was merely playacting—for if it was, he belonged on the stage at Covent Garden. He kissed her as though he really meant it. Thoroughly. Wonderfully. Endlessly.

She had not risen to her current state of prosperity by missing an opportunity when it presented itself. She fisted her hands in his lapels and pulled him closer. He made a tiny sound of surprise in his throat, and then went in for a second. And when, after an aeon in which the world tilted off its axis and began to spin in a whole new direction, the kiss broke and he lifted his head, it was to gaze into her eyes as though he had never seen her before.

He blinked.

She released his coat, self-consciously patting the abused lapels back into place.

And then his gaze lifted, over her shoulder, watching something. Not her. She could not speak, could only look into his face, seeing the way the winter sun gilded his lashes and made his blue eyes even more intense. But he was breathing heavily, as was she.

"What is it?" she finally managed, when she was sure her mouth would work properly. "Who did you see?"

After a moment, he nodded, but for some odd reason, did not step away as she expected. "I am not quite sure I would have believed it, if not for the evidence of my own eyes." His gaze dropped to her lips ... whereupon he blinked again and hastily met her eyes. "It was Gerald Meriwether-Astor. He just got into the steambus from which we removed Andrew's parcel."

He must be hallucinating. Could kisses do that to people? "Gerald Meriwether-Astor is forbidden to set foot on English soil. And even if he had the nerve to do it, he would never ride a steambus. The man is as rich as Croesus. He could hire a six-piston Bentley."

"I agree on all points. And yet, there he is, you see? Dressed as a country walker—at this time of year." He slipped an arm around her and moved around until she could gaze past his shoulder yet remain mostly concealed. Sure enough, there he was, a fireplug of a man wearing a tweedy jacket, heavy walking boots and the kind of tweed cap into which one sticks flies on hooks. With one hand, he used the pole in front of the steam pipe of the bus to help pull himself up as he climbed the steps. The fingers of the other were looped through the straps of a rucksack.

Alice sucked in a lungful of air. "Ian, we have to leave. If that's really him, we can't let him see us on the road. And we have to tell the others. Heaven only knows what this means—but it can't be good."

She leaped to re-ignite the boiler, and before the bus could get up a proper head of steam, they were out of the station yard and away down the road as fast as the acceleration bar would allow.

Two miles passed in a panicked blur before he spoke. "Alice—about what happened, there in the station yard—please allow me to apologize."

She slowed their headlong rush slightly, but not much. "Why? I enjoyed it—and so did you. Though I don't imagine Gloria will if she ever hears of it. We shall have to be clear it was necessary so that we wouldn't be spotted."

The landau plunged into a pothole and out again, but instead of grabbing the nearest stationary object, he gripped her arm. "What the devil does Gloria have to do with anything?"

She couldn't shake him off or she'd lose her grip on

the acceleration bar. Besides which—to her shame—she rather liked the feel of his hand.

"Well, nothing right now, maybe. But once she is safe, I expect she'll have quite a lot to do with you."

"You are speaking in riddles, woman."

His testiness allowed her to be a little more frank than she might have been ordinarily. "It's no riddle that she's the woman you've had your eye on since Venice. Everyone knows it—except maybe Gloria. She's a good choice for you."

"For me?"

Goodness. Did she have to spell it out for him? Fine, then.

"She's smart, and pretty, and knows how to dress for all those fancy occasions you and Claire are in the habit of going to. She's got buckets of money, and you have a title. If I didn't like her so much, I'd hate her, because she's going to have—" She stopped.

"Have what?"

"You."

"Is she?"

"Isn't she?"

"No, she bloody well isn't! I'll thank you to allow me to do my own choosing."

"Well, fine. Just hurry up about it, will you?"

"Hurry up? I've only just realized it myself."

"Realized what?"

"I'm not going to tell you that when we're tearing down a road in a landau!"

Oh, the big bumble of a man! She hauled on the braking lever and the landau careened over to one side, where thankfully there was not a bank. Or a tree. "There. Are you happy? You have two minutes to tell me what on earth you're talking about before that steambus catches up to us, so spit it out."

He glared at her. "I have never in all my life met such a headstrong, maddening woman." He checked himself. "Except for Claire." The glare returned. "I'll have you know that I am not going to court Gloria Meriwether-Astor. I've never had any intention of doing so. The only reason I'm up to my neck in this business is because she is your friend. I am doing this for *you.*"

She gaped at him, while the landau's boiler bubbled, and steam pressure built.

"You are not."

"Do not contradict me! I am helping to rescue your friend. I am offering you my airfield for as long as you need it. I would offer you my hand and my home, too, if I didn't think you'd shoot me on the spot for my impertinence!"

He couldn't be serious.

But yet, he must be. He was certainly furious enough to be.

Wordlessly, holding his gaze, she reached into the pocket of her pants and took out the lightning pistol she had made. She laid it on the seat beside him, and he took it up, resting it on his knee.

"We have to go," she said at last.

"This conversation is not finished."

"I know. Hang on."

She retained just enough presence of mind to remember what Claire had said about letting off the pressure, and the landau leaped ahead like a deer.

When she had it under control, she realized that he had chosen to hang on to not the handles or even the seat, but her hand, though it was wrapped around the acceleration bar in a white-knuckled grip.

Her heart filled and lifted with such amazed, crazy joy that if the landau had suddenly tilted up into the air and taken flight, she would not have been a bit surprised.

19

Gloria lay upon her bed, fully clothed and wide awake, her head turned upon the pillow so that she could see the moon rise through the tall windows. She couldn't remember ever caring about where the moon was prior to this, but tonight, she had opened the drapes the maid had so carefully closed, every nerve strung taut as she waited for the slow silvering of the sky that would tell her it was time.

Saturday night, when the moon was full, just as the crinkled invitation under her pillow had said.

In the meanwhile, her brain ran riot, running over every possible scenario for rescue.

For it was a distressing fact that while she knew the *when* of a rescue, she did not know the *how*. Even though she knew it was ridiculous, she had waited through dinner and the interminable evening that followed with bated breath, in case they decided the bold approach was best, and came dressed in evening clothes, ready to introduce themselves and sit down for a game of cowboy poker.

But they had not. So that left a few other options.

Would they come by road, in the landau? Certainly not—they would be spotted before they drove halfway through the park.

From the windows at the back of the house, she had seen walkers and hunters in the hills, the former somehow managing not to be shot by the latter in their pursuit of game. Perhaps her friends might disguise themselves and come that way, pretending injury so that they would be admitted to the kitchen, from whence they would promptly lose themselves in the house until they located her.

To her knowledge, that had not occurred either.

And so she lay there, wondering what other plan Claire and Ian might come up with. But every option seemed impossible. After the mysterious gunman's single shot, more gentlemen from the Walsingham Office had arrived to scour the estate. They had found nothing save a flattened space in the grass under the trees opposite the house, where presumably he had lain to take his shot. Subsequently they had not seen so much as a hair of him, which made her even more certain it must have been a poacher with terrible aim, who had frightened himself so badly he was probably in Ireland by now. If it had not been for the patch on the drawing-room wall where the portrait had been removed and the plaster repaired, she might have thought she had dreamed the entire incident.

If only she could shimmy down the wistaria vines and run! But Barnaby had taken her at her word—every window was guarded, every door had a man posted next to it. Nameless, pleasant men whom one would forget instantly if one were not forever tripping over them in passages.

Her very soul yearned toward the hills in the south—to fly over tree and wall and garden and land in some nameless village where she could buy a ticket on the milk train and disappear. Or perhaps she would simply fly to London, while she was at it, and—

Gloria caught her breath, sat up abruptly, and flung her feet over the side of the bed.

Fly. Of course.

Claire flew an airship, didn't she? That's how they'd come to Venice. How they'd come to England. And very likely how they'd come to Hollys Park, for who would drive on roads as poor as the ones in England?

Every man Jack in this house was watching doors and windows, bushes and trees, waiting for her father to arrive. No one was looking up. No one was guarding the roof.

No one had been more surprised than Gloria to see the note that had come by pigeon this morning, in response to the letter she had written a few days ago.

Gloria,

I will not dwell upon the utter hell you have put me through during the course of this escapade. I will not elaborate upon the letters I have sent to your friends, and the letters they have sent to their friends, all in an effort to locate you. We have all been convinced you were dead, and instead you are running off with a scoundrel with not even a thought for those who feel responsibility for you.

I utterly forbid you to marry the bounder. If you do, not a single penny of your inheritance will you ever see. I will donate the lot anonymously to a foundlings' home in Philadelphia, so you will not even have the satisfaction of your name upon a plaque above the door.

You may expect me by train on Saturday, when I will deal with this man and take you back to the Fifteen Colonies. My ship is waiting in France and we will quit this side of the Atlantic immediately. You may inform your erstwhile suitor that the only reason I do not have his head, his property, and his career is because I must enter and depart the country quietly. If he has laid so much as a finger upon your person, he will deal with the consequences.

Your father,
Gerald Meriwether-Astor

He never signed his letters *Dad* like a normal person. He always signed them with his full name, as though she had never met him before in her life.

He had not turned up on schedule, but that did not fuss her much. With any luck, he had been arrested in Bath, which would save Barnaby and the pleasant men some exertion. She did not care. As far as she was concerned, she had become an orphan the moment she learned about the French invasion of England.

So she had put him through utter hell, had she? Say rather that, like the Famiglia Rosa, he did not allow anyone to take what was his. The only emotion he likely felt was outrage, not love or fear for her safety. Even his reply had been about his rage and his money, not about her happiness or well-being.

Well, she had disappeared quite successfully against her will. She would disappear even more successfully under her own steam, and despite all his millions and his seemingly endless supply of men and ships and guns, he would not be able to find her then, either. Perhaps Claire would help her find work to keep a roof over her head, and then she could live her own life instead of pretending to be content as a mere appendage—or inconvenience—to his.

The house slept, as much as the pleasant men working their rotating watches could be said to do. Having no coat, since she had not been out of doors since she arrived in her suit and shirtwaist, she pulled a woolen blanket from the back of the chair next to her bed and wound it about herself as a shawl. Her rings and her little bit of money were already tucked into her corset.

She crept into the corridor, which was carpeted, and up the back stairs, which were not. The servants had gone to bed, so there was no one to see her slip up a set of stairs so narrow they practically formed a ladder. A short corridor served several storerooms, which she only knew because she had prowled about up here the other day for want of anything better to do. She did not dare light a lamp, for the guards posted outside in the garden would surely see it glimmering in the topmost row of windows under the roof, and send someone to investigate.

The door to the roof was in a tower so short it was more like a human-sized barrel, so she unlatched it by feel and stepped out, closing it carefully behind her.

Air! Sky! Freedom!

Gloria dragged lungfuls of frigid air deep into her lungs, then scanned the sky for anything resembling an airship. But nothing crossed the sky but banks of woolly clouds, moving in from the north. It felt like snow.

Surely they would come soon. Surely she would not have to retreat to her room, half frozen, and spend the rest of the night contemplating yet another day of imprisonment.

Claire, are you out there? Are you really coming? Please don't leave me here.

*

"We must leave soon, or she will think we are not coming." Cautiously, Claire leaned out of the basket, craning upward as she attempted to see Andrew in the touring balloon's rigging. Except that it was not really a touring balloon anymore. It was something quite new.

"There—that's got it," came Andrew's voice from above. "Ignite her, Claire, and we shall see if this will work." Nimbly as any midshipman, he climbed down the rigging and landed in the basket beside her. "I had the Membrane laid out in the sun all day and its energy clusters are fully charged—how fortunate the weather has cooperated until now."

"Let us hope all these cobbled-together parts will cooperate with one another, as well," she observed, her hands moving quickly from switch to lever. "It has been so long since I ignited a vessel without Seven that I have quite forgotten how—to say nothing of the fact that we have no coal or fire."

"It seems strange, I agree. And—now."

He pushed forward the final lever and to her immense satisfaction, the power stored in the Membrane made its way to the automaton clusters, each of which featured a small, modified version of one of Dr. Craig's power cells, and thence to the makeshift gondola. The propellers began to turn.

She clutched Andrew's arm. "It works!"

He caught her against him in a hug of triumph, and kissed her soundly.

"Now, now," said a voice from below. "None of that out in full view."

Claire detached herself from Andrew and leaned over the rim of the basket. "That will be enough of your impertinence, Jake Fletcher McTavish," she said, smiling. "You may cast off."

"Sure you don't want one of us along?" Tigg said. He hadn't been happy about this excursion from the moment he'd learned that Claire and Andrew would attempt it alone.

"I want both of you along," she said, "but as you can see, the addition of Gloria's weight on the return journey will be as much as this poor old wreck can manage. You know your part. I count on you to carry it out."

She had every confidence that they would, for she had no confidence at all that the ancient touring balloon would survive the journey. Jake and Tigg were to follow as best they could in the landau, keeping them in view as much as possible during the ten miles between Hollys Park and Captain Hayes's house, in case something went wrong and the little vessel went down. Claire was not afraid of an outright crash, for unless the gasbag ruptured altogether, it would behave as larger ships did, and land on a long, slow approach. The part she did not relish was being stranded in some farmer's field and having to abandon their precious Membrane, with miles to walk and Gerald Meriwether-Astor who knew where in the neighborhood.

Jake and Tigg released the ropes, and the touring balloon with its silvery cover rose gracefully into the sky. As the ground fell away beneath them, Claire controlled the amount of energy going to the propellers and the homemade vanes, while Andrew did his best to steer by controlling the propellers' direction.

Awkward, yes. Inefficient, certainly. But they were flying!

One mile, two, and Claire caught a glimpse of the road and the double glow of the landau's running lamps far below. So far, so good. Four miles. Five. Eight ...

And there it was.

Andrew patted her arm, since he couldn't be heard over the beating of the propellers, and made a downward motion with one hand. Claire nodded, and leaned on the lever that throttled back the energy. The balloon sank toward the house.

Now came the tricky part.

She could feel the balloon's trajectory as Andrew controlled vanes and propellers with both hands and one foot. The still night was perfect for flying—with one difficulty. They were too loud. Which was why speed and accuracy would be paramount, and she must judge this very carefully ...

Now. She pulled back again on the lever and the propellers fell silent, still turning for a last few rotations as the balloon drifted toward the roof. The large square area in the middle, near the short tower, might have seemed enormous to someone standing on it, but for them, it was a bull's eye all too small, and they had only one shot.

Someone stepped out of the shadow of the tower—a bulky, shapeless mass—and Claire's heart nearly failed in her chest.

But it was too late now. They must land. With her free hand, she unfastened the strap of the lightning rifle in its holster on her back.

The bottom of the basket scraped on the gravel of the roof. Andrew leaped out to hold it steady, his body positioned protectively between her and the unknown person. Claire thumbed the switch of the rifle and it began to hum.

The person hurried toward them, tearing something from its head—a blanket! The moonlight struck—

"Claire! Andrew! Thank God!" Gloria said with a gasp, and flung herself upon Andrew in a hug.

"Gloria—yes—no, wait—"

Claire leaped from the basket and pulled her away, then both she and Andrew whirled to catch at the ropes before the whole rig floated away, unmoored, into the sky.

"Oh, I'm so sorry!" Gloria clapped her hands over her mouth until they moored it to one of the crenellations of the parapet. "I'm just so awfully glad to see you—alive—well!"

Claire turned and wrapped her arms about her in joy. "And we are equally glad to see you. Come. We will have only a moment once the propellers begin to turn. Someone will hear."

"You're quite right. The place is crawling in government men," Gloria said.

Andrew held the basket while she and Claire clambered in, then ran to untie the rope. "What possessed you to come up here?" Claire whispered. "I had thought I would be searching the house in evening dress." She indicated her ensemble under her coat—which Ian had unearthed from a trunk in the attic, made in the fashion of a hundred years before.

"I've been waiting all day, and finally concluded that you would come by air. Anything else would be too risky."

"There is no shortage of risk even yet." Rope in hand, Andrew barrel-rolled over the side of the basket and the balloon began to float upward. "Claire, ignition, please, quickly."

Again the ignition procedure, her chilled hands moving with difficulty now, on switches and levers.

"Halt right there!"

Gloria gasped and Claire lost her balance for a moment on the tilting floor of the basket.

Below, several men emerged from the tower and fanned out on the roof. One leaped for the bottom of the basket, his fingers barely scraping its wicker floor under their feet. "Stop, in Her Majesty's name!"

Claire braced her feet and flung her weight against the lever, and power flowed to the propellers. They sputtered into action, and Andrew threw the vanes full vertical.

The touring balloon labored into the sky, the weight of three people clearly forcing it to its limits.

"Stop, or we will be forced to bring you down!"

"Andrew," Claire gasped. "Vanes full horizontal, propellers north and east!" The lightning rifle was ready now, blue and white tendrils of light flickering impatiently in its globe. "I dare not fire—Gloria, what does this mean?"

"They laid a trap for my father—I'm the bait." Crouched in one corner, Gloria clutched the edges of the basket, her back pressed against the wicker. "But heaven only knows where he is. It doesn't matter—get me out of here!"

20

Tigg would never have imagined that following a touring balloon would be so dad-blasted difficult. He would have had more success putting a steering mechanism in the Lady's walking coop and taking it across country than he was having presently in her landau.

"Ow!" Jake cursed as they jounced into a pothole and back out again. "Are the roads this bad in the rest of England?"

"No idea." Tigg hauled on the acceleration bar to slow the vehicle down. "Sensible people fly. Spin the wheel, would you, and get us back in the middle." Nothing like on-the-job instruction to hammer something into one's head. Jake had wanted to learn to pilot the landau, but this was not the classroom exercise Tigg would have chosen.

"They've landed!" Jake exclaimed a moment later, when the sorry excuse for a road crested a hill and they could see Haybourne House in the distance. "They must have. The balloon is gone. No, there it is—rising, see?"

"Something's wrong," Tigg said tightly, hauling on the wheel himself to turn them around in the narrow confines of the road's high banks. "They can't have even got inside the house—we only lost sight of them for a moment."

"Heading north and east."

Tigg leaned on the acceleration bar and the landau shot back down the road toward Hollys Park. "Now?"

Jake craned to see. "Tigg! They're firing on the balloon from the roof! Look!"

Even over the puttering of the boiler, Tigg could hear the sound of the rifles' reports. Icy cold fear poured into his gut, and he spun the wheel left, sending them diving down a farmer's lane that with any luck would take them on an intersecting course with the balloon if it fell. Then he pushed the bar as far forward as it would go, the landau rocking and jouncing down the dirt lane at a horrific pace.

"Slow down or you'll crash us!" Jake shouted. "We'll be no help to them dead in a pile of metal!"

Hauling gulps of air into his lungs, Tigg controlled his panic and dared a look up into the sky. "Where are they?"

"Can't see—"

A bolt of silvery blue light flashed, seeming to come from nowhere and everywhere under a ceiling of woolly clouds. "That's the Lady's rifle! Heading!"

"Two points west," Jake said. "We'll have to go overland and hope there are no walls."

It was a vain hope—but Tigg urged the landau up and out of the lane and into a meadow that stretched down a slope toward a line of trees. The Hay bourne. The river.

"Where are you?" he demanded of the sky.

Two more shots was his answer.

"There!" Jake rose in his seat and pointed. "They're almost down!"

Past the line of trees, Tigg could just make out the diffused light of the obscured moon as it reflected off the silvery Helios Membrane—before the balloon disappeared from sight.

"Jake, triangulate," he ordered. "I need an approach and an exit strategy."

It took five seconds of bouncing, frantic flight down the slope before Jake's focused stare came back to earth and he nodded. "Stay on this course for two hundred feet. There's a wall three-quarters of the way down; we'll leave the landau there where it's protected, and get across the river on foot."

Tigg nodded. "They dropped fast. If anyone is injured, we'll use the Lady's driving coat behind the seat as a hammock and carry them back."

He hauled the landau to a rocking stop next to the wall, half of him relieved he hadn't gone right through it. The machine was heavy, and with the slope … He shook the thought away as they clambered out.

Crack!

Instinctively, both he and Jake flung themselves to the ground, out of sight behind the wall. "Are they still shooting from the roof?" Jake said incredulously, raising his head for a look. "Are they mad? It's half a mile off!"

That couldn't be right. But there was more. "Look!"

Hunched close against the old stones, Tigg pointed to the hills that rose gently behind the estate. Dark shapes bounced and jogged down the stalking trails. Human shapes. "It's a bloody army!"

Only one person could call up an army in a country where he was forbidden to set foot.

"They're coming for the Lady and Andrew—and Gloria, if she's with them," Jake said, vaulting over the wall. "But not if we get there first!"

Tigg and Jake pelted down into the river bottom, leaping over rocks and tussocks of sedge. The river widened here, and clearly the farmer used it as a ford, for the bottom was shallow and graveled. Splashing through, soaked to the knee, the two young men dashed up the opposite slope into the trees.

"This way." Jake's internal compass hadn't failed him, from the speed with which he ran through the brush, pushing branches aside. The dark seemed thicker here, though the trees were bare of leaves. After a hundred feet of slapping branches and tripping over fallen logs in the dark, Tigg's eyes had adjusted enough that he could see where the trees began to thin out.

"There!" He pointed at a struggling hillock of silvery fabric on the near slope.

"And none too soon," Jake panted. "Vultures at ten o'clock, a thousand yards off."

And to the left, in the distance, lights were coming on all over Haybourne House. If only the balloon had been able to stay aloft another half mile! They'd have been behind the hill and out of sight of the riflemen on the roof. But now the men would have told their companions in the house exactly where the balloon had gone down, and Gloria's captors would come from that quarter to join the army coming from the other.

They didn't have much time.

The silvery cover was flung back and Andrew crawled out from under it. Claire and Gloria, on hands and knees, emerged right behind him.

"Lady!" Tigg shouted. "Into the trees, quick!"

Claire's head lifted at the sound of his voice, and she clutched Gloria's arm. The words had barely drifted away on the wind when there came a *crack!* and a bullet pinged off a bent propeller right behind them.

Claire flung herself to the ground, dragging Gloria down as well, and Andrew dove on top of both of them.

"Where did that come from?" Jake demanded. "We're out of range."

"Behind us," Tigg said. "It's impossible."

Jake's curses this time were truly spectacular.

By now the three next to the downed balloon had commenced crawling on their bellies, moving as fast as they could up the slope, using hillocks and rocks as cover. Tigg could hear the Lady murmuring encouragement to Gloria, hear the sound of fabric tearing as their skirts were caught up under them.

Another bullet sang and pinged off an outcrop of granite.

Andrew grasped the waistbands of both women and hauled them up the slope, hunched over, Claire and Gloria using both hands and feet in a headlong dash for cover.

"Show yourself, you beggar." Jake's whisper was harsh, his lightning pistol out and humming as he cast about for a target. "How can we cover them if we can't see him?"

"Jake, don't!" Tigg grabbed his shooting arm. "The

vultures don't know we're here. Don't give us away."

"But—"

"Come on!"

He burst out of the trees and grabbed Gloria. Andrew seized the Lady and together, they half-carried, half pushed them up the remainder of the slope and under the eave of the trees.

"Tigg, thank God," the Lady gasped.

"Is everyone all right?" Jake demanded.

Gloria couldn't speak, between gasping for breath and crying, but she nodded. The Lady and Andrew both managed to say yes before Andrew demanded, "Where did that shot come from? It can't have been the house."

"It wasn't." Jake stood, pistol at the ready. "It was from the trees, to the east and behind us, but we ent got time to search him out. There's a teeming horde of vultures pouring down that hill, and we have about half a minute to get to the landau before they catch us."

"Vultures?" Gloria squeaked. "I'd welcome vultures."

"He means men," Claire said briefly. "Run."

Back through the whipping darkness of branches and trip holes and traps for the feet, Jake led their little party, his unerring sense of direction their only advantage. At least the vultures would have these woods to negotiate as well, and with any luck, they wouldn't have a Jake in their party to help them.

"Perhaps it was only the farmer, thinking we were poachers," Andrew panted. "I cannot imagine there are three parties of gunmen in the Somerset hills. It beggars the imagination."

"The ones in the house are government men," Claire

said, hauling Gloria out of a hole and over a fallen log. "But who are the vultures?"

"I'd lay money they're mercenaries, hired by Gloria's dad," Tigg said. "Watch that bough." Andrew ducked, and the rest of the party ran under it. "Not far now."

"The walkers," Gloria said unevenly. "All the walkers in the hills. In November."

"Ah," the Lady said. "We should have guessed. They have been watching you for some time, then."

"No one ... can second guess ... my father," Gloria got out between breaths.

They emerged from the trees and now there was only the river and the far slope to manage. "Landau's behind that wall over there," Tigg said, conserving his breath. "Not far now."

"Gloria," Claire said, "you must tell us—what is the situation with your father? If Jake's vultures are indeed sent to fetch you to him, why should we not throw in our lot with them?"

"Claire, there is no time!" Andrew's tone was urgent, and even now they could hear the crashing of branches in the distance.

"I'm sick of them all!" Gloria said, bent over and holding a hand to her side. "Sick of being bait. Sick of my ignorance about the French invasion and some stupid telescoping cannon. Neither Barnaby nor my father wants me for me. They just want me for what I can do to further their political schemes."

"Right, then," Claire said. "That clears matters up somewhat."

"Lady, if you cover us with the lightning rifle, Jake and I can get Gloria to the landau," Tigg said urgently. "You and Mr. Malvern have a better chance of hiding than all five of us do."

"A good plan," Andrew said. "A better one is if I cover you with the rifle and the four of you go."

"I think not," Claire said with some heat. "You and I remain together or we do not remain at all."

"If you lovebirds have finished billing and cooing, can we hurry this up?" Gloria demanded, clearly having regained both breath and nerve.

"Now." Tigg grasped her elbow and she, Jake, and Tigg hunched over and began a zigzag run down to the bourne.

Crack! A rock shattered into pieces not five feet from Jake's boot, making him jump back as his leg was struck by a shard of it. A bolt of blue-white light sizzled across the gap, aimed vaguely in the direction from which a shot might have come.

"Why shoot at us?" Gloria panted. "We haven't done anything."

Another rock exploded ten feet in front of them, and a tiny propeller arced into the air, broken off by the force of the impact.

A propeller!

"Wait—that was a—" Gloria said.

"We're not going to make it," Tigg said grimly. "He'll pick us off one by one as we cross the bourne."

"It's him!" Gloria staggered to a halt.

Crack! Jake cried out, spun, and fell to the ground.

"Jake!" Gloria screamed.

"I'm shot! Back to the trees!"

She dashed to him and hauled him up by an arm— the wrong arm, from the resulting howl of pain. Tigg grasped the good one and together they got him back under the sheltering cover of the trees.

"Jake, how bad is it?" Gloria demanded. "I'm so sorry—the acid—"

"Dunno. Don't care. We have to get out of here, and the direct route ent going to cut it."

"We can't go east," Claire and Andrew ran up. "That's where the gunman is. Jake, my dear—"

"I'll be fine, Lady," he said through his teeth. "For now, we have to run."

"But the acid!" Gloria was practically in tears. "If nothing else, we must get him to the river to wash it away!"

"Are you mad?" Jake glared at her.

"Stop right there," said a voice behind them. "Here they are, boys!"

Tigg plunged his hand into his pocket and thumbed on the lightning pistol. Jake's right arm was immobile now, so Tigg leaned over to breathe into his ear, "Not a word, mate," and pulled the humming pistol from his pocket. Behind the cover of her skirts, he slipped it into Gloria's hand.

A swift intake of breath told him she understood. There was no time to show her how to operate it—he could only hope a girl raised by a munitions manufacturer would know a trigger from a teacup.

"Now then, who have we here?" the voice said. "Let's have some light, then."

This was a nightmare. Someone was firing propelled bullets—

Suddenly, Tigg realized what Gloria's panic about acid meant. The *bullets.* Propelled bullets containing acid that would burn away the evidence once they entered the body. "Jake—Lady, he was shot with a Meriwether-Astor bullet. The kind we saw in the Canadas, when he tried to assassinate the count."

"You see?" Gloria yelped. "Can you blame me for trying to run away?"

By now they were surrounded. Several men held up moonglobes, and in their light he could see they were dressed in tweed walking costumes. But their eyes were not the eyes of men interested in spotting meadowlarks and plovers. They were the eyes of mercenaries, hardened in battle, and prepared to do whatever it took to accomplish their goal.

Gloria had tugged Jake's jacket off his shoulder. "Let me see. There might still be time."

"Step away from him, young lady," the ringleader snapped.

Gloria told him what he might do with that suggestion, and when his eyes widened in shock, she pulled Jake's shirt aside, revealing his bare shoulder. "Oh, thank God."

Someone with a moonglobe moved in out of sheer curiosity, and Tigg could see that while the shoulder was torn and bleeding, the bullet had not lodged in the flesh. It seemed to have passed through his sleeve, if the size of the hole was any indication, and the tiny, sharp propellers had done some damage on their way past.

Gloria heaved a huge breath and attempted to restore him to rights. "It did not break. The arm is cut, but no acid was released. Oh, thank heaven, Jake."

Jake appeared much more startled by her concern than he did by the evidence of his close escape. "Thank you, miss," he mumbled, and shrugged his clothes back into place, clearly embarrassed at her seeing even an inch of bare skin.

"What's this now? Acid?" The leader of the walkers

was clearly a little slow on the uptake. "Never mind. Miss Meriwether-Astor, I presume?"

"No," she snapped. "My name is Madeleine Aster, and I am a guest of Captain Hayes at Haybourne House."

"Really," he drawled. "And I suppose you and your friends are merely out for a walk?"

"We were taking a midnight flight in our touring balloon," Andrew said with such dignity that Tigg might even have believed him if his heart hadn't been pounding so hard. "I and my fiancée and Miss Aster."

The leader's gaze narrowed on the Lady. "And who might you be besides this gentleman's fiancée?"

"I should think that when you are sent to collect someone, you might at least be able to identify her correctly," she said in what was quite possibly the worst attempt at a Colonial accent Tigg had ever heard. There was no mistaking its tone of frigid offense, however. "I am Gloria Meriwether-Astor."

Andrew's hand convulsed on her sleeve, but there was no help for it now. It was a mad idea, but it was done now and the Lady must play it out, for good or ill.

"This is Captain Hayes. And since what brings you all here *en masse* is undoubtedly Papa's hearing of our engagement, then I suppose I must assume our elopement is off?"

"Cl—Gloria, no," Andrew managed.

She patted his arm. "I knew he would never permit it. For you are penniless, and he believes you to be a scurrilous fortune hunter."

"All right, all right. Enough," snapped the ringleader. "Our instructions are to bring the young lady to her father, so I suppose you'll have to come, too, Captain Hayes, and explain yourself to him. Don't envy you that one bit."

"And what of my friends?" Claire asked, tilting her nose in the air. "Miss Aster's driver has been injured. Their vehicle is at the farmhouse, there." She nodded toward the river. "I suggest you allow them to take him to the nearest doctor, or at the very least, to ask for assistance of the farmer's wife."

The ringleader looked a little put-upon at this wrinkle in his plans. But before he could reply yea or nay, there was a commotion in the woods—swearing—and in the next moment a barrel-shaped figure burst from between two fir trees and stomped into the circle of light cast by the moonglobes.

"Great balls of fire, Gloria!" Gerald Meriwether-Astor shouted. "What in the name of Zeus are you thinking?"

21

Claire gasped and clutched Andrew's arm. Gently, he lifted it and laid it across her shoulders, where subsequently she felt a tiny tug as he released one of the fastenings that held the lightning rifle in place. A moment later there was another tug as he slid the switch forward and the rifle began to hum. She did her best to play the helpless damsel while inside, she rejoiced in having a man by her side who not only recognized her capabilities, but meant her to use them.

Gloria had frozen in place, but as one man, Jake and Tigg stepped protectively in front of her to block the fuming progress of her father, who, it seemed, would like nothing better than to haul off and backhand her.

"Gloria?" one of the men murmured. "Oo's 'e talking to, then?"

"Well, girl? Out of my way, blackamoor. I want an answer from my daughter."

Tigg stared him down—literally, for the man was at least six inches shorter. "I am Lieutenant Thomas Terwilliger of Her Majesty's Air Corps, and I'll thank you to address me that way. I am not moving until I am certain this young lady will come to no harm."

Gerald swore with such imagination that Claire apprehended exactly where Gloria's repertoire had come from. But none of it moved Tigg an inch. He merely folded his arms, alongside Jake, whose left hand had moved to rest casually on the haft of the Texican blade at his hip. His right hand, considering the injury to his shoulder, lay casually in the pocket of his flight jacket.

"This is your daughter?" The ringleader of the vultures gave Claire a look that could have seared a side of bacon, to which she returned a sunny smile.

"Of course it is, you dolt," he snapped. "I don't know what game you're playing now, missy, but the jig is up. You're coming with me and we're going home, pronto."

Instead of meekly admitting that the jig was indeed up and going with her father, Gloria's chin took on an obstinate firmness that eerily reflected that of her parent. "No, I'm not, Dad."

"What?"

"You have to get out of England immediately. We don't have time to argue. They'll be here any moment."

"Who will?"

"Barnaby Hayes, Dad, and the government men staying at his house."

"I'm not afraid of that bounder! I don't care how many men he's got with him—he deserves to be shot on sight for aspiring to my daughter."

"He doesn't aspire to me, you fool," she snapped, losing her patience in a rush. "He suggested I write that letter to get you to come here. It's a trap, Dad, and you've sprung it. They're agents of the Walsingham Office and I was their bait!"

Claire imagined this was likely the first time Gerald Meriwether-Astor had ever been struck dumb by anything his daughter said. He stared at her, his mouth working as though he were chewing tobacco. "I don't believe it."

She threw up her hands and slipped through Tigg's and Jake's protective shield. "Believe it or don't, but it's true. Didn't you see them firing on our touring balloon? Claire and Andrew were trying to *rescue* me, and all your stupid henchmen have done is slowed us down—and injured Jake!" She gripped that young man's wrist, and he winced. "I know what you've done. I know about the convicts in Venice. How you supplied the weapons and ships for the French invasion. About the attempt to shoot down the Prince of Wales. I know it all, and I'll tell you right now, if this is the man you've become, then I wash my hands of you."

The ringleader stiffened in shock, and around them, men began to mutter among themselves.

"Shut up!" Gerald snapped over his shoulder. To Gloria, he said, "None of that is your business, except to spend the money those deals made."

"I'm not spending that money. It's blood money. Not that it will make any difference to you, but I'm leaving this place with my friends and making my own way from here. I doubt I will ever see you again."

"Nonsense, missy. Hatch, Corling, take her and bring her along."

"My name is *Gloria*, not *missy*, and I tell you, I won't go."

"Hatch!" Gerald whirled to find that his team of burly men tasked with rounding up one slender young woman had backed away into the trees, leaving them under the eave of the forest, where it opened on the slope. "Corling, what is the matter with you! Obey my order at once!"

"That were you," said a voice behind one of the moonglobes, "what engineered the French invasion? You?"

"What of it, you dolt?"

"I didn't know I was signing up with a bloody Bourbon lover when I took this job," someone else said.

"Me either. Shot down the Prince o' Wales? That's treason, that is. What's next, 'er Majesty?"

"The Californias, actually," Gloria said.

"I don't care about no Californias," Hatch said, branches cracking under his boots as he took another step back. "But I ain't havin' it noised about that I'm a Bourbon lover. I'd never get a drink in these parts ever again."

"My cousin died on the beach during the invasion," came another voice, injured, with a foreign accent. "I've a mind to knock you down and take what's in your pockets for his widow!"

Beside Gloria, Tigg stiffened, and his head swiveled sharply as he sought the source of the voice in the dark.

"Hold," Hatch told whoever it was. "No time. We'll leave 'im for Her Majesty's men and a fine justice that will be. Come on, lads, we still got time to scarper—they've half a mile to cover."

And just like that, the moonglobes winked out and

the vultures faded into the trees until nothing could be heard but the sound of cracking branches. Then silence. A few snowflakes drifted down, as if the commotion had shaken them out of the clouds.

"How dare you? I paid you!" Gerald shouted after them.

In the distance, Claire heard the sound of an answering shout, but it meant nothing. For a dark shape stepped clear of the trees holding a heavy, double-bored pressure rifle.

Tigg sucked in a breath. "No," he said, the word sounding almost like a moan. "Oh, no."

"Nice to see you again, boy," the man said pleasantly. "And your friend, too."

Jake swore under his breath, and his hand jerked on his knife.

"Try it, and I promise you I will no longer be playing cat and mouse."

"Where did you get that gun?" Gloria said sharply.

"It's one of ours," Gerald said at once. "The Astor fifty-five caliber with the—"

"I know what it is, Dad," Gloria said impatiently. "What I want to know is whether this man is, as I suspect, the one who fired at me through the drawing-room window the other night."

"Know your ordnance, do you?" the man inquired. "That's refreshing in a lady. Pity you don't play the piano as well. All of you, step back."

"Who are you?" Gerald demanded. "If you're the only loyal one of that miscreant crew who just deserted me, I'll pay double your price and we'll be off."

"I don't work for you. Step back, away from the young lady. Now. I have as many cartridges as I need to

deal with all of you, but I prefer to keep things clean."
The double bores of the Astor .55-calibre did not move
from between Gloria's eyes.

"I say again, who are you and what have you got to
do with my daughter?" Gerald shouted.

"His name is Thomas Terwilliger," Tigg said, "and
he's an assassin for the Famiglia Rosa in Venice."

The man's eyes glinted above the bores of the rifle.
"Quick on the uptake, aren't you, boy? Wish I could
take credit for that, but I suppose I can't."

"You both have the same name?" Gloria asked.
Then her eyes widened as well. "Tigg, you can't mean
this is—"

"Looks like we'll both be disowning our fathers tonight," Tigg said, his steady gaze never leaving that of
his parent. "Unless they intend to make better choices
than the ones we've seen up to now."

"If you know what I am, you also know why I'm
here," Terwilliger said. "Stand out of the way and you
won't get hurt."

"But why?" Tigg demanded, doing no such thing.
Instead, he stepped in front of Gloria. "What has Gloria
ever done to you—or the Family, for that matter?"

"Gloria? Don't know a Gloria. My medallion is for
Alice Chalmers. Now step back. I won't ask you again.
You'll get the first barrel, and I'm not in a temper to
miss."

"I'm not Alice Chalmers!" Gloria shouted. "I only
wish I were, being courted by Ian Hollys and having a
dadburned future to look forward to! I'm Gloria Meriwether-Astor."

The business end of the double barrel dipped an
inch, the only indication of the assassin's surprise.

"You've got the wrong girl, mate, and the right one is on the other side of the world, running cargo out of the Royal Kingdom of Spain and the Californias," Tigg said.

How clever and brave he was! Claire could hardly breathe, the tension was so thick in the air. No one dared move, for the first to aim a lightning pistol would be the first to ensure Gloria's instant death.

"I don't believe you. How many girls of her description and acquaintance can be in this part of England?" Terwilliger lifted the barrel once more. "The Ministry of Justice was very specific. My ... client ... is a blond Colonial named Alice Chalmers, seen in the company of Captain Ian Hollys, whom she set free illegally from his lawful imprisonment. I am here to administer justice on their behalf. But if you force me to it, and obstruct the Doge's justice, I cannot answer for the consequences."

He did have them mixed up, Claire thought in despair. Herself, Alice, and poor Gloria, who of them all was the least guilty of any crime.

Gloria made a sound as her eyes rolled up in her head, and her knees buckled. As she fell forward between Jake and Tigg, a sizzle of lightning arced past the assassin, who had already begun to move in reaction to his target's fall.

The blast of the pressure rifle sounded like Gabriel's last trump, and a tree behind them cracked, split, and toppled. The reverberation rattled Claire from heels to skull, but it did not stop her from whipping the lightning rifle over her shoulder and taking aim at Terwilliger.

But she could not pin him down. Moving like a dancer, he aimed at Gloria's recumbent form. His finger slid into the second trigger guard, and pulled.

"Gloria!" screamed Gerald Meriwether-Astor, and flung himself across his daughter's unconscious body.

The bullet caught him full amidships, and he screamed again as the force of it flipped him over her, straight into the legs of Jake and Tigg, who went over backward under the weight of his body.

Lightning arced into the trees as Jake attempted a shot as he fell. A tree branch the size of a human being crashed down, and Andrew grabbed Claire, swinging her out of the way.

When she regained her feet, the rifle cradled in both arms, she sighted down the barrel and swung it in the direction of her last sight of the assassin.

The slope lay empty.

Snowflakes landed silently on the ground—as silent as the man who had vanished into the night.

In the distance, she heard the shouts of Her Majesty's men.

22

Being grounded had never sat well with Alice. Being grounded while waiting for other people to pull off a rescue was making her plumb crazy. "There must be something we can do, Ian, besides sitting here biting our nails."

"I am not biting my nails." Indeed—they were in the crew's quarters on *Swan*, and he was knotting a rope ladder for the fuselage. It wasn't difficult work, merely time-consuming, and she ought to be helping him.

If she could bring herself to sit still for two minutes together.

"We should take her up," she suggested. "Just a fast sail over to Haybourne House. They might need us."

"We all agreed that the safest place for you is here." He laid the long grid of the ladder along the deck and considered its length, then, satisfied, turned to her. "In fact, I suggest we remove to the house, which is more defensible."

"More defensible than a military-grade airship?" Her eyebrows rose in disbelief.

"The gondola may deflect a bullet, but the fuselage will not—and *Swan*'s crew are quartered in the fuselage."

"You don't have to tell me the layout of my own ship."

"I am simply pointing out that while *Swan* is nearly unbeatable in the air, on the ground I would rather rely on the greater safety that granite and brick provide. In fact, why don't we go up into the tower? At least there we might be able to see their return."

As suggestions went, it wasn't much, but maybe all the steps up into the tower would take the edge off the nervous energy burning her up inside.

They crossed the park on the gravel walks, Alice's shoulder bumping his from time to time, and she wondered if he had forgotten all about the things he had said in the landau a few days before. Yes, he'd said they'd discuss this—this *thing* between them once everything was over and Gloria was safe, but still ...

Alice sighed. Everything seemed to be conspiring to teach her patience.

"There are eighty-four steps," Ian informed her cheerfully as he unlocked a door off the dining room, which she had for some reason assumed merely opened into the library. "After you."

By the time they reached the top and he had ushered her out onto the open roof of the tower, she was winded enough to admit that this had accomplished one thing, anyway. She walked to the parapet and leaned on the roughly hewn pale stone to catch her breath.

Alice lifted her face to the woolen sky. "Look—it's snowing."

"I hope it will not lessen their chances of returning safely." Ian joined her, his hands clasped over the edge of the parapet, one shoulder leaning comfortably against hers. "Are you warm enough?"

In her flight jacket, she could cling to a fuselage in a gale, and he knew it, but it was kind of him to ask. "Yes. So how far do the Hollys holdings extend?"

"You will have to come up here with me in daylight so that I may show you. But in practical terms, the estate is nearly a thousand acres, with six tenant farms and half a mile of fishing rights on the river, which is on the other side of the first farm."

"A thousand acres," Alice breathed. "I've heard of ranches owned by the Californios in the Royal Kingdom of Spain ten times that size ... but things are more spread out there. How does a person get used to owning so much property?"

The sum total of her ownership was half of *Swan* and what she could carry in her valise. Which, she supposed, was a lot more than she'd left Resolution with. At least this airship wasn't stolen. It had been ... recovered.

"It is a responsibility," Ian replied, "and I suppose one grows into it. As a child and a young man, I helped on the farms during harvest, planted roses with my mother, and flew over all of it in the touring balloon— cows and sheep tend to be hard on fencing, and until I left to join the Corps, my job during holidays from school was to repair it."

"So you didn't grow up taking dancing lessons and gambling?"

He laughed. "Hardly. Though I do aspire to Claire's skill at cowboy poker."

"Don't we all—though I give her a run for her money. Or toothpicks, as the case may be."

"Does the property—the house—do *I* make you uneasy, Alice? Is that the real source of these questions?"

"Not uneasy, no. It's just ... not what I'm used to, that's all. And if—" She stopped. What if she was mistaken and her inexperience had led her to read something into his words the other day that wasn't there? What if she'd dreamed the whole thing? What if it never happened at all?

"And if I meant what I said that day in the landau, could you become used to it? Is that what you were going to say?"

"*Did* you mean it?" There was no sign of the touring balloon as far as she could see, which wasn't very far in the dark. She turned to him. He was solid, visible. Close. And radiating warmth, the way people got when they were laboring under strong emotion.

"I did," he said. "This is hardly an appropriate time, when our friends are in danger—when *you* are in danger—but I feel like champagne shaken in a bottle. I must speak, or explode." He took her shoulders in both hands, so that they faced each other square on. "Alice, is there any hope that you might feel for me what I have come to feel for you? Sometimes I think there is— at the station, for instance, when you kissed me in that *highly* inappropriate manner—"

"Don't tell me you didn't like it."

"I did like it. It shocked me to the core, and gave me hope that I might—that you might—that we—"

Was this really the arrogant, commanding Captain

Hollys, this man who had been through hell and survived … and now could hardly get his words out? She felt exactly the same way—as though there was so much to say that it was all backing up in her throat, and all she could manage was a whisper. "That we what?"

"That we … might be more to each other than merely comrades in arms. That you might truly believe me when I say I want to offer you all that I have."

She could hardly speak over the pounding of her heart. "I don't want all that you have. I want the man who kissed me at the train station. The man who flies as well as I do—and who trusts me to take the helm when he can't. The one who puts me first—me, an air pirate's daughter with nothing to her name but half a ship and the clothes she stands up in. That's what I want."

He released a shuddering breath, as though he had been holding it. "I am not the man I was, Alice."

"We would hardly be having this conversation if you were."

"I do not think I would have survived these weeks since Venice without you. Even now, I—"

"Shh." She put a finger to his lips, then slipped her arms around his neck as his hands slid to her waist. "You will get better. We'll see this through together. And after that …"

"After that, will you marry me?" His voice was a whisper of hope in the silence. "Will you, Alice?"

She opened her lips to answer against his mouth. But the word never came out.

Crack!

The granite crenellation two feet from Ian's elbow

exploded in a thousand pieces, and without a second's hesitation, he rolled her to the rooftop behind the parapet.

*

Claire thrust the lightning rifle into Andrew's hands and dashed to Gloria's side. With some difficulty, Jake and Tigg helped each other out from under Gerald Meriwether-Astor's not inconsiderable weight, and Tigg laid a gentle hand on the man's neck.

When Claire's gaze met his, he shook his head.

Jake gazed down at the man's body—and at the damage the propelled bullet had done. "Guess he won't be invading the Californias after all."

So many emotions and panicked questions were ricocheting inside Claire's skull that the fate of the Californias was the least of her worries. "Gloria! Gloria, wake up. Oh, bother—why do I never think to carry smelling salts?"

"Because our friends do not tend to faint?" Andrew knelt next to her and snapped the rifle into its holster on her back while she patted Gloria's cheeks.

A snowflake fell on the young woman's eyelid and her lashes fluttered open. She groaned and closed them again. "Am I shot? Am I going to die?"

"No, darling," Claire said. "Not for many years yet."

Her eyes opened slowly and then she looked about her and sat up. "What happened?" Then her gaze fell on Gerald's body. With a gasp, she said, "Dad! What's wrong with Dad?"

Rolling to her knees, she reached for him—and then saw the black stain under his ribs. She reared back, both hands pushing at the air as if to deny the very evidence of her eyes. "What happened?"

Claire took her in her arms and pressed her shivering body close. "He saved your life, darling. You fainted and the assassin fired at you. As he pulled the trigger, your father threw himself across your body and took the bullet himself. And as you know, there is no surviving those bullets."

Gloria gulped air, and pressed her face into Claire's shoulder. "He died to save me?"

"Without a second's hesitation," she said softly into her friend's hair.

Gloria shivered, and began to sob—great heaving sobs that seemed to come up from the very ground on which they knelt. "I was wrong—oh, I thought such terrible things—said such terrible things of him—and he—oh, Claire!" A shudder of breath, an attempt to gain control, and then she gave up under the onslaught, buried her head, and wept.

Long moments passed and Claire did not move, absorbing her friend's distress. Sometimes there were simply no words that did justice to a situation. Sometimes only action would do, and sometimes the only action possible was a hug.

When the flood of her tears had at last been reduced to a trickle, Gloria straightened slowly, wiping her nose inelegantly with the hem of her skirt.

Andrew knelt beside them. "Claire," he said quietly. "I do not like it that the assassin has disappeared with his mission unfinished."

"I do not like it either," she admitted, sitting back on her heels. She helped Gloria up and stood with one arm about her waist, lest her knees should give out again. "How could he conclude anything but that he had the wrong girl when her father sacrificed his very life with her name on his lips?"

"Precisely. Which leads me to conclude that he will certainly go after Alice."

"But does he not believe she is in the Californias?"

Tigg rounded Gerald's inert walking boots and touched her shoulder. "I don't think he does, Lady. When Miss Gloria said she'd rather be Alice, being courted by Ian Hollys and having a future—begging your pardon, miss—it gave him another lead. He's bound to follow it. It means his death if he doesn't—a man with a medallion must carry out the Doge's command, or die trying."

"But—"

"It's true, Lady," Jake said. "I heard him tell it just so. And it wouldn't take but a few enquiries at one of the inns along the post road to get directions straight to Hollys Park."

"Because nobody expects a Venetian assassin," Claire moaned in despair.

"So it's true?" Gloria asked, her tone hollow with horror. "What he said? Because Dad proved that I was me, he now means to kill poor Alice?"

"He does, and Ian and she do not know for certain he is in Somerset." Andrew took Gloria's hand and squeezed it. "We must act quickly. Jake will go with you back to the touring balloon to wait for the Walsingham men and inform them of your father's demise."

When Gloria began to protest, he shook his head. "If they do not see his body *in medias res*, as it were, and hear the facts, you will never be free of them. It must be you, and you must not be alone. Claire, Tigg, and I will take the landau at once to Hollys Park, for Tigg is right. That is certainly where he has gone."

"Mr. Andrew, I would rather help Jake and Gloria," Tigg objected. "I am also in Her Majesty's service, to say nothing of Lady Dunsmuir's service. Even in the Walsingham Office, that name will carry weight."

Claire's mind cleared, and she saw all at once why Andrew had divided them this way. And also that she must be the one to explain. "No, dearest. You must come with us. You are—he is—"

Understanding lit Tigg's eyes, and a weight seemed to settle at the same time in his shoulders. "He is my father. Do you think I have any influence with him? That anything I say will stop him, when he fired on Gloria without hesitation?"

"No, I do not. But if the worst comes to pass—" Oh, how could she say this? But she must. "If there is a fight, and tonight is to be his last on the earth, it is right that your face should be the last one he sees."

Tigg's whole body stiffened, and she could not read that beloved face in the dark. "You aim to kill him?"

"He aims to kill Alice, and already did for Gloria's dad," Jake pointed out.

"My only aim is that Alice should live to see the morning." Claire forced the words through chilled lips. "Anything else is in God's hands. Come. We do not have much time."

For a moment, she thought Tigg would refuse. His presence was not, after all, strictly necessary. But something—some instinct—some knowledge of him that her years as companion and mother figure had given her told her that *necessary* could have more than one meaning.

"All right, Lady," Tigg said quietly. "I only hope the landau will ignite on that slope."

"Let us find out, then, as quickly as we can."

23

"He's found me!" Alice pressed her face into Ian's shirt front. "Dadgummit—how?"

"Of greater urgency is the firepower he carries," Ian said grimly. "That was a seventy-five-yard shot. Come. Stay low. Though the doors and windows are locked, we must see to the servants' safety."

The two of them still recumbent upon the gravel roof, he wrapped Alice in his arms and kissed her hard. It was just her luck, to be shot at and have the most wonderful moment of her life ruined with a vengeance. Claire and Andrew had such a romantic engagement story. How would she tell hers?

First, she supposed, she had better live through it, and worry about the telling later.

They scrambled to their feet, and, running hunched

over, gained the tower door and slipped inside. The trip down took about a tenth of the time of the trip up, aided by sliding along the ironwork rail and taking the steps two and three at once. Ian shot the bolts and closed off one entire wing of the house, as well as the staircase that led to the floor where the Boatwrights and the maids slept.

"If he does break in, at least we shall limit his movements as much as we can. And while Boatwright was a fine shot in his day, I would not want to risk his safety if he should walk in on that gun."

"How are we going to watch for him—the assassin?"

"We shall arm ourselves to the teeth and retreat to the second floor. There, you will stay away from windows and watch the hall from the gallery. He must cross the hall to gain the stairs, and you will have a clear shot."

"You will stay away from windows, too, you hear?" Alice said, the anxiety in her tone rather spoiling the order. "I have an answer for you and you're not getting it until this is done."

"Then I will do my utmost to make this the briefest siege in the history of England."

Even in the midst of mortal danger, he could make her smile.

She thumbed the switch of the lightning pistol that had never left her pocket since she'd returned from Venice a wanted woman, and as it hummed into life, she took up her post crouched behind the marble rail of the gallery that overlooked the entrance hall below. After a moment's debate about whether or not to douse the electricks, she decided she needed light for a shot as much as the assassin did. She would just have to be faster on the draw.

Smoothly, Ian moved from window to window, slipping in and out of the rooms on the west side with the ease of long familiarity. How long would it take her, too, to feel that this house was home? How was she going to manage it all—staff, grounds, enough rooms to put all of Resolution in? How was she ever going to live up to the legacy of beauty and grace that his mother had left, when the only legacy she had of her own mother was how to take a man down with one shot, and how to stretch a penny until it squeaked?

She supposed she ought to be grateful for the first, since without it, all the rest might not be possible.

Ian moved farther away, and soon her quick hearing lost even his quiet footfalls on the polished wood and thick rugs. He must be working his way around to the south side, which opened up on the gardens and would provide any number of places to hide. Terwilliger might even conceal himself until morning, thinking she might be foolish enough to step out of doors.

He might even have gone out to *Swan*.

Alice's stomach leaped and sank. The ship was only partially provisioned, but she had no doubt an assassin would be as good at stretching food as ever her mother had been. All he would have to do was wait until she pulled up ropes, and she'd be trapped on her own ship until he was good and ready to shoot her. Maybe he'd even fly it back to Venice with her body in the hold, and poor *Swan* would be stuck forever in the impound yard on the Lido where Alice had found her, her brief bid for freedom scuttled.

No, no. She couldn't think that way. She needed to stay alert and remember that she and Ian were each other's first line of defense. She mustn't let the tension get to her, or she'd start to gibber the way he had during those first few days after their escape.

"Alice Chalmers, I presume?"

Her heart practically leaped from her chest at the sound of a man's voice. Not Ian. Not Boatwright.

Foreign.

Him.

"Who's there?" Her whisper was harsh with fright.

"I am the representative of justice."

Where in tarnation was he? In the corners the electricks didn't reach, the dark was complete. He could be anywhere, his voice whispering in the gallery, seeming to come from every direction. She must scream.

No, she mustn't. Ian would come running, and Terwilliger would pick him off like a pheasant flushed out of hiding.

"You are charged with illegally freeing lawful prisoners of His Serene Grace the Doge of Venice, with grand theft of a legally impounded ship, and with failing to pay your transfer fees before leaving the country."

"Those last two are worthy of death?" She couldn't help the incredulity in her tone. "That's a bit extreme, isn't it?"

"The Doge does not take slights to his authority lightly." He was moving, she realized suddenly. His voice seemed to be coming from—

There. An inky shadow moved on the side of the gallery adjacent to where she stood, the north side, where they'd just come down from the tower.

"How did you get into the house?" He knew where she was, so she might as well ask questions while she could. Her only advantage was that he didn't know she knew where *he* was.

"I came prepared with a rocket rucksack. Even the best security never quite seems to extend to the top of a house. After I missed my shot up on the tower, I made a wager with myself that you would be in too great a hurry to lock the door behind you. I rarely lose my wagers."

"We didn't think of a rocket rucksack," she admitted. One step. Two. Just a few feet and an enormous ceramic urn would give her partial protection. While it likely wouldn't slow the bullet much, it might deflect it enough that she could get a shot off. "Was it you shooting at Gloria Meriwether-Astor?"

"Sadly, yes. It strains credulity that there could be two blond Colonials acquainted with Captain Hollys within ten miles of one another, but here you are. I will remember next time not to make such assumptions."

He must be very confident in his ability if he could yarn on like this, giving her a better bead on his location. She had almost made it to the urn when he said, "Halt there, if you please. Take your hands out of your pockets and raise them. I will make this as quick and painless as I can. I have no fondness for a woman's suffering."

"Don't count your chickens," Alice said through her teeth, and, her hand still in her pocket, where it had been wrapped around the grip of the lightning pistol, she pulled the trigger.

A bolt of blue-white light burned through the front of her pants and arced across the space dividing her side of the gallery and his. She saw at once that shooting from the hip had caused her to aim low. The bolt burned away part of the marble railing and spent itself at last in Terwilliger's leg, where it burned his pants and some of the flesh right down to his boot.

He screamed, and in his convulsion of pain, pulled the trigger of the huge double-barreled pressure rifle that the lightning had revealed he carried. Alice dove for cover behind the urn, and it exploded in a million pieces that rained down for twenty feet onto the parquet floor of the entrance hall.

Simultaneously someone banged on the front door and shouted. Ian burst out of the corridor to the guest bedrooms, skidding on the polished wood and diving to the floor, rolling and coming up next to her. "Alice!"

"He's down but not dead," she said, barely able to get the words out for shaking.

"Not for long," Ian said, gathering himself for a rush along the gallery.

"No!" She grabbed his arm. "That gun has two barrels—he only shot one! I saw where he went down— there. Cover me."

To her everlasting amazement, he did not argue. He, an experienced military man, simply calculated the odds, saw that they were greater if they did as she said, aimed his Corps-issued pistol across the gallery, and fired. At the same time, she ran like the hounds of hell around to the next side and saw Terwilliger lying on the floor, propping himself up with the stock of the pressure rifle.

Ian fired again—glass shattered on the floor below— and Alice aimed the lightning pistol and let off another bolt as she flung herself to one side, against the wall. Simultaneously, the pressure rifle barked, deep as a bloodhound's baying, and a painting fell off the wall and landed with a crash on top of her.

As she struggled to get it off—it had to weigh a hundred pounds—footsteps passed her at a run.

"Lay down your arms in Her Majesty's name!" Ian demanded. "Or I'll shoot you where you lie."

Which was all Alice heard before someone hauled on the painting and Claire's voice said, "Alice! Oh God, Alice, are you alive? Speak to me!"

"I'm fine," she managed. "Dadburnit, I missed and that villain is still alive!"

"Ian and Andrew are tying him up with their belts," Claire said breathlessly. "Dear heaven, is this painting lined in lead?"

"Gold, probably. Umph!" With a final push, she was free, and Claire hauled her to her feet.

"Oh, I am so glad you are unharmed. So happy—" Her voice wobbled and she burst into tears.

Alice put her arms around her. "Hush. It's all right. Between the two of us, Ian and I brought him down. Now I suppose it will be up to the Admiralty to deal with him."

"And you and Gloria will be safe at last," Claire wailed, completely gone to pieces.

With a quick breath, Alice remembered that she wasn't the only one in danger tonight. She patted her friend's shaking back urgently. "Gloria! What happened? Is she here? Did you get her out?"

Claire raised her head, drew a shuddering breath in a clear effort to regain control, and scrubbed the tears off her cheeks. "We got her out and they shot us down. Her father and his mercenaries found us—and when Terwilliger shot at Gloria, Mr. Meriwether-Astor flung himself in front of the bullet."

"Then—"

"He is dead and Gloria is alive and explaining all of this to the gentlemen from the Walsingham Office."

"The *who?*"

"Never mind, we'll explain it all later. The important thing is that you are both safe!"

"Alice?" Claire stepped back to allow Ian to take her into his arms. "You're all right? He didn't hurt you?"

"The only thing that might have hurt me is this ruddy great painting." She craned her neck to look up. "Oh dear. It looks like you'll have to replaster your wall. And the painting's done for, I'm afraid. The canvas tore clear across."

"The devil take the painting. It was my great-uncle George and he was a crashing bore. The only interesting thing he ever did was fall on you."

She grabbed his lapels, a sudden urgency compelling her to speak, though Claire was standing just on his other side. "Ian. *Yes.*"

Despite the fact that his gallery was in ruins and an assassin lay not ten feet away, he understood at once. Or perhaps he understood not the words so much as the emotion gleaming in the tears in her eyes. His face softened in a smile and he whispered in her ear, "I understand, my dearest, bravest love. You have made me eternally happy. And great-uncle George notwithstanding, I want no other partner by my side."

"Tigg?"

At Claire's soft question, silence fell upon the gallery, broken only by gasping attempts to catch their breath. Alice pulled herself out of her own chiefest concern with an effort, and focused on the young man approaching slowly along the gallery.

Tigg knelt beside his father, who had been trussed

hand and foot by Ian and Andrew. "So," he said quietly.

"We meet again," Terwilliger agreed, his face pinched with pain from his burned leg. "Can't say I'm sorry."

Tigg gazed at him. "I wish it hadn't been during your attempts to kill my friends."

"If your friends hadn't offended the Doge, they'd never have met me. But that's all clouds under the keel. You're a fine young man, Tommy. I know I haven't a right to be, but I am proud of you."

"No. You don't. It's my friends here who have that right—Lady Claire. Captain Hollys. Alice. Andrew. It's them you should thank for helping me along." Tigg paused, and leaned down. "Dad?"

Alice leaned in to see better over Ian's shoulder. The man's face was working, as though he was in greater pain than could be accounted for by the burns, and a bubble of liquid frothed between his teeth. "Nice ... to hear that word on your lips, son. I won't go to prison. Won't even go to trial."

"You don't have much choice," Tigg pointed out. "We'll be sending a tube to the Admiralty in a minute, to report the capture of a foreign assassin and a deserter."

"A man always has a choice," Terwilliger choked. "Always. Mine were bad. I have regrets. But I don't regret Nancy ... and I don't regret ... you ..."

His voice faded into silence and his body went limp.

Tigg whipped off the belt and grabbed his wrist, and in doing so, revealed a ring on the man's hand. A ring with a hinged top that lay open, revealing a tiny empty chamber.

"Dad!" But his fingers on Terwilliger's wrist revealed the truth—as did the froth issuing from the man's lips. Tigg raised his head, his gaze meeting Ian's. "Poison, sir. Must've taken it before you reached him."

"Oh, Tigg," Claire breathed, and moved to touch his shoulder. "I'm so sorry."

Slowly, he stood, gazing down at the body of the man who might have fathered him, but who had never been a father to him. Almost blindly, his hand covered hers on his shoulder. "Don't be sorry, Lady," he whispered. "I never knew him long enough to grieve him."

"But you can grieve the loss of what might have been," she said softly. "You can grieve the man who loved your mother, and who made her smile so beautifully in that daguerrotype."

Tears swelled in Alice's throat, and instinctively she slipped her arms around Ian's waist, under his coat. He pulled her closer, his arms about her shoulders.

And when Tigg, all six feet of him, turned to Claire and buried his face in the crook of her neck to weep, his shoulders shaking as she hugged him tightly, no one begrudged him his tribute to what might have been.

24

Three rosebushes had managed to bloom in the conservatory at Gwynn Place, so Maggie had gathered several blooms and buds into a nosegay with some glossy camellia leaves, some sea-grass, and one or two golden sickle feathers from the majestic Buff Orpington rooster who was the pride of the small breeding program with which she and her grandfather were experimenting. Titan had obligingly moulted in time for Claire's wedding, which all parties concerned felt was most considerate of him.

Now Claire stood in the porch of the tiny chapel whose windows overlooked the sea. It was indeed a white Christmas, she thought with satisfaction—no, more than that. It was a sparkling, glorious, silver-and-gold Christmas. The sky was a brilliant blue and the light peculiar to Cornwall glimmered on glass and snowdrifts alike. She had not, after all, been able to convince the parish priest at the Baie des Sirenes that she ought to be married there, so she had taken her mother by the horns, as it were, and wrestled the Christmas Eve wedding she really wanted from her, practically by main force.

"Are you scared, Clary?" piped six-year-old Nicholas, Viscount St. Ives, resplendent in his very first morning coat and topper, at her side. "Your flowers are shaking."

"A little," she confessed in a whisper meant for his ears alone. "It's rather momentous, getting married. One doesn't do it every day."

"Lady, after all you've faced?" Snouts, resplendent in the most astonishing embroidered waistcoat on her other side, grinned. "This will be a piece of cake."

"There is cake?" Nicholas looked deeply interested in this new information.

"There is indeed, darling. Weddings are known for cake, you know, and you shall have the first piece once we have our breakfast. But now here is the curate to tell us that they are ready for us."

The tiny organ began the wedding march and Maggie and Lizzie, holding matching prayer books bound in trailing ribbon and ivy, stepped into the aisle. The chapel only held twenty, so Claire was able to see nearly everyone through the door. Her family. Andrew's widowed mother, already dabbing at her eyes. All the inhabitants of Carrick House under Lewis's watchful eye. Lord and Lady Selwyn, holding hands and looking so adorably happy that Claire's heart rejoiced. Captain Hollys and Alice, sitting in the second row, an heirloom sapphire on the fourth finger of her left hand. Peony Churchill, lovely in bronze silk, batting her eyes at Maggie's cousin Michael Polgarth, though she had no business to do so. Polgarth the poultryman and his daughters and grandchildren. Her solicitor Mr. Arundel and his wife—and next to them—

She drew in a breath.

Nicholas looked up, and Snouts leaned in. "What is it, Lady?"

"The Count and the Baroness," she breathed. "I did not think they would come."

"I did," Snouts said, nodding. "They landed an hour ago, while you were dressing. You know the man does not hold a grudge, nor can he refuse you anything."

Claire could think of a number of things he had refused her, but today was not a day to dwell on them. Today was a day for happiness and celebration, and if she could number Count von Zeppelin among her friends again, then the day was truly complete.

"Our turn," said Nicholas when Lizzie and Maggie passed the halfway point down the aisle, and reached up to take her hand. She slipped her right hand into the crook of Snouts's arm and together, the three of them stepped forward.

Her dress rustled in the most delightful way as she paced slowly up the aisle. The only person missing from the happy scene was Gloria, who had shaken her head and hugged her at the suggestion that she stay another month and join in the celebrations.

"I would love nothing better," she told Claire regretfully at the airfield at Hampstead Heath, where she was to board *Persephone* and connect with a Meriwether-Astor airship in Paris. "But every day I get another message from the bankers and the board members demanding my presence in Philadelphia, so for my own sanity I must go. But you can expect a wedding present in a week or two."

Claire had kissed her and bidden her a safe journey, but she did not say good-bye. Between the three of them—Alice, Claire, and Gloria—there existed a bond so fine yet so strong that even oceans could not separate them. Sure enough, two weeks later, when Claire had forgotten all about it, came a box from the Atelier Worth in Paris containing the most beautiful wedding gown that she—or anyone in Cornwall—had ever seen.

When she had put it on this morning, she thought her mother would faint. "Oh, why would you not let me invite all of the County families with whom we dine?" she had wailed. "Every woman in Cornwall must see this dress. It must have cost a thousand pounds, Claire."

Truly, it was lovely, with pleating and sashing and fans of beaded embroidery in which the discerning eye might detect either the curling of waves ... or the graceful tails of chickens. It also possessed a waist so small that Claire had a feeling she would be giving her piece of cake to Nicholas, to say nothing of the array of sweets and delicacies that had been prepared.

But best of all was Andrew's face as she approached the altar and he saw her in the gown for the first time. Even through the mist of her veil she could see the moisture glistening on his cheeks—tears of sheer joy.

Which made her own eyes brim over, too.

Snouts kissed her cheek, and Nicholas, having been briefed on his duty, solemnly conveyed his sister's hand into that of Andrew.

"Dearly beloved," the rector began, "we are gathered here today in the presence of God and this company to unite this man and this woman in holy matrimony."

As Claire and Andrew said their vows, knelt for the blessing, and Andrew lifted her veil to kiss her for the first time as her husband, Claire felt as though she were in a dream. But then, after they had signed the parish register, the rector said, "May I be the first to congratulate you, Doctor Malvern, and offer my very best wishes for your happiness, Mrs. Malvern."

A wave of happiness broke over her. It was not a dream. She was really Andrew's wife, and he her husband. Together, they would face the joys and triumphs and sorrows and dangers of life, with the confidence that each held the other's heart in safekeeping.

She took his arm and laughed with sheer joy. In the first pew, Mama looked scandalized. But Andrew put his hand over hers and they walked down the aisle together, her thrown-back veil trailing like a banner of light. Jake escorted Maggie, and Tigg, of course, took Lizzie, holding Claire's bouquet. Little Viscount St. Ives offered his hand to his mother, and Snouts took Mrs. Malvern. The guests began to cheer from the sheer exuberance of the recessional, and as the curate flung open the doors and the light poured in, Claire saw that Holly and Ivy were there, too, busily snapping up the seeds thrown into the air by the crowd of staff from the manor house. She was quite sure that somewhere in heaven—probably sitting on God's knee—Rosie the chicken knew that all was finally as it should be, and was content.

The light burst over them and Andrew flung propriety utterly to the winds. "I love you," he said, and kissed her again, right there in front of God and everyone.

"I love you," she whispered, "and always will, no matter what our lives hold in store."

Hand in hand, they ran down the steps and into the bright silver and gold of the first day of their lives together, the sound of the cheering and laughter of their friends and family rising like music into the sky.

Epilogue

January 3, 1895
Philadelphia, the Fifteen Colonies

Claire, my dear heart,

Thank you so much for the account of your wedding, for the piece of wedding cake (which I ate instead of putting under my pillow to dream of the man I will marry, which was much more satisfying, believe me), and for the lovely little watercolor painting from Maggie of the chapel on the cliffs, so that I might imagine it all. I am very happy that the dress arrived in time. I am sure you looked a perfect princess in it—and being that heavy cream color, you know, it can easily be worn on formal occasions afterward.

A GENTLEMAN OF MEANS

I can just imagine Julia's and Catherine's faces should they see you in it at the reception to which you've invited the Prince Consort. That alone would be worth the price of a transatlantic fare.

You'll never guess whom I heard from in a letter this week—Captain Barnaby Hayes. If you can believe it, he wishes to press his suit! Well, I am sure you know the tenor of the reply I returned, for who could trust a man who had deceived one and treated one so abominably? It is a shame, really. He is so handsome and so kind. But such a man may smile and smile and be a villain, so I will put him out of my mind.

My mind is quite occupied, thank you, with business matters. It is going to take me some time to untangle the labyrinth of my father's business dealings. The first thing on the agenda was to recall the fleet of undersea dirigibles from the Adriatic. Now that Captain Hayes has no doubt turned Neptune's Fancy over to Her Majesty, I suspect they will use it as a prototype and this new method of transportation will become popular in the seas about England, giving me some competition. I am determined that the Meriwether-Astor name shall henceforth be known for its honesty and integrity, which means the dirigibles will be plying the waters off the Fifteen Colonies like good little vessels, with no more dealing in convicts and contraband.

This matter of the Californias has me a little worried, however. I am investigating just how far my father's plans had gone in that regard, with a view to nipping them in the bud. Goodness knows how long that will take, or how complicated it will be, but rest assured that I will prevail in the end over board members and family connections alike. In moments when I doubt my-

self, I think of you and Alice, and my courage returns to me threefold.

I am sorry that the Admiralty continues to be obstinate about Alice captaining Swan. Actually, I am not sorry at all. For my devious plan is to encourage her to register the vessel here so that she may join my fleet. I will not only have her fly as captain, I will pay her handsomely to run cargo between here and England, once I am successful in having the embargo against us lifted. If Ian is to settle down to the life of the landed gentleman, it will be up to the women of his acquaintance to keep our various ships in the air, don't you agree?

I simply must see you at least once before spring. Either you and Alice and Andrew and the girls must come to me, or I shall come to you. We will contrive it somehow. Your friendship is like a good wine, and I have become quite fond of it!

With my best regards to that dashing man of yours,
I remain your friend always,
Gloria

THE END

A Note from Shelley

Dear reader,

I hope you enjoy reading the adventures of Lady Claire and the gang in the Magnificent Devices world as much as I enjoy writing them. It is your support and enthusiasm that is like the steam in an airship's boiler, keeping the entire enterprise afloat and ready for the next adventure.

You might leave a review on your favorite retailer's site to tell others about the books. And you can find the electronic editions of the entire series online, as well as audiobooks. I'll see you over at www.shelleyadina.com, where you can sign up for my newsletter and be the first to know of new releases and special promotions.

About the Author

RITA Award® winning author and Christy finalist Shelley Adina wrote her first novel when she was 13. The literary publisher to whom it was sent rejected it, but he did say she knew how to tell a story. That was enough to keep her going through the rest of her adolescence, a career, a move to another country, a BA in Literature, an MFA in Writing Popular Fiction, and countless manuscript pages.

Shelley is the author of twenty-four novels published by Harlequin, Time/Warner, and Hachette Book Group, and several more published by Moonshell Books, Inc., her own independent press. She writes romance, paranormals, and the Magnificent Devices steampunk adventure series, and under the name Adina Senft, also writes women's fiction set in the Amish community.

Shelley is a world traveler who loves to imagine what might have been. Between books, she loves playing the piano and Celtic harp, making period costumes, quilting, and spoiling her flock of rescued chickens.

AVAILABLE NOW

The Magnificent Devices series:
Lady of Devices
Her Own Devices
Magnificent Devices
Brilliant Devices
A Lady of Resources
A Lady of Spirit
A Gentleman of Means

Caught You Looking (Moonshell Bay #1)
Immortal Faith

The Glory Prep series
Glory Prep
The Fruit of My Lipstick
Be Strong and Curvaceous
Who Made You a Princess?
Tidings of Great Boys
The Chic Shall Inherit the Earth

Coming soon

Caught You Listening, Moonshell Bay #2
Caught You Hiding, Moonshell Bay #3

Everlasting Chains, Immortal Faith #2
Twice Dead, Immortal Faith #3